Poppy

BORN RECKLESS

THE BORN SERIES

BJ ALPHA

BJ Alpha
x

Copyright © 2022 by BJ ALPHA

All rights reserved.

No part of this book may be reproduced in any form or by any electronic or mechanical means, including information storage and retrieval systems, without written permission from the author, except for the use of brief quotations in a book review.

This book is a work of fiction. Characters, names, places and incidents are products of the authors imagination or used fictitiously.

Any similarity to actual events, locations or persons living or dead is purely coincidental.

Published by BJ Alpha

Edited by Amy Briggs

Proofread by Dee Houpt

Cover Design by Haya In Designs

Photographer RafaGCatala

❊ Created with Vellum

AUTHOR NOTE

WARNING: This book contains triggers. It has sensitive and explicit storylines. Such as:
Violence.
Pregnancy loss.
Strong language.
Scenes of past traumas.
It is recommended for readers ages eighteen and over.

For those of you who find my writing offensive, clearly you are reading the wrong book.
Close the book now!
I suggest you ALPHA MIKE FOXTROT!
In other words, Adios Mother Fuckers.
To the rest of you, I truly hope you enjoy Born Reckless.

BORN RECKLESS

THE BORN SERIES
BJ ALPHA

PROLOGUE

CAMERON

The atmosphere here is electric. The floor is vibrating from the crowd and heavy bass of the music. The scent of weed and sweat fills the air as body upon body grind on one another.

Me and my best friend Joel are at a warehouse on the wrong side of Hawks Town. It has taken us over two hours to get here, but the fights tonight are known to be some of the most fierce and competitive in the state. I've slowly been gaining my own reputation in my hometown, Trent Valley, but I'm eager to gain a little more diversity and experience. Something outside of my usual kicks.

The warehouse is completely unlike anything we've seen before. Sure, women dress sexy back home, but this is something else. This is off-the-fucking-charts hot.

Pole dancers line the bar, overturned crates are being used by topless dancers, and the air is thick with weed, and the whole warehouse is full of every origin of the world—a complete contrast to back home.

Joel and I are from a prestigious town north of here, and I can count on one hand the number of kids who aren't white in our school. We attend a prestigious private high school where rich, white privilege is the norm. Growing up, we were always taught anyone outside of our inner circle is below us and are outsiders. *Fucked up, I know.*

But right now, we are most definitely the outsiders, and I can honestly say it doesn't feel good. I swallow thickly at the realization.

"You sure about this?" Joel asks, obviously feeling the same angst. He's bouncing from one foot to the other, clearly riddled with anxiety and excitement.

"Yeah, I'm sure, I need experience, man. You know, see what different techniques are used." I shrug, bluffing my confidence, and wave my hand around the warehouse for effect.

"Yeah, I get that, but do you need *this* kind of experience?" he says, cringing and gazing around wide-eyed with uncertainty and nervousness.

I laugh and try to downplay the nerves starting to flow through me. For some reason, I can't shake the feeling in my gut that something is off, it just doesn't feel right, like something is going to go wrong . . . very fucking wrong.

I pat Joel on his back and pull him toward the bustling bar. "Here, get yourself a drink and unwind a little." Joel grins in agreement and wriggles his eyebrows. His jokey actions make me throw my head back on a laugh.

The bartender has his back to us as he tends drinks. I glance left and instantly zone in on a girl around my age with long dark hair in waves down her back. I watch as she approaches the bartender. She has an oversized hoodie on and jean shorts with battered Converse sneakers; she turns to talk to the barman, gifting me with the perfect view of her ass cheeks hanging out the bottom of her shorts.

I swallow deeply but snap out of it when Joel releases a groan of approval, his eyes transfixed on the little hottie too. *How the fuck can someone look sexy dressed down like that?* I'm used to girls dressing up to impress me and putting on a display for attention, not dressing to blend into the crowd.

Looking around, I realize once again how different our environments are, at least how people are dressed. Like literally anything goes. There's no conformity here; shirts are untucked, dresses are long, short, see-through. Men and women alike wear makeup, jeans hang low. Tattoos and piercings adorn bodies in a variety of places. Everyone is accepted.

For the first time in my life, I begin to feel comfortable, and my shoulders relax at the thought. *What the fuck is all that about?*

"Yo, dude, can I get a beer and a water?" Joel all but bellows, prompting the bartender while leaning farther over the bar. Jesus, he can be such a dick sometimes. I mean, the guy could have a fucking gun for all we know. I scrub my hand down my face in frustration. *I can't take him any-fucking-where.*

The girl turns around at the same time as the bartender, and her eyes automatically hit mine. They're fucking beautiful. They shine bright green, and I must be staring, because the girl laughs and raises her eyebrows in question. I'm truly mesmerized. She takes my fucking breath away. I feel my face heating when I realize I'm busted. *Shit, am I embarrassed? What the hell?*

"I'll get them, Dev; you serve someone else." Great fucking answer, sweetheart. "A beer and a water, right?" she questions with a playful smile, biting her bottom lip as she approaches.

"Yeah, thanks." *Fuck, what the hell do I say to her?* My mind is blank. Shit, this has never happened. Jesus. My heart beats frantically in my chest as I watch her work the bar.

"Never seen you guys in here before." It's more of a statement than a question as she delivers the drinks to us.

"No, we're here to watch some of the fights. Heard they're pretty brutal." I try to respond casually.

"Yeah, they can be. There're some good ones scheduled for tonight. They can be pretty entertaining." She laughs as she speaks, and her whole face lights up. She has plump suckable lips and a small scattering of freckles on her nose. She slowly pushes her hair behind her right ear, and I notice she has several piercings and a blue star tattoo behind the ear. She sure as shit isn't anything like my usual type, but fuck, I'm getting hard just looking at her as we stare at each other, mutually captivated.

"What do we owe you?" Joel breaks the fucking stare. *Goddamn cockblocker!* I glare at him in annoyance. The guy is oblivious, *how the hell is he my best friend again?*

"Oh, it's fine. My treat. Enjoy your night guys," she says with a flirty wink. At that, she waves us off and proceeds to move along the bar to another customer.

We sip our drinks in silence while we sit back and observe the crowd, and generally just watch the whole setup. We're both equally transfixed on our surroundings.

"Listen, I'm gonna go take a piss, see where I change and shit, you wait here, okay?"

"Yeah, dude. I'm good here." Joel nods, agreeing with me while not giving me eye contact at all. I feel like I'm leaving a kid alone with a bunch of strangers. I brush my hand through my hair with anxiety while he's watching what appears to be a three-way kiss. Jesus. I decide to leave him to it.

Looking around, I figure it's time to make my way to the back of the warehouse.

I push through the heaving crowds until I reach a bald scrawny guy covered in tats, who's sitting beside a side door on a stool, clipboard in hand.

"Hey, man, I'm here to fight tonight. Where do I piss and change?"

He eyes me up and down, and his lips tighten in displeasure before he huffs. "Sure, what's your name?"

"Cameron Donovan."

He flicks through the sheets attached to the board, and his crooked smile raises in the corners of his mouth. His spine straightens, and his demeanor seems to have changed. He's a fucking weirdo, that's for sure. "Yeah, I got ya. Through this door here, first door on your left to change, last door on the right to piss. Here, I need to stamp your hand for you to access the changing rooms." I hold out my hand as he stamps my fist with a blue hawk.

"Thanks, man." I nod at him.

He smiles eerily and proceeds to light a joint. "Good luck, kid, you're gonna need it." He winks at me. *Weird fucker.* I shake the odd vibe off.

I push through the door and walk down the darkened corridor where a few people mill around, making out. I'm just about to turn into the restrooms when a door slams abruptly beside me.

I spin around and find myself hit by a person who walks straight into me. They aren't paying attention to where they're going, and their phone has scattered noisily across the floor, spinning for extra effect.

"Shit!" The voice is soft and trembly. I scoop up the phone and as I hold out my hand to return it to its owner, I come face-to-face with the hottie from the bar.

Only this time, she looks fucking distraught. Tears are racing down her face; her body is vibrating with shakes. I glance into her eyes to see pure devastation. *What the hell has happened to her?*

"Fuck, are you okay? What happened? Did someone hurt you?" I panic the words out while scanning her up and down, trying to assess her for any damage.

She pushes her hair from her face and slowly tries to compose herself. She's breathing deeply, as if trying to gain control of her emotions. While staring at nothing, she looks . . . broken.

The sheer expression on her face panics me. My heart races wildly in my chest, desperate to find out what's happened to her. I don't know why but I don't like seeing her appear so hurt, so distraught. A need to protect her overwhelms me. I swallow away the foreign feeling.

I once again quickly scan her body for something out of place. *Has someone hurt her?*

She's as still as a statue, in a trance. In shock?

"Do you want me to get someone? Can you speak? Are

you okay?" I'm firing random questions at her, anything for a response. Anything for her to tell me what to do.

She gently shakes herself as if trying to pull herself out of whatever bubble she's in.

Her eyebrows knit together in concentration as she clears her throat. "I'm fine, thank you."

Nah, sweetheart, not buying it. She isn't fine. "You don't look fine. You want me to get you the bartender? A drink or something?"

She stares at me, frozen, as though I'm an alien, her eyes searching for some hidden agenda maybe? "No, I'm fine, thank you," she says a little more confidently. She's trying to convince herself, that's for sure.

She holds out her hand for her phone, and my hand meets hers, and our fingers touch as she grasps the phone.

Tingles spread through my body, and I know she feels them too. Her hand jerks away quickly, almost like she's not wanting to acknowledge the feeling.

I swallow heavily as the tension blocks my words. "Is it broken? The phone?" I gesture toward the phone in her hand, breaking her from her frozen state.

She glances down at the phone, and her body jerks. She stumbles backward and hits the wall. *What the fuck?*

I look at her in question. "What's wrong? Is everything okay? Do you need something?"

Her hand meets her mouth and then she tugs on her hair dramatically, pulling it back, "Fuck!" she screeches. "Motherfucker!" Her eyes are wide in what seems to be shock.

I move toward her, but she puts out her hands in front of her to keep me back. "I've got to go." She seems bewildered and panicked. Turning on her heel, she starts to walk away, leaving me fucking void, confused, and empty. *What the fuck just happened?* I stare behind me for answers before turning toward her again.

I watch as she strolls down the corridor, unsure whether to follow. Before she reaches the door, she turns around, her woeful eyes meet mine. "I'm sorry, Cameron!" Then she darts through the doors into the thick crowd, leaving me feeling a little fucking lost.

What the hell was she sorry for? Knocking into me? Did I tell her my name? Did she overhear Joel? What the hell! I shake off the whole experience. Tonight, I need to focus, put this shit behind me and get my A-game on.

But I can't help this niggling feeling something is going to go wrong, very fucking wrong.

1

SIX WEEKS LATER...

CAMERON

I shift quietly into the seat in the balconies of the courtroom, with a cap pulled low on my head and a hoodie pulled tight around my neck. I'm hoping to disguise myself and blend in. I've been looking forward to this day for almost two months now, and finally, I'm going to get some justice and retribution for the shit storm that occurred while in that shithole, Hawks Town's, warehouse.

I watch down on the proceedings, and my blood pulses with vengeance and anger at the disrespectful little shit that smirks at the lawyers on both sides. She lazes casually in a chair, not a care in her miserable little world.

Luckily for me, I've bagged some of the best prosecution lawyers in the state. Sure, it's out of my own pocket, but it will all be worth it to see the deceiving, thieving, little bitch sentenced for a decent stretch of time.

My eyes dart to three guys who are obviously there in support of their friend. The one in the middle is the cheating scumbag that kicked my ass that night. He wears a wifebeater, short dark wavy hair. He's physically impressive with tattoos adjourning his biceps, and he chomps on a toothpick and appears to be the one in charge. His presence screams arrogance and dominance.

The Latino guy beside him also wears a wifebeater, has a shaved head with tribal tattoos running along both the sides of his head, and his eyebrows are pierced, framing his sharp features. He appears a force to be reckoned with.

The other guy seems oddly out of place: lean with a clean white T-shirt that hangs loosely from his body. His hair is blond and long to his shoulders. He fidgets nervously with his fingers, his palms clasped together, almost praying.

I watch closer at the trio, scrutinizing them, trying to find something but I'm not sure what. Then I see it on the middle guy, the leader, the one I know as "Bale." If that's even his fucking name.

He sports a blue star tattoo behind his ear, the same one the girl has.

The case is well under way by the time I've arrived. I'm just hoping to watch the sentencing. Let's face it, that's the most important part.

The defense lawyer approaches the judge with a manila folder, and I try to listen in. They're calling a character witness on behalf of the girl's defense. *This should be interesting!* I roll my eyes.

The doors open and in confidently strolls a tall, lean

guy with light-brown hair, cut clean but longer on the top. He's dressed smartly in a gray three-piece suit and tie. Credit where it's due, the guy looks the real deal. He has an air of confidence and importance about him, and my first instinct is he's probably a cop.

I watch the trios' eyes bug out, and Bale's fists are clenched, causing his knuckles to turn white.

The blond has his hand on Bale's back as if calming him down while the Latino whispers into his ear. They clearly don't like the guy taking the stand.

I glance to the girl, and her head is downcast, her whole demeanor has changed in an instant, almost like she's crawled into herself.

She suddenly appears so very vulnerable. As I start to think this, I want to fucking hit myself. *What the fuck am I thinking? Vulnerable? Yeah, she deserves to feel that way!*

I listen intuitively as I hear the guy explain he's the girl's teacher, and she's an excellent student who's excelled in all areas.

Yeah, I can imagine! Grade-A student in deception and robbery, amongst other things.

"It's an honor to teach Francesca; she is a role model amongst her peers. She shines in all her subjects and has a specialty for the sciences and languages, something not many students with her underprivileged background can achieve. She has a bright and talented future ahead of her, and I can only hope that this small mindless act of teenage recklessness will not hinder her future."

Is this guy for real? I've previously met with my lawyer who assured me the girl has a rap sheet a mile long. *Shines? In what?*

Bright and talented my ass, the only thing bright will be her fucking orange jumpsuit she wears behind bars.

This is utter bullshit!

As the teacher steps down, he glances over toward the trio, and they look through him with narrowed eyes, glares, and pointed stares.

The teacher sighs as if defeated, and he turns and walks to the chair alongside the courtroom. It's then I catch the tattoo on the side of the guy's neck, right below his ear, a blue star. Yeah, you can guarantee the other guys have the same tattoo.

The lawyers finish their closing statements, and the judge clears his throat as he announces his verdict. The trio are on tender hooks, the girl nonchalant and seemingly unfazed. *What a fucking idiot.*

My spine straightens with gleeful anticipation as he begins his speech, and I watch in satisfaction as he delivers his words . . .

"Francesca Starlight Vadetta, I have listened to both sides of the arguments today and have received information from both parties proclaiming your indiscretions and notabilities. I have decided that at your current age and the fact you have only recently turned eighteen, that in the interests of your future, it would be unjust to serve you with a sentence that will tarnish any form of further positive progression in your life. Therefore, I will not be proceeding with the prosecution's recommendation of six years imprisonment . . ."

What the actual fuck!

My blood boils and I'm livid. Absolutely mother fucking seething!

The girl's eyebrows shoot up in surprise, and the trios'

postures have altered to one of hope. The cocky fucking pricks.

The teacher sits bolt upright, head tilted to the ceiling as if praying.

The judge continues, "I will, therefore, impose my own sentencing, one that you will continue serving in the confines of a juvenile detention center until you finish your senior high school year. Should I receive word of any unruly behavior or criminal activities, then I shall reverse my decision and sentence you to the original six-year incarceration. That is my final decision." He slams the gavel down.

Effectively slamming my expectations along with it, the bitch might as well have got off completely. *What a fucking joke.*

The cheers and jeering break me from my utter shock. *What utter fucking bastards.* My head pounds with rage, and I clench my jaw so hard I'm surprised my teeth haven't shattered.

As the courtroom clears, I'm still in shock, the lawyer told me it was in the bag. She'd get what she fucking deserved. *What the hell?* He said it was a done deal for Christ's sake.

Reluctantly, I make my way down the stairs.

In the corridor below, I hear a commotion and raised voices, so I jump the last few steps and open the door, sneaking into the dim-lit corridor, my body masked by the shadows. Bale is calling after the teacher. "Yo, teach, a word." He's broken away from the other two guys who were trying to hold him back, and he appears to be storming toward the teacher.

"Fuck off, Bale, I just came to help!"

"Help? You're the one that's gonna need help!" Bale slams his fist into the teacher's face repeatedly. As he falls to the ground, the other two guys race over and drag a deranged Bale from the teacher. Bale holds his arms up in defeat, and stops above the teacher and spits at his face. "You're lucky I don't kill you, you piece of shit!" He turns and storms away from the others, they turn and follow.

What. The. Actual. Fuck!

2

TEN DAYS AFTER SENTENCING . . .

FRANKIE

I'm sitting in the visiting office at Wood Creek Juvenile Detention Facility; who and why the fuck would anyone want to visit me, is beyond me. I huff out in annoyance.

I've been here for a few weeks now, ever since that night, and to be honest, it's actually quite nice. I miss the guys and our lives, but it isn't as bad as I expected.

My social worker walks in with a man behind her. "Hello, Francesca, nice to see you again." She's always so polite, prim, and proper. I roll my eyes.

"It's Frankie, I've told you a hundred fucking times it's Frankie!" I snip back.

"Of course, your visitor . . ." She waves her hand toward the door as my eyes move from the table in front of me to meet the brown-eyed, slick-looking suit in front of me.

Holy. Fucking. Shitballs.

"No fucking way!" I choke on a laugh.

The man laughs gruffly. "I've changed a bit, mm?" he muses.

"No fucking kidding, you've got hair! A suit!" I wave my hand at the clothes he's wearing, completely surprised.

"I have. Smart, mmm?" He pulls proudly on his suit jacket; he has a dazzling white smile and reeks of money and confidence.

He lowers himself into his chair opposite me. "Where are your tattoos, Jimmy? I remember you had them all over your fingers?" I point to his hands clasped in front of him.

He smiles back broadly. "You're right, I did, but they don't quite go with the businessman image I'm going with now." He laughs forcefully.

I shake my head. "No, you're right, they don't. So, Uncle Jimmy, what are you doing here?" I ask him, a little confused at his sudden reappearance.

"I'm here to save your ass, my dear niece!" He grins broadly.

I scrunch up my nose. "How so?"

"I got you out." My eyes jump in surprise as excitement bubbles through me, and I sit forward in my chair, eager to hear more.

"Out?"

He holds up his hands to stop the excitement bubbling further. "Yes, out, Frankie, but there's some stipulations," he practically hisses.

"Stipulations?" My body and excitement drop. *Fucking stipulations?*

"Don't be too down, I can assure you it's all good." He sounds optimistic.

"Explain," I nonchalantly ask, while throwing myself back in the chair, annoyed as hell.

"You're coming to live with me, in Trent Valley." He sounds . . . happy?

I choke. "Trent Valley? You're kidding me, right?" Annoyance wavers through me. *Why the hell would I go there?*

"No, I'm not." My anger is starting to rise, just because he left Hawks Town doesn't mean every fucker wants to. He thinks he's too good for us, that's why he never visited; well, he can just go fuck himself!

"Yeah, I think I'll pass!" I fake a smart smile and throw myself back in the chair once again.

His jaw drops. *Yeah, you weren't expecting that, were you? Prick!*

"Frankie, you don't have much choice." His eyes meet mine again as he tries to give me a soothing voice.

"Wrong, I'll stay here instead." I raise my chin in defiance, my jaw ticking in anger.

He shakes his head with a small laugh. "It's already been agreed to; another inmate is arriving to take your bed today, it's done."

What the hell! I'm being thrown out of the fucking detention center?!

"I'm not going to some fucking swanky town with a prissy, posh school full of people who wear clothes like this." I wave my hands, gesturing to how him and the social worker are dressed, not even trying to erase the look of utter disgust on my face.

My uncle laughs, his voice turning stern. "Frankie, unfortunately for you, the decision is out of your hands. I'm now your acting guardian, and what I say now goes. I've spent a great deal of time and money on your case, and I can assure you with the amount of evidence against you, it was pretty fucking difficult to get you off. Now, I'm offering you a fantastic opportunity to accelerate your future into something positive. I will provide everything you need, and you will want for nothing, all I ask is for you to wipe the slate clean with me and give me a chance to prove myself."

I fidget uncomfortably, my voice low, I'm determined not to show any emotion to this prick. "Why now?"

Jimmy drops his head and hangs it in shame before swallowing sharply. "I assumed you were doing okay; I didn't realize it had come to this. Honestly, Frankie, you can fight me all you want but this is a done deal. You can make things as easy or as difficult as you like, but it's happening either way. You're coming home with me."

I sigh in defeat. *Fuck. My. Life!*

3

FRANKIE

The driver pulls the car up in front of huge wrought iron gates. A security booth located beside them; the security guard waves the car on as the gates open toward a vast estate.

Manicured lawns and beautiful flower beds adjourn the paved driveway. The mansion itself is nothing more than ostentatious, absolutely fucking ridiculous. I shake my head as I stare out of the window, gaping at the scene before me. *What the ever-loving fuck?*

My uncle chuckles beside me. "Quite impressive, isn't it?"

I roll my eyes. *Am I meant to be thrilled? Impressed? In awe?* No, I'm fucking fuming. *He abandoned us, his family, for this?* For show.

I scowl back at my uncle. "Well, you seem quite impressed with yourself, Jimmy. I take it you're proud?"

His eyebrows knit together in confusion. "Shouldn't I

be? I've worked my way up from rags to riches, Frankie, surely you can appreciate the enormity?"

I think on the matter, a little lost in my own head. If it meant losing my family to achieve this? Fuck that, there's no question or doubt in my mind, family always comes first. Always.

The car comes to a stop outside the grand pillars of the front doors. My uncle breaks the silence, clearing his throat. "Listen, there's a few things I need to tell you before me go in." He takes a deep breath as his face turns serious.

"Firstly, I'm married to a beautiful, kind woman named Josie, and I have adopted her son." He sighs before going on to explain, "He's not mine by blood but in all other ways, he's my son, I'm very proud of the young man that he is today. Secondly, my family doesn't know much about my previous life, and I'd prefer to keep it that way. I'm known as James, therefore I prefer you to use that, also my surname is Donovan now. I had to reinvent myself and therefore, anything in my past is void. I'm sure you understand." He says the words, but his voice gives out unease, he's not as confident in what he's saying as he'd like to be. He watches me, nervously awaiting a response.

"So, let me get this straight. Your family, your blood family, are in your past. You've created this businessman persona, married, and have an adopted son? Who know nothing of my existence, and what, you expect me to be comfortable with all of this?" I'm seething, and if I am being honest, a little crushed too. *What the hell?*

His veins bulge at the side of his head, and I'm unsure if its rage or guilt from my words that's tipped him over the edge.

His words are boarding aggressive. "Frankie, I realize me leaving Hawks Town left you somewhat in the lurch. But I can assure you I had to do what was best for me at the time. I've worked incredibly hard to achieve my success, I've adapted everything to do so, even my goddamn appearance." He blows out a breath to calm himself. "Listen, I came back for you, didn't I? Obviously things escalated since my absence, but I'm genuinely trying to make amends, Frankie. Please, I want to offer you all the opportunities that were never available to me and your father." He sounds desperate. *Desperate for me to comply or desperate to make amends?*

His words soften me slightly, but I'm still pissed. "I wouldn't quite say you left me in the lurch."

He laughs awkwardly, thinking he's won me over. *Big mistake, prick.* "You did much worse than that, James, you left me in hell."

On that little note, I open the door and exit the car with a swift slam of the door. Gifting him with a smug smile.

The front door opens, and out walks a man in a butler outfit. Jesus. I shake myself because if the guys could see this shit, they'd die laughing.

I can feel James standing behind me as my eyes drift up at the house and butler. "Frankie, this is Grant, he is the head of the house staff. Should you require anything, speak to him. He will show you to your room and collect you for dinner in an hour. That should give you time to dress appropriately before meeting my wife and son." He nods at me as if to prompt me to follow this Grant guy.

"This way, Miss." Grant points toward the mansion.

I follow behind Grant like a lost puppy. I am lost, lost

for words. I can confidently say that never happens, I need to get my head back in the fucking game.

We walk into the foyer of the mansion, a.k.a. *show-the-world-I'm-a-rich-prick mansion.*

The foyer has marble floors, and a winding staircase to my right flows above the length of the foyer, with a balcony over the top, giving a full, uninterrupted view of the foyer below.

"Miss, follow me."

We walk up the stairs and along the corridor a little. Grant stops at the first door on the right. "This is your room, Miss, I'll leave you to get settled and fetch you in an hour."

"I'm sure I can find my own way." I smile back softly.

Grant seems a little uncomfortable as he fidgets on his feet. "I prefer to do as Master James requested." My face must give away a look of shock because he softens his voice. "I think Master James would prefer you didn't run into Madam Josie and their son until you're formally introduced, that's all." I nod in understanding—fair enough.

I step into my new room; a huge white bed is in the center of the room. Dressers on either side. To my left are two doors, and on further inspection, the first is a massive fucking bathroom and the second is a walk-in closet. I walk back out, there's no fucking way I have enough clothes to fill that space. I laugh to myself; in my old home, I didn't even have my own dresser.

I busy myself unpacking the few items I've brought with me, then I decide to try out the shower.

Oh my God. Fucking bliss! Credit where its due, rich people know how to shower. Hot water instantly and all these posh shower products that leave your skin silky, so freaking lush. Ah!

Before I know it, there's a knock on my door. Grant has come to take me down to dinner.

Oh, goody.

4

CAMERON

My dad had given me a heads-up this morning I had to be around for dinner tonight. I was pissed because I was supposed to be going to Stacey's house. I needed my dick sucked. She'd been tormenting me all day at fucking school and wouldn't give it up.

With promises of me spending time at her house tonight, she was going to give me head. About fucking time, she's always so hot and cold. One minute she wants it, the next she doesn't. She knows I'll fuck some other girl over the weekend, and that's why she's stretched it out all week, then she was going to blow my load tonight to keep me sweet. She plays too many games, and there's always an agenda with the girls at my school. Hell, even the parents have an agenda. Some poor saps are even married off before they're old enough.

Sometimes I still find it hard to believe parents arrange marriages. They're treated like business contracts in our circles. Thank fuck we're not one of those families.

Anyway, to appease my father, who has been pretty stressed just lately, I agreed to attend this urgent family meal. Mom said it's important to him. When I asked more, she informed me that his niece was coming to stay with us for a while. I didn't even know he had a niece.

Well, here's hoping she's some fucking eye candy. I smile to myself at the thought.

I briskly open the door to the dining room to find my father standing in front of the table, blocking my view of the girl in question.

"Ah, Cameron. I'd like to introduce you to my niece, Frankie." He gestures with his hand and moves to the side.

As my eyes land on the girl in the chair, I can hardly breathe through my rage and growing shock. I'm literally shaking inside. Big green eyes look up to me, and at first, they bug out in surprise and the color drains from her face. Clearly, she's as shocked as me. Then her face morphs into one of amusement. She smirks—fucking smirks!

"So nice to meet you, Cameron," she smugly says.

I'm fuming; *how in the fuck did this happen? His niece?* I dart my eyes to James who is standing watching our interaction.

Her smirk is growing bigger when I realize that I need to close off my shocked, angered emotions. I can't show anything that might give off how I feel.

Pissed, annoyed, intrigued, and apparently my dick thinks it's horny. I clear my throat. "Are you fucking kidding me?" I glare at my dad.

His voice deepens. "Enough. Don't speak to me like that. Sit your ass down and show some damn respect!"

I glance back at Frankie, and her eyebrow is raised in amusement and maybe challenge? Her smile is sly, and her lips curl up at the corners of her mouth; she seems pretty proud of herself. *Bitch.*

I'm contemplating my next move when my mother walks in the door behind me.

I sit down at the first chair, directly opposite the little thief. If she thinks she can outsmart me, she can think again. She chuckles to herself, shaking her head. The venomous glare I throw her should make her toe the line, but she finds it funny. Fuck, I need to mask my contempt, she's getting off on this shit.

"Frankie, this is my beautiful wife, Josie," James proudly introduces my mom.

Mom walks around the table, giving James his medication, then moves to Frankie.

"It's lovely to meet you, Frankie, dear," my mom's sweet voice greets her.

Frankie stands and welcomes my mom's hug, although she's tense, clearly uncomfortable with the interaction. Her back is ramrod straight, and her arms barely squeeze my mom, who has gone in full-blown hugging mode. I roll my eyes at the interaction. I'm trying to control my breathing and slow the anger inside me. I can't let her see how much she's affecting me. She doesn't deserve the satisfaction.

As I sit watching them, I take a closer look at Frankie from behind. She's smaller than I remember. Her dark wavy hair is pulled back into a messy ponytail, and she's wearing tight jeans that fit her ass perfectly. She's wearing a black vest top. On her shoulders, I can see some ink, but her hair hides what it is. Her arm is littered with random words. The tattoos aren't neat, they look like someone has been practicing on her; they're a mess. *How fucking ridiculous.* I seethe while eyeing her up and down.

I've never seen a girl our age with ink before. I've never even imagined it on any woman in my fantasies, but for some reason, I'm intrigued. As soon as the thought enters my head, I shut it down. I seriously need to stick with the hate; that's all the bitch deserves.

My mom has finally finished fussing around her and comes to sit next to me.

As Frankie sits down, I glare at her with repulsion masking my scrutinizing gaze. Small waves of hair flutter into her face, and those big gorgeous green eyes shine, her lip curls in amusement. I scowl at her, hopefully distaste in my stare. She has several piercings in her ears. Her top is pulled tight across her chest, her tits bulging. She has ink across her chest, near her right breast, in some script writing it reads, *family forever*. Her right arm has numerous tattoos. Not even girlie shit like roses and butterflies. No, this idiot has: cars, guns, and phrases on her arms, she's a fucking abomination. My lip curls up in disgust.

My dad coughs, and I realize I've been staring at Frankie too long; she gives a smug, white-teeth smile that makes me want to throttle her. I regard my dad with a glare. *What the fuck does he expect?* Bringing the likes of her into our house, he's actually gone crazy.

Mary, our housekeeper, places the plates down in front of us—it's a steak with a side of salad.

Frankie shifts in her chair uncomfortably. I imagine

nobody has ever served a meal to her before, and her idea of a restaurant is probably some fast-food joint. The thought makes me chuckle at how out of her depth she is. *This is going to be fun; the bitch is on my turf now! Fucking bring it!*

5

FRANKIE

When Uncle James first introduces me to Cameron, to say I'm shocked would be an understatement. I'm utterly fucking dumbstruck.

I survey him, and he's wearing fitted jeans with a belt and a tight black T-shirt stretched across his broad chest. His golden skin fucking glows like one of those models in swim shoots. His brown hair is wet and has a wavy curl in it. He looks delicious. Hazel eyes sparkle before he realizes who I am and then they turn to stone. A spiteful, piercing stare boring into my soul, or lack of.

Then I quickly remind myself the prick is probably out to get me with some sort of vendetta. I close my immediate attraction down and turn it into intrigue at his reaction to me. His obvious and clear contempt for me is actually somewhat amusing. He can't help but look down his stuck-up, arrogant, rich-boy nose at me. He's openly checking me out, scanning me up and down with a vicious snarl. I'm not even sure he realizes he's doing it until Uncle James coughs, and then hethrows James a vile stare. His lip is curling up in disgust as if to say where the fuck did you drag her from?

Well, my dear little stepcousin, I've been dragged from the depths of hell, and I'm going to thoroughly enjoy being in this prissy little world of yours. I may as well make the most of my life as a fancy fucking princess. *Bring it on.*

The room is quiet, apart from the chiming of cutlery against the plates, when Josie breaks the uncomfortable silence after what feels like a lifetime.

"So, Frankie, James tells me you lived with your mother in Hawks Town, how was that? Did you get along well?"

I stare at her, open-mouthed, unsure how to play this one out.

Fuck it, I go with the truth. "I hated the dumb bitch, and the day she died was the happiest day of my life." *There you go, how do you like that answer?*

Josie's mouth gapes open, her fork clatters to her plate. Cameron's fork is stilled halfway to his open mouth, and James is sitting bolt upright, tension radiating from him. Josie glances to James in question. "Your mother passed away?" she asks meekly, a quiver to her voice.

"Yeah, she died when I was thirteen," I state.

Josies annoyance and anger bores through toward James. "I thought you said Frankie was living with her mother?" she scolds James.

"That's what I thought," he replies, panic lacing his voice.

I laugh at the tension, waving my hand around to ease everyone's discomfort. "It's fine, seriously, the bitch died. I'm over it." I shrug to emphasize it's no big deal.

Josie and Cameron look at me as though I have three heads.

Then my dumb ass uncle asks the most stupid of questions. "Are you sure she's dead?"

I cut into my steak and ignore him, placing a bit in my mouth, and I continue eating, savoring the tenderness; this is some good steak.

But quizzical eyes drill into me from each direction, encouraging me to elaborate further.

I throw myself back into my chair with a huff, and I drop my utensils. I'm pissed. *Am I sure she's dead? How fucking stupid is he?*

"Of course, I'm fucking sure she's dead. What a dumb question for someone who's supposed to be so goddamn smart!" I snap back, glaring at him. Josie's spine straightens at my tone and no doubt my colorful language. Poor dear isn't used to someone like me.

"How do you know?" Cameron prompts, but his eyes are low as if he's struggling with the conversation. He swallows thickly, making him look uncomfortable in his questioning.

I visibly breathe out heavily so they know I'm pissed. "I know because I was there."

James shuffles awkwardly with the line of conversation. "How did she die?"

And then . . . I snap. I'm sure my face appears like it's going to explode, but I bite my lip between my teeth and breathe deeply, just how my anger management classes have taught me.

I take a moment before schooling my anger and tone. Gently, yet patronizing, I address him. "I can assure you, Uncle James, she's one hundred percent dead; drug overdose, obviously." I roll my eyes and stare back at him.

"Your mom's dead?" Cameron repeats, softly, more like a statement than a question.

"Jesus, yes, she's fucking dead. I walked into the trailer to a fucking awful smell; like seriously, it was toxic. Anyway, she was there on the floor, rock hard, green vomit coming from her mouth and nose, all dried up, of course. Needle still in her arm. But she was a white color, like a wax thing. Blue lips and she fucking stunk! Like I said, one hundred percent dead!" I'm trembling trying to keep my temper.

I close my eyes and soothe myself before I reopen them and pick up my knife and fork and continue with my meal, hoping it hasn't gone cold.

I chance a peek at Josie, and she has tears running down her face; clearly, she's melodramatic. James is still surveying me with uncertainty, and I'm not quite sure what Cameron's problem is, his scrutinizing gaze is unnerving. *Is he trying to assess me? Fucking weirdo.*

"Did you call the police?" James asks.

"What do you think?" I raise my eyebrow.

James nods back in understanding; he knows this isn't something that we'd do. We don't ever call the badges, ever.

Josie uses a tissue, then makes a noise at the back of her throat, then she speaks louder for me to hear her. "Where've you been living, Frankie?"

"I moved in with family." I throw James a smug grin as

Josie smiles at me, happy with my reply, but I can feel the death glare from James.

"Who?" he snarls.

"Excuse me? What the fuck's it got to do with you?"

"I'm your guardian. Of course it's got something to do with me!" he demands.

I choke in annoyance. "Oh, you're my guardian now, are you? Well, you haven't been doing a very good job of guarding me, have you?" I'm seething, and my blood is boiling. How dare he, the prick.

I look from each of them and find only myself still eating.

James's tense body starts to relax, as if he's talked himself into staying calm. "Where did you go after your mother died, Frankie?" he asks me in a nice, placating voice, almost condescending.

A voice that I replicate when replying. "Well, Uncle James, when I found the decomposing body of my mother, the whore, I quickly packed a bag and made a run for it before her pimp arrived to collect me as overdue rent payment. I then hot-footed it to the only decent home I've ever known. My friend Aiden is in foster care, and I stayed there with his foster mom, Mable." I smile sweetly.

Josie has her hand to her chest, and the poor woman looks like she's going to faint. I watch her from the corner of my eye, and I can't help but feel sorry for her. Cameron catches my gaze and must see my concern. He takes his mom's hand and squeezes it. "It's okay, Mom, Frankie says she was in foster care, right, Frankie?"

I nod in agreement and smile at Josie. "That's right, I was, but it wasn't official or anything." I waft my hand in the air.

Josie glances at James. "What does that mean?"

I peek at her and speak softly to placate her. "It's fine, it just means, I didn't have an official place to stay. You know she didn't get paid to have me, so I didn't get a bed or anything." She gasps, tears fill her eyes. *What the fuck did I say? What's wrong with her now?* I shrug and back track. "I mean I got a bed, it's just Aiden would have to take the couch if there wasn't a spare one in the house, you know, if it was a busy time."

"Did you have a funeral for your mother?" she asks gently.

I laugh to myself. "No! She was probably bagged up or wrapped in a carpet or something when the Johns or pimp found her; they probably set her on fire or something, right?" I gaze toward James for assurance. He nods his head, agreeing with what I'm saying. James knows too well that someone in our circumstances would have been disposed of like rubbish. Like the trash society lets us believe we are.

She pushes her plate away as I continue to finish my meal. Clearly the ungrateful fucks can't be bothered to finish their meals; they've barely even touched them.

"We need to talk!" she snaps at James, who sits there stoically.

He turns to me. "Go to your room, Frankie. I'll speak to you in the morning. You too, Cameron."

Cameron jolts in disgust. "It's eight o'clock!"

"Then do some schoolwork, watch TV, play video games, but find something to do and go to your goddamn room!" his sharp voice bellows.

I jump up from my chair and leave the room. I can't quite help myself as I spit the word out at him. "Prick!"

6

CAMERON

I've sat through some enlightening and boring meals in my eighteen years, but never have I sat through one that repulsed me the way this one has. Frankie gave insight into her life, and it sounds like it's been complete and utter turmoil. Worse, it's been a fucking living hell.

The girl didn't even have a bed for Christ's sake. And here her uncle is, living as a millionaire in a fucking mansion.

I study James, and for the first time in a long time, I don't want him to be my dad—he doesn't deserve the title. He's let his own flesh and blood down, and I can completely understand and agree with the animosity Frankie feels toward him.

How the hell can he not have realized her mother died? And why the hell was she living with her in the first place if her mother was a drug user? A whore? The woman had pimps and dealers around her and her teenage daughter? Jesus. The thought turns my stomach.

I go through the meal in my mind again, recalling Frankie's body language. Understandably, she was getting frustrated with the questions regarding her mother but what shocked me the most was the concern and shock evident on her face when my mom was getting emotional. Frankie seemed like she couldn't understand why my mom would be upset or sympathetic toward her. She referred to her "family" as one of her friends, and I assume that's one of the guys who attended court. *I wonder which one?*

My mom's sharp and irate voice stops my thoughts. "What the hell is going on, James? Is it true? Is Frankie's mom dead?"

My dad acts uncomfortable, fidgeting with his hands in his lap while looking down, he's struggling to make eye contact with us. "I'll hire a private investigator first thing in the morning. I hate to admit it, but, Jodie, her mother was pretty reckless," he says, grimacing.

"Then why the hell would you leave her with her mother?" I spit.

James's head shoots up from studying at his hands. "Get to your room, Cameron, like I asked!" He thumps his fist on the table, making the plates clatter.

I stand and push my chair back, glaring at him in disgust. "I have to agree with Frankie, you are a prick!" He bristles at my words, and I storm out of the dining room, returning to my room.

I throw myself on my bed and stare up to the ceiling. Fuck—what a day!

I decide to call Joel; he's been wondering if James's

niece is a hottie, and he warned me to call him with a low down. Well, he's not going to believe me when I tell him who she is.

"Hey, man, how'd it go?"

I scrub my hand down my face. "Bad, real fucking bad."

Joel laughs. "Is she a dog?"

I laugh at his words. "No, unfortunately not. Fuck, it's complicated." I exhale deeply.

"Man, you're killing me here. Was she hot?" He's chuckling to himself, as usual.

I breathe out. "You remember the girl the night of the fight?"

"Yeah, course, is she as hot as her?"

I chuckle, disbelieving my own words. "It *is* her!"

"What? The girl who took your car?"

"Yeah."

"No fucking way! The girl who set you up?"

"Yeah, her, man. It's fucking her!"

"No fucking way!"

"Believe me, I couldn't believe it myself. I was like a fucking fish with my mouth flapping open. Jesus, I still can't believe it!" I rub my hand through my hair in frustration.

"Did she recognize you?"

I smile to myself when I remember Frankie's eyes meeting mine. "Yep."

"What did she say?"

"Seriously, Joel, all fucking sorts of things. I mean nothing about that night, thank fuck. But my mom went all fucking maternal on her and was asking her all sorts of personal shit."

"How personal?"

I laugh at my sex-obsessed buddy, he's constantly fucking horny. "Nothing like that dipshit. Anyway, the shit she was telling us . . . Jesus, man, she's like a walking fucking psychotherapy patient."

"No shit. Did you expect anything otherwise for a girl living somewhere like that?"

I nod, even though I know he can't see me. "No, you're right. She's bound to be fucked up."

"Yeah, she is. Anyway, is she still as fuckable?"

My body goes still. If Joel thinks he's going to fuck her, he can think again. There's no fucking way that's going to happen.

"We aren't going to fuck her, man. We're going to fuck with her!" I grin inwardly.

Joel laughs, and in a mocking begging tone, says, "No, please, my dick's ready for some new pussy."

My voice sharpens. "No, Joel, I'm serious. I need some fucking revenge for that night. The bitch has landed on her fucking feet here, and you can guaran-fucking-tee my dad has enrolled her at Trent Valley High."

"Okay, game on, so what do you suggest?"

I smile to myself as I start to formulate a plan.

7

FRANKIE

I slept like a queen in this ridiculously humungous bed. Never in my life have I so much as sat on a bed as big as this, let alone slept in one. The sheets are like silk or something—whatever the fuck they are, they're amazing.

I stretch my arms above my head like a cat.

There's a gentle knock at my door, and I quickly scan my eyes around to remind myself where the hell I am.

"Who is it?"

"It's Grant, Miss. Master James asked you to join him for breakfast."

"Okay, I'll be right down."

I throw the blankets off of me and quickly make use of the bathroom, freshening myself up as I wash my hands. I inspect myself in the mirror and decide to put my hair in a messy bun. I glance down at my sleepwear and a small scheming smile graces my lips. My camisole top is tight around my breasts, exposing my tattoos. It's short enough to ride up my waist, offering a peek of my belly button stud and below that, a tattoo that reads *Nate* across my lower stomach.

My sleep shorts ride high, leaving nothing to the imagination, I turn in the mirror and see my ass cheeks hanging out. *Perfect!*

I practically skip down to breakfast.

As I enter the dining room, Cameron is seated in the same place with his back to the door. My uncle peers up toward me and chokes on his coffee with a "Christ" mumbled under his breath.

"Morning!" I singsong as I saunter toward the same chair as last night, directly in front of Cameron. I can feel his eyes on me as I walk past him. Then I notice the fruit on a plate to his left and decide to double back. I approach Cameron and purposely reach over him, brushing my breast against the back of his shoulders. I help myself to an apple from his plate. I feel him go rigid beneath me. *Mission accomplished.* My uncle's eyes bore into me as I move back to my seat.

"I slept so fucking good last night!" I tell them as I munch on the apple nonchalantly. I'm well aware their eyes haven't left me, but I make sure not to let them know I notice.

The door opens and in walks Josie with a tray of food. She's beautiful, her brown hair tied in a bun on her head. She has the same hazel eyes as her son. Where her soft smile is genuine and graceful, her son seems to have a cold permanent scowl. Her eyes peek at me in shock, but she quickly masks it with that same sweet smile.

"Morning, Josie, I was just telling the boys how well I slept last night." I smile sweetly.

Josie maneuvers around the table, setting plates down, and her simple elegant dress flows beautifully as she works around the table. "That's wonderful, sweetheart, I'm pleased to hear it. We both are. Aren't we, James?"

"Yes, of course." His sharp, deep voice tells me otherwise.

I glance toward him and decide to ask him, rolling my eyes. "Go on, what's wrong?" I cross my arms over my chest, emphasizing my cleavage even more.

He pushes his plate back and takes another sip of his coffee, careful not to make eye contact with my chest. "I'd prefer you didn't wear nightclothes to breakfast, Frankie."

I innocently peek down at myself. My nipples are erect, and honestly, it's because of the air conditioning. I gaze back up at Cameron, and his eyes meet mine in a smug smile. He thinks he can intimidate me by blatantly checking me out. News flash . . . I don't give a shit.

"Well, I'm sure you've seen worse." I shrug.

"What I have or haven't seen is not the issue. The issue is I want you to wear more clothes at the dining table." His I-mean-business voice is on.

"Well, maybe the issue is . . ." Before I can say anything else, Josie interrupts me.

"I'm sure Frankie understands, don't you, sweetheart? It won't happen again." She nods at me as if I'm to agree.

I smile back at her. "Sure."

James picks up his pills and swallows them, and as I glare at him, I silently hope the fucker chokes on them.

"So, seeing as I'm abiding by all your archaic rules,

how about you give me something in return?" I ask with a raised eyebrow.

Cameron looks at me and narrows his eyes, he's trying his best not to stare down at my tits, and it just makes me smile all the more.

James sighs as if he's expecting this conversation. "Go on." He motions with his hand.

"I need a phone and a car."

Cameron erupts from his chair. "A fucking car? You're kidding, right? Tell me you're not getting her a fucking car!"

"Sit down!" he spits at Cameron. "You can have a phone, Frankie. I've actually already got you one. But it will come with stipulations."

"Of course it will," I snipe sarcastically.

"You're not to have any contact with your old friends."

My head fucking explodes. "You mean my family? I'm not to have any contact with my family? Is that what you're saying, James?" Anger is radiating off of me. *How dare he?* How fucking cruel to try and extinguish them from my life. He can turn his back on his past, but I sure as hell can't.

I concentrate on my breathing exercises when all I want to do is whip his coffee out of his hand, poor the boiling water in the silver jug over his fucking face, and then stab the butter knife through his eyes, gauging the smarmy little suckers out.

Breathe, Frankie. I close my eyes and think of the guys.

"You know what, Jimmy . . ." I softly snarl, and his back goes rigid at the nickname from his former life. "I'm not sure your new family know all that much about our past; shall we share some old stories?" I ask him as I push the cereal around my bowl. I view him from the corner of my eye, his body is now full of tension. He knows he's pushed too far; he knows I'm about to let it out and let rip.

He clears his throat and waves his hand. "We can negotiate on the phone; the car is a no."

"How the hell am I supposed to get around?"

His head turns toward Cameron, and I almost choke on my cereal at Cameron's mortified reaction. "No fucking way!" He shakes his head furiously.

"We'll discuss the matter after breakfast, Cameron." Cameron's body sinks into his chair, poor guy.

"Maybe we can work toward a car?" Josie politely suggests.

Cameron grumbles to himself, and I can't help myself. "Maybe I can work toward a license too?" I smile, knowing full well he'll be pissed.

Cameron pushes forward in his chair, leaning over the table. "You mean you don't have a fucking license?" he sneers.

I smile and shrug my shoulders. "Nope. I mean I can clearly drive. Just not officially, you know?"

His face is mortified, and its fucking hilarious. I bite my lip to stifle my laugh.

He gapes at James and then back at me, utterly shocked, mouth agape.

I lift my glass of orange juice and wink at him before taking a sip. He's too easy. Poor boy acts like he's going to explode.

Cameron spends the remaining time stabbing his food and giving me disgusted death glares. His mother seems oblivious to his little tantrum, and James is not biting either.

James gets up and walks over to a cabinet behind him, he opens the drawer and returns to the table with a new laptop and iPhone box. He slides them toward me. "Here. I expect you to use them wisely."

I slowly pick the phone up and make eye contact with him. I can clearly read between the lines, and I'm not sure if he's purposely telling me the phone is monitored, or if he's trying to give me a subtle warning.

Whatever. I decide to go with an innocent response and to keep my phone interaction clean. "Thank you, James. I can't express how much I appreciate this." I tap the phone box and smile at him. He nods and graces me with a genuine smile. Fucker has definitely tapped this phone.

James clears his throat. "Frankie, tomorrow you start at Trent Valley High School. Cameron will see you arrive there safely and return you home."

Cameron has stilled in his movement; it's obviously news to him. I actually feel a little bit sorry for the rich dick. I mean, James never has a conversation, he just demands, and you do as you're told, end of story.

My body sags at the thoughts of going to a new school, especially a posh, prissy fucking school. I peer up from my cereal and see Cameron smiling at me. Yes, the fucker is already planning my demise.

Josie begins clearing the dishes away and offers to take me shopping with her. I decline and decide to hang out the house today. I've yet to explore the mansion.

"Your uniform is hanging in your closet. Be ready to leave the house at eight in the morning." James speaks sharply to me, as though dismissing me and telling me he won't see me for the rest of the day.

I narrow my eyes at him. "Are you not sticking around today? Won't you be here for dinner tonight?"

He straightens his shirt collar. "No, I'm going away on a business trip for a couple of days; you'll be in capable hands. I expect you to behave." He doesn't meet my eyes, and I'm not sure if he's being sincere or feels guilty for leaving.

I focus on Cameron for guidance but he's still wearing the smug grin.

So, I decide to do what I do best, put my I-couldn't-care-less-what-life-throws-at-me face on. I shrug at him as I rise from my chair. "Of course I will behave, I always do!" I wink at him as I leave and throw Cameron a sly smile back. His face drops, and he decides to glare at me instead. He can't work me out and doesn't like it.

CAMERON

Frankie leaves the dining room, and I'm relieved and pissed. Relieved because sitting opposite her with her fucking nipples on show is making my fucking cock ache at the side of my zipper and pissed because, what the hell? She stole my car and doesn't even have a fucking license to drive it? How fucking dare she.

"You can't buy her a fucking car!" I snap at my dad.

His head rises slowly from his breakfast. "I don't answer to you, Cameron. You don't get to tell me what I can and cannot do!"

"I understand that, but I'm just saying, I don't think she should be trusted with a car."

He studies me sharply. "Is this you still being pissed at the fact she stole your car?"

My body stills, and ice runs through my veins. *What the fuck? He knew? All this time and he hasn't said a word to me!* I can't mask my shock quick enough. I thought I managed to cover the car going missing as a theft. I paid my investigator to keep it quiet.

He laughs. "Please, Cameron, give me some credit. Of course, I knew. You were actually the one to help bring Frankie back into my life. I just wasn't aware of how far she'd fallen"—he shrugs—"but I will tell you this, Cameron, as I've told you before, I am aware of your activities, inside and outside of school, and I'm warning you now . . . *No more illegal fights.* Do you hear me?" He points at me with emphasis, the veins at the side of his head bulging. When he acts like this, I don't recognize him at all. He's so Jekyll and Hyde.

The silence between us is stifling, and my jaw tenses. I bite the inside of my mouth in annoyance. The only reason he doesn't want me to fight is because he wants our family to portray a clean-cut persona. *What a joke.*

But what really pisses me off is he knew all along where my beloved Bugatti Chiron was, in fucking pieces, thanks to the little bitch he calls a niece. Not only that but the only piece I have left of my father is gone with it!

I'll never forgive or forget the trailer trash piece of shit for that, and with James away for a couple of days . . . I might start getting a bit of my own revenge.

"I'm expecting good things from Frankie when she starts school. I'm sure given the opportunity of a good education she can reform herself. I'm sure you'd agree everyone deserves a second chance, Cameron." He looks at me pointedly.

His eyes bore into me as he watches me closely, assessing me, waiting for me to acknowledge his dig, so I appease him. "Of course I do." I nod in agreement.

James smiles at me but it doesn't reach his eyes and then he claps his hands together. "Good, that's settled, then. Oh, actually, I'd like to just mention I expect the feud between you and Chad Wilder to be finished by now, am I right?"

Of course he expects that, he plays golf with his father every other weekend.

I give my own patronizing smile. "Of course me and Chad are on speaking terms."

"Good, I don't want any more embarrassment coming from you." He points at me once again.

I glare at him and nod before I make a quick exit. I'm desperate for a fucking joint and to get the hell out of this fucking show home.

8

FRANKIE

I'm awake early Monday morning and recalling the conversation I overheard Cameron have with his father yesterday morning. James knows I stole Cameron's car, and he also knows Cameron has been doing illegal fighting. I'm sure the fighting thing pissed him off more than anything. More than the trouble I got in and more than the fact his son's car was destroyed. James obviously likes to keep up appearances, and his son fighting isn't one he wants to maintain.

I've made a mental note to find out who Chad Wilder is. Sounds like Cameron had some sort of disagreement with him, and you never know when I might need one of his enemies, either former or current, on my side. If nothing more, I'm sure it'll piss Cameron off for me to make friends with this Chad dude.

I decide to shower and pamper myself a little in preparation for the day ahead. Anxiety is flowing through me, and I seriously need to psych myself up. I could do with a joint, and that's going to be one of my first things to sort out at school today. I need a hit desperately.

I glance down at this pompous fucking uniform: a pleated navy-checked skirt with red detailing, a long-sleeved white shirt and red tie with a navy *TV High* logo on the bottom, followed by a navy blazer. I've also got to wear navy stockings and navy glossy high heels, all uniform. Even the backpack is school issued. *What the actual fuck!*

I've also read in the handbook that only one set of earrings are allowed, no tattoos, hence the long-sleeved shirt, no belly button rings, no other jewelry, apart from a Christian cross necklace—*yeah, right*—no makeup, which is not a problem because I rarely use any.

I spray myself with perfume and apply some lip gloss, grab my bag, and go down to the kitchen to grab something to eat before school.

In the kitchen, surprisingly, Josie is bustling around. I sort of expected the staff to be making breakfast and serving it. I climb onto a barstool. "Hi."

Josie spins around to face me with a sweet smile. "Oh, morning, Frankie. Wow, darling, you look beautiful!" I blush at her response; I don't think I've ever been called beautiful before. Hot! Sexy! Fit! Fuckable! But not beautiful.

She smiles softly at me and offers me a plate with pancakes. "Oh, thank you."

"Would you like some fruit with those? Or maple syrup?"

"Fruit, thank you." Josie passes me a bowl of fresh berries to pour onto the plate.

I eat them quickly as she stands over me smiling at me with her hands on her hips, clearly pleased with my clean plate.

Before long, I hear Cameron's shoes on the marble floor. I turn around in my chair. "You ready?" He glowers.

His tone of voice tells me he's still pissed so I decide to play extra nice. "I am. Thank you for taking me, Cameron. I can't tell you how much I appreciate it." I smile to Josie who smiles back at me. She's happy I'm trying to win the rich, pretty boy over, and his glare tells me he knows exactly what I'm doing.

"Come on, then, I don't like being late!" he snipes the words out, and I roll my eyes, causing Josie to giggle at me.

"You two have a good day!" she calls out as we leave the house. I turn around and give her a beaming smile and sweet wave.

The red Audi R8 is waiting by the front door as Cameron strolls to the driver's door and gets in. I follow and get in the passenger side, dropping my bag between my feet. He swiftly pulls away from the house and down the drive.

We're about five minutes into the drive and utter silence, not even any music on, and I make no attempt to hide watching him. He's seething about something, and he's also hiding behind his sunglasses, which, of course, had to be Ray Bans. So fucking predictable. His hair is wet as though he's just showered, body gleaming. *Does he bathe in baby oil? So fucking hot! God, he smells good.*

"What the fuck are you staring at?" he spits out with venom.

Ah, so the stubborn prick has noticed I'm watching

him. I sigh. "Just trying to figure out why you're in a pissy mood."

He scoffs. "You're kidding, right?" He gives me a sideways glance before his eyes snap back to the road, annoyed with himself for even peeking at me.

"Nope, not kidding."

His knuckles are white on the steering wheel. "I'm pissed I have to drive your sorry ass to school, for a start."

I roll my eyes. "I could have drove if you'd have preferred." I smile to myself, knowing it'll piss him off a little more.

Again, he shoots me a look. Shame I can't see those damn sexy hazel eyes, though.

"Are you trying to piss me off more?"

I shrug, unsure if he's seen the gesture. "I mean, it's not difficult, you're a little uptight, are you always like this?" I poke.

His body tenses, and he chokes on his words. "Fucking uptight? I'm not uptight!" His veins in his neck protrude.

I wave my finger at him mockingly. "Yeah, you are! You either need a joint or a good fuck. That's what I do when I'm uptight."

His head spins toward me sharply, he studies me up and down, then his head snaps back to the road. His fists tighten on the steering wheel, his body is radiating anger, and I've noticed he's driving faster. Probably can't wait to get to school.

"I'm pissed I have to share a car with the girl who stole from me, for a start, then having to listen to your bullshit and share a house with you, really fucked me off. And for the record, I get plenty of good fucks, so I don't need any."

I shoot forward in my seat, raising my voice. "For the

record, I wasn't fucking offering! And the whole 'you stole my car' bullshit, seriously, buy another. I'm sure good old Uncle Jimmy has plenty of money to throw at you. Seriously, you need to get over it!"

"It wasn't just the car," he says calmer, so softly I almost miss it.

"So, you're pissed about the fight? The money? Well, Bale won that fight fair and square, and the money, you shouldn't have bet that much if you weren't prepared to lose it," I nonchalantly explain.

He laughs. "Fair and square? Really? I shouldn't have even been fighting that guy and you know it!"

I slink back in the seat. I'm getting annoyed and it's getting us nowhere. "Well, you weren't the only one who lost a lot that night, Cameron, so stop with the pity party."

He steals a glance at me again. "Yeah, well, I lost more than you think."

I turn my body and gaze out the window. My voice is a whisper, in the hope he doesn't hear me. "Me too, more than anyone could ever imagine."

Cameron turns the car into a driveway, and I sit forward to take in the parking lot. I've never before seen so many supercars. Ferraris, Lamborghinis, McClarens, Aston Martins, you name it, they're here.

They even have fucking limousines parked up. Chauffeurs in Bentleys line the left-hand side of the school. It's a true show of wealth. *What complete spoiled dicks.*

He pulls into a spot, and I notice students around us have turned to watch us, and he grabs my wrist as I go to get out the car. "Don't fucking talk to me at school and be back here by three forty, otherwise get your own ass home."

I peek up to him and smile sweetly. "Not a problem, thanks for the ride." Then I slam the car door with spite.

The school is beyond ridiculously beautiful. It's red bricked with ivy growing up the sides, the driveway and front are pebbled, flowers line the walkways, no litter or graffiti in sight. They even have a fucking water fountain. *How pretentious!*

I make my way to the entrance, two large wooden brown doors are opened inwards, so ignoring the stares and whispers, I lift my chin and make my way inside.

CAMERON

I stand beside my car as I wait for the onslaught of students to approach me and find out who the hot new girl is. Leaning against the car, I ignore everyone and scroll through my phone. Joel texted to say he'd be here in five, so I pretend to be focused on my phone, while really, I'm replaying this morning in my head.

As soon as I woke, I was pissed at Frankie, because the first thing I thought of while my dick was rock hard, was her and her big green eyes shimmering when she smiles, even though it's usually a cocky smile. Then her fucking tits, they're not even fake, I'm sure of it.

I shake my head and try to dispel the thoughts, the last thing I need is another fucking hard-on, because as determined as I am to not give in and fuck my hand while thinking of Frankie, I fucking failed epically.

Being close in the car didn't help, she smelled all citrusy and fresh, with those fucking heels on and her skirt riding up as she sat in the car. Yeah, my dick was at half-mast just being close to her. I wore sunglasses so I could hide the fact I was watching her. The more I crave her, the more I hate her.

The moment she mentioned the fact she stole my car, my blood boiled. She thinks I'm pissed at her for smashing it and me losing the fight and money. She's wrong! So fucking wrong! But I'm not going to tell her why I'm pissed. It would make me appear weak and vulnerable, fuck that.

Then she goes and mentions I'm uptight? Me? And I need a fuck because of that? Like she does? What the hell? I'm fuming, she fucks when she's uptight? That just pisses me right off, the thoughts of her fucking people. And she says it as though it's nothing.

Then I tell her not to speak to me at school, and she replies "no problem"? What the hell? Girls normally beg to speak to me, they throw themselves at me and our friends, yet she's happy not to speak to me?

Fuck, I can't figure her out, and you know what? That pisses me off.

I shake my head to dispel the thoughts. "Hey, dipshit, I'm talking to you!" I snap my eyes up and see Joel sauntering toward me. "Cam, seriously, I've called you three fucking times and you were staring into space. What the fuck is wrong with you?"

I narrow my eyes, I hadn't heard him calling me. "Sorry, I've got things on my mind."

"Sure. Like the sexy little stepcousin?" His eyebrows wiggle in jest.

I laugh and shake my head. "No, not her." *I'm such a fucking liar.*

"Fuck, watch out, Stacey's on her way over here!" I roll my eyes at Joel and wait for her bitching to begin.

"Cameron, where the hell have you been all weekend?

And why the hell haven't you returned any of my texts or calls? And Delia said a girl got out of your car this morning? What girl?"

I sigh as I listen, I can't quite catch on to what she's babbling about because she's firing that many questions at me. "Are you listening to me, Cameron?"

I brush my hand through my hair with a sigh. "Yeah, you're pissed I haven't been around this weekend!"

She throws her platinum blonde hair over her shoulders—it's fake like the rest of her, like most of the girls in this school, fucking fake. Fake nose, fake hair, fake lips, fake tits, and fake personality. And me? I'm fed up with fake. My mind darts back to the foulmouthed, sassy, tattooed, pierced, fucked-up hottie I'm living with who is anything but fake.

My fists clench in my hand, pissed at myself for thinking about her.

Stacey's arms wrap around my waist and my spine jolts. "What's wrong, Cammy?" *Fucking Cammy? Jesus.*

"Nothing's fucking wrong, apart from the amount of bitching you're doing!"

She moves and stands in front of me, hands on her hips, probably fake. I mean, I know she wants ass implants for her birthday. She pouts her big red lips, and she looks hideous. "Who was the girl getting out of your car this morning?" She stomps her foot to emphasize how pissed she is.

I breathe out. "Her name's Frankie, and she's my stepdad's niece."

"Well, what is she like?"

I watch her before answering honestly. "She's not like you."

She smiles a megawatt fake smile with the fake teeth, happy with my response. It wasn't meant as a compliment though.

She throws her arms around me and stands on her toes, kissing me gently with her big lips. She grinds her waist into me, trying to get me hard. *Yeah, not fucking happening!*

I glance at Joel who is eyeing me with amusement. I flip him the bird and throw my arm over Stacey's shoulder. If I'm playing all lovey dovey with her, she best fucking blow me tonight.

9

FRANKIE

I'd half expected to be given a tour guide around this prehistoric place, but I'm relieved to find the app on my phone gave me all the information and maps I require; it literally has a little dot showing me where I am and a dotted line showing me where to go next.

My mind is blown that people would waste money on shit like this, yet back home we didn't even have enough chairs in the class for all the kids. I shake my head as I think about the differences.

So far today, I've endured English Literature, Chemistry, and History. Luckily, I haven't shared those classes with Cameron—the blatant stares and whispers are bad enough, I really don't need any unnecessary drama. I can't say I've made any friends, and honestly, I couldn't give a fuck, I'm here to get the work done and get out.

Thank God it's time for lunch. I follow my little mappy

through the corridors, ignoring the obvious silences, cat calls, and giggles as I go, and walk into the . . . cafeteria?!

I gaze around in awe. It's like a fucking restaurant with servers delivering food to the tables. *Where the hell is the counter with the food on display?* I watch people on their phones and realize I need to pull the app back up. Yeah, you order your freaking food on your phone.

I scan the room and look at the groups of people milling around, the usual setup, popular jocks, nerd group, odd group, cheerleader group, then I spot the table I'm going for—the outcasts.

There are three kids sitting at a table for about twelve, one black guy, one olive-skinned girl, and a messy-haired dude that does not belong in this school, he's grungy-looking.

I drop my bag and plonk myself down on a chair opposite the fit dark-skinned guy as I finalize my food order.

"Did I say you could sit there?" He's pushing a salad around his plate.

I smile at him as his dark eyes meet mine. "Nope, but I didn't ask."

He watches me curiously, as do his friends. "Why are you sitting at this table?"

"Why the hell not!" I cross my arms defiantly.

He watches my movement and smirks. "You're new." He points his finger at me.

"I am. Observant, aren't you." I grin back at him cheekily.

He throws his head back and laughs. "I wouldn't say I'm observant, but I'd have noticed you." He shrugs. "What's your name, then? Seeing as though you've invited yourself to sit with us."

"Aw, seeing as though my invite has been accepted, my name is Frankie. Who are you guys?" I ask waving my hand between them.

The girl beside me speaks up first. "I'm Jess, this is Ollie with the crazy hair, and the dude giving you rude attitude is Leo."

"For the record, I don't fuck white chicks, if that's why you're over here," Leo declares with a bright smile.

I crack up laughing. "Well, thank you for that enlightening, but I can assure you as gorgeous as you are, I sure as hell am not interested! No offense but I've had my fair share of dramas, and I don't intend on having any more."

Leo beams his megawatt smile on his sexy face. "Then I'm sure we'll get along just fine." He nods in approval.

"Is he always like this?" I ask Jess.

"Yeah, he's pissed because every white girl in this school must have thrown themselves at him, just to have a taste of the only black guy in school. It's a status thing with them."

My eyes bug out. *Is she serious?* "You're kidding me?"

Jess shakes her head and chuckles sweetly. "Nope."

I don't know if I'm more shocked at the fact that Leo is the only dark-skinned kid, or the fact that these bitches make him feel like he's some sort of trophy.

I clear my throat. "Well, you probably don't get laid too often, then, am I right?" I ask as I regard the room, absolutely mortified at the amount of white rich kids there are here.

Leo laughs. "I go to parties and shit but it's still hard to find someone outside of these." He motions with his hands, but his face and voice are clearly oozing disgust.

"Well, my friend, I think today may be your lucky day.

Because where I'm from, white kids are probably the minority and I have a heap of friends who would kill to hook up with you, so tell me, Leo, what floats your boat?" I smile a sly, knowing smirk.

Leo's face is a mixture of shock and joy, and he chokes on a chuckle and sits back in his chair, draping his arm over the empty seat beside him. "I mean, I'm not opposed to a white girl, just none of these. I've got a thing for Latinas but as you can see, we're in a major shortage of those." He stares around the room in disappointment.

"A very good friend of mine just so happens to be a Latina, Leo, and I'd love to hook you guys up. Apparently, she's got a mouth like a hoover and fucks on the first date, assuming you ply her with tequila!" I wink at him.

Jess starts choking on her meal, as Ollie starts rubbing her back, laughing at her response. She takes a drink of water. "Ar . . . are . . . are you serious?"

I eye her quizzingly. "Are you serious you can hook him up, for, you know what?" she asks sheepishly.

I study the girl beside me, confused. "For a fuck?"

Her eyes widen, and she swallows hard. *Jesus, is this his girlfriend?* "Oh shit, are you two a couple or something?"

"What? NO!" Jess screeches, and Ollie chuckles beside her. "No, we are not a couple! I don't date guys, that's all."

"Oh, are you gay?"

Her eyes bug out even wider. "No, I'm not gay." She's getting all flustered now.

But now I am confused, and my face must read it. My meal appears in front of me, and the server is gone before I get to thank them. *This is fucking crazy!* I start eating the burger and fries and motion with my hand for Leo to explain what's got Jess's panties in a twist.

He laughs to himself. "She's celibate, a true good girl, Christian."

I gawk at Jess, the beautiful olive-skinned girl with tight curls and plump pink lips, she's a little goddess and she's never jumped on one of these pretty rich boys? "You're shitting me?"

She laughs nervously and tucks a lock behind her ear. "No, I really am." She sits a little straighter, proud of herself.

"Well, I mean, cream your jeans. Good for you if it makes you happy." She seems to like that because she gives me a genuine smile and hugs my arm?

I'm sitting in silence a few minutes, minding my own business, munching on my fries when Ollie interrupts my thoughts. "So why've we got a table of pretty boys glaring at us. What did you do to cause their frown lines?" He mocks and gestures with a nod to the front of the cafeteria.

I move to the side and peer over Leo's shoulder the same time Leo turns around to regard the pretty-boy table, he stares back at me with a raised eyebrow.

I sigh and sink back into my seat, because, sure enough, I have attracted the attention of a table of pretty boys and overly pretty fake girls.

Outright glaring at me with pure hate in his eyes is Cameron, he has a fake-as-fuck girl sitting on his knee, even though this school has enough chairs for all the kids.

Anyway, she's playing with his hair, which to be honest, seems like its pissing him the hell off. His head keeps moving away from her, and his body is tense and straight, although I'm sure that's more about the anger he's got radiating toward me than anything else. Next to him is the guy from the bar the night of the fight. He's smiling over at me with a mischievous glow. His hair is long on top and short at the sides, and he appears broader than Cameron, and I must admit he's hot too. They must have different water here.

Fuck my life, why the hell do they all have to be so fine? They're surrounded by a few more guys and half a dozen girls all flirting and fawning over one another, it would be amusing if it wasn't so sickening.

I smile tightly back at Leo and then throw a sideways glance at Jess and Ollie, taking a deep breath, I explain, "Long story short, I'm from Hawks Town, stole pretty-boy Cameron's car, crashed it. I got sent to juvie, my uncle bailed me out, moved here to live with him and he just so happened to be married to Cameron's mom." I openly exhale.

Leo cracks up laughing, Jess's mouth is wide open, and Ollie can't get his words out quick enough. "N-no fucking way!"

"Yes way. I fucked up and now I'm sent here as punishment to reform my character!" I gesture quotation marks on this last part.

Ollie starts laughing. "I'm sorry but that's fucking hilarious! No wonder Cameron is throwing you the evils."

I twiddle my fries into the ketchup. "He's an uptight motherfucker, that's for sure. I'm talking legit grumpy; he needs something to loosen him up!"

Leo dips his head, shaking with laughter. "Let me guess, you've got a few friends he could fuck to loosen him up?"

"I have actually, but according to him we're trailer trash, so he can go and fuck himself or those bimbo, fake-looking Barbie girls over there, he needs to stick to his own." I nod toward his table.

"Couldn't agree more, that table is like a fucking orgy, seriously, they've all fucked the girls, and they just pass them around. The girls act as though they're all better than everyone else but they're just sluts, rich, fake, sluts!" Leo says.

I nod in understanding. "Anyway, I need a favor." I bat my eyes at him.

He shakes his head. "Should have fucking guessed, go on . . ."

"I need a phone and some joints, desperately!" I plead.

Ollie responds first, "I can sort the joints, no problemo. You do realize you have a phone, right?" He motions toward my phone on the table.

"Yeah, it's from my uncle, and I'm pretty sure it's got a tracker and he'll be monitoring and reading all my texts."

"Absolutely, if there's one thing I've learned in this school, it's you can't do a fucking thing without someone knowing about it. You need to watch yourself with Cameron, though, he can be a sneaky little fucker, and if he's got it in for you, his littles bitches will be right there in front of him."

I sneak a peek at Cameron, and sure enough, the whole table, including the girls, are staring right back at me. "Shit," I mumble, realizing that my time at this school is not going to go as plain sailing and easily as I'd originally planned.

Leo snaps me back out of my worries. "I can get you a phone by tomorrow, if that's good? Be about a hundred bucks."

Relief waves through me at the thought of contacting my boys. "Yeah, that's great, thank you."

The bell rings and over the tannoy a posh, strictly spoken woman informs us that our relaxing lunch hour will be concluding in ten minutes. *Seriously?!*

CAMERON

From the moment I walk into the cafeteria, I'm searching the room for Frankie; I haven't had any classes with her so far, and if I'm being honest, I was a little disappointed.

I sit in my usual seat, and Joel drops his bag down next to me. Neo, our IT geek, sits opposite me. He's a whizz in technology, and his mind has no bounds with the knowledge it holds. Not only is he an asset as a friend but he's also loyal and trustworthy. Joel may be my best friend but Neo is a very close second. We're pretty much a trio, the only difference between us and Neo is he doesn't like how we are with the females. Sure, he fucks them, but he goes in for a relationship, not the whole one-night thing or the usual guy locker-room chat. He doesn't like hearing or sharing shit on girls, and that is Joel's favorite subject.

"So, Dane was telling me he's got a fucking hot piece of ass in his history class!" are the first words out of his mouth, not even a hello. My spine goes rigid at Dane's description of her. Neo watches me studiously.

I don't reply to Joel's little comment, and continue my

observations of the cafeteria. Neo's openly watching me and then he glances over his shoulder, probably to see what I'm looking for. His eyes narrow at me, he can't read what he sees, so instead turns his attention to his meal in front of him.

My pasta is delivered, and I'm just about to put the first forkful in my mouth when Stacey drops her ass onto my knee and wriggles herself onto me. I have to push my chair out to make room for her. I hate the fact she sits on my knee when there's plenty of spare chairs. She does it to try and make it look like we're a couple. The whole we're-together thing. I shake my head away from her as her fingernails make their way up my neck. She's all over me in public but goes cold when we're alone, unless she has alcohol, then she'd fuck anyone or anything.

Joel's excitement snaps me out of it. "Fuck, she's there!"

All our heads whip in the direction of Joel's gaze, of fucking course she'd sit at their table. I can feel my blood boil as I watch Leo Nessia laugh at whatever she's saying, followed by Jess and Ollie. Frankie's eyes sparkle as they all interact, the group are clearly in awe of their new friend, and I can't help but feel jealous at whatever it is they're sharing. I swallow the jealousy down.

"Oh my God, it's that girl who was in your car this morning, isn't it?" Stacey spits out with hostility.

"Who is she?" Taylor, Stacey's fake-redheaded friend, asks. Both girls now glaring daggers at Frankie, purely because the guys at our table have now erupted in comments about "new girl has got a great rack, she's got a mouth that needs fucking, her ass is so tight. Chad is going to try and fuck her first?" *WHAT.THE.FUCK!*

Over my dead body is Chad fucking Wilder going anywhere near Frankie.

"She's Cameron's stepcousin!" Joel declares, wriggling his eyebrows with a broad, proud smile on his face.

I sigh, as the table falls silent and all eyes land on me for confirmation. "Yeah, she is. She's also out of fucking bounds; she's a lying, thieving, little trailer trash tramp who won't be around for long, so by all means have fun fucking with her, just not fucking her!" I point at them all with narrowed eyes.

"Ew, you have to share a house with her?" Taylor asks in disgust.

"Yeah," I muster back and continue eating my pasta while openly firing death stares at Frankie. Her table seems to be reveling in something amusing because they haven't stopped laughing with one another, and it pisses me off all the more.

"I can feel your tension, Cammy, do you want me to help you out?" Her nickname for me prickles at my nerves, and I feel like swatting her roaming hands away from me as she runs her fingers through my hair and down my neck.

I stare up at her and her pouty mouth, her long straight hair touching her knees. "Yeah, for fuck's sake, stop calling me Cammy. What class do you have next?"

She fidgets in her seat, she doesn't like being told what to do. "I have Home Economics, why?"

I smile back at her. "You don't need that shit, do you? You can blow me in the locker room when the bell goes."

I glare at Joel, he's smirking, digging into his burger, stealing another look at Frankie as she shovels fries in her mouth. I glance around our table at the girls, and most aren't eating, the ones that are, they're eating salads, not a burger or fries in sight. *Why does she have to be the complete opposite?*

"Why is she wearing a long-sleeved shirt like a weirdo?" Stacey asks. Her voice is whiney, and that's another reason why I'm excited to shove my cock in it, to get her to shut the fuck up.

"She's got tattoos down her arm, so she has to wear it due to school policies." I shrug at my answer but sneak a peek at Joel whose eyes are alight.

I roll my eyes and shake my head at him, and Neo chuckles. "Fuck, this girl is going to cause some shit around here!"

Joel sits forward on his seat and leans over me. "What sort of tattoos?"

My eyes snap back up to meet his. I'm fucking annoyed at the interest he's paying her. "How the fuck would I know?"

"Ugh, who has tattoos? And on a girl, what a fucking tramp!" Stacey glances to Taylor who is nodding in agreement, and her comments rile me.

Once the bell rings, I make my way to the empty locker room. I'm supposed to be in Double-Languages, but I might as well be bilingual, so it doesn't matter, what matters is Stacey is going to give me a blowy instead of sitting in a boring-as-fuck class. I stand behind the door, hearing the corridors clear out, scrolling on my phone as I wait.

The locker room door swings open and in sashays Stacey. I lock the door behind her and grab her arm, spinning her around. She releases an exaggerated fake laugh, but I try not to acknowledge it. "I want you to take me to

Jenna's party on Friday, can you do that, Cammy?" And just like that I'm back to being pissed off. *Fucking Cammy!!!*

I'm tense again and fucking annoyed that she won't listen. "Take your top off and get on your knees!" I snap.

She looks at me and pouts. "Only if you agree to take me to Jenna's, as your date?" she asks before glancing away, her attention on her long painted fingernails.

I roll my eyes at the game she's playing, she wants to parade me around in front of her friends as her boyfriend, even though I've told her that's not what we are.

"I'll take you but not as your boyfriend."

She plays with her hair now, twisting it, pissing me off that she's wasting time. "And you won't fuck anyone else?" Her eyes watch me from under her thick fake lashes.

I throw my head back and laugh. "I won't fuck anyone else on Friday, even though we aren't together, happy?"

She smiles gleefully and claps her hands together; she can't be fucking serious. I cringe.

"Do you have a condom?" she asks as she starts unbuttoning her blouse.

That piques my attention, my dick starts getting hard. "We gonna fuck?" The words leave my mouth so fucking fast I can't disguise my excitement.

"No, I'm not going to fuck you at school, Cammy. Jesus! I just don't want to get your cock juices all over my mouth. I have an ulcer in my mouth, and I can't deal with it, so it's either a condom or no blowy," she whines again.

I sigh and tug at my hair. *Why the fuck does she have to be so goddamn difficult?* If I wasn't so invested in a blowjob right now, I'd tell her to fuck it.

I dig into my wallet and pull out a condom, taking my cock out of my boxers. I have to help it along with a few tugs, and luckily Stacey is now on her knees before me, and I can see her bare tits poking straight ahead. I grimace, that should help the visual but the fact they are so fake is not helping me at all. I try shaking my head to rid me of the visions of her fakeness.

I'm fucking annoyed when thoughts of Frankie's tits enter my head. I slide the condom on and move toward Stacey's open mouth, her big eyes stare up at me robotically, like she isn't into this at all. "You sure you want this?" I have to ask to be sure. She nods her head eagerly, like a nodding dog, too fucking eagerly. I sigh.

I shove my dick in her mouth so fast it makes her choke, and I smile to myself. I hold onto her head, and she immediately pulls out of my mouth with an obnoxious scowl. "Can you not touch my hair, I only had it done yesterday!" She glares at me in contempt.

Is she for fucking real?

I grab the back of her head and push her forward to my dick again. Once I'm in, I let go and look down to the girl moving her head backward and forward on my cock. I'm struggling to get fucking excited and close my eyes. Swallowing hard, I let thoughts of Frankie consume me.

Perfect fucking face that lets me unleash on her mouth, fucking it harder and faster, her groans escalating my pace. She moves her hand between her legs and starts touching herself, faster and faster her hand moves. All the while pushing her face further into my groin, all the way to the back of her throat. She's such a dirty girl, enjoying this as much as me, greedily lapping the juices in her mouth, her tongue working over the head of my cock. Her other hand massages my balls as they tighten in anticipation, my own groans joining hers as we climax together.

Fuck yes, my dirty girl. I bite my lip on a groan.

"Fuck, yesss! Suck it all the way down!" I've grabbed her head again without realizing, shooting my come into the rubber.

My body sags when I open my eyes and see a disgruntled fake platinum blonde looking up at me. "Did you have to touch my hair, Cameron? Jesus! You've no idea how long it takes to have this perfection created."

I roll my eyes and pull off the condom, marching toward the bathroom, dumping it into the toilet, flushing it down. I make my way out of the bathroom to find the locker room already empty. For some reason, I deflate. Clearly Stacey got what she wanted. *I guess I got what I wanted, didn't I? Then why do I feel so empty?*

I scrub a hand through my hair in annoyance. I best get to Languages and show my face.

FRANKIE

Double Fucking Languages?! What the hell was my uncle thinking?

I can speak various languages but read them? Write them? Yeah, that's a big fat fucking no.

The teacher introduced herself as Mrs. Adams, she's nice enough but a little too interested in me for my liking. I'm not sure if I'm her new little project but I sure as hell don't like the attention she's giving me. She's given me a test paper to see where I'm at with languages, and I'm not surprised to realize I know fuck all.

I'm halfway through the test when the door to the class swings open and in waltzes Cameron. He's very windswept, his golden hair unruly, his shirt half untucked, and quite frankly, he's sporting the just-fucked look. I bite my lip as I think how incredibly fuckable this guy looks.

He sees me straight away and smiles a smug smile before eyeing the empty seat beside me and a cocky grin graces his pretty face. Mother. Fucker. I groan internally.

"Mr. Donovan, where have you been?" Mrs. Adams snaps.

"Been busy in the locker room." He shrugs, feigning innocence.

The class erupts in laughter and fist bumps. They're childish behavior makes me roll my eyes as he drops his bag down beside me and proceeds to slump into the chair next to me. This is the closest we've been to one another, and it makes me a tad uncomfortable.

Cameron's lazy body language screams "can't be bothered."

"We're working on course three, section four, get to work, Mr. Donovan!"

Cameron huffs and drags his workbook out of his bag, dropping it on the table we're sharing with a thud. He flicks through the pages and sets about his work.

I can feel his eyes on me and the paper I'm working on, he's watching me from the corner of his eye. Making me self-conscious.

"What?" I snap, narrowing my eyes at him.

He uses his pencil to flick the hair beside my ear out of the way. "What's with the star?" He's referring to the blue star tattoo, the one me and the boys all have.

I smooth the hair back over the tattoo. "Nothing to do with you."

Cameron chuckles, enjoying the fact he's riling me. He continues to watch me and the answers I'm writing, his scrutinizing gaze unnerving me.

"I thought you were meant to be good at languages?" He chuckles to himself.

I frown and look at him, confused. "When did I say

that?" I've never said that, we've never had a proper, civil conversation.

He shrugs in response. "Hate to inform you but you're shit at languages."

I turn toward him and give him my attention. "I'm sure you don't hate to inform me I'm shit at languages, Cameron. But," I point out, "I never claimed to be good at them. Besides, maybe I'm just shit at these languages. Maybe, I'm amazing at other languages, there are over six thousand languages, after all." I smile a patronizing smile back at him.

"Huh, I doubt that. Doesn't take a mastermind to figure out the answers you're giving there are because you're that uneducated and dumb, the only language you speak is that Hawks Town's slang you spill." He smiles a patronizing smile back.

He starts laughing to himself in a mocking tone, then points to my sheet. "You don't even know the basic French words."

"Je connais beaucoup de mots de base pour t'appeler, en commençant par l'un de mes favoris, ta bite!" *I know a lot of basic words to call you, starting with one of my favorites you're a dick!* I snark back at him.

He stares at me open-mouthed, gobsmacked. I can't help but widen my grin.

"Miss Vadetta, you are not to use foul language in my class, do you hear me?"

I nod at Mrs. Adams, and she gives me a knowing soft smile. *Yep, I think I like her.*

"What the fuck did you just say to me?" Cameron whispers so close to me I can feel his breath on my neck.

I shrug at him. "I'm sure being the amazingly educated bilingual rich boy that you are, you can figure it out."

The rest of the lesson is pretty much in silence. I can't believe the contrast to my old school, the rooms were alive with some hustle and bustle or another. I gape around the room in wonder.

How many kids from my old school would actually achieve something given the same opportunity as these kids here?! It's sad to think how worlds away our education systems are. I lower my head in shame. I'm here and I don't even want to be, yet some poor kid would give anything for this opportunity. I swallow the guilt down thickly.

"What are you thinking about?" Cameron asks, breaking me out of my little pity party for one.

I clear my throat, unsure whether to be honest. I go for a different take on my original thoughts. "Just thinking how different this is from my old school. You know, the no fucking each other in the classrooms, the teacher teaching the class not the TAs, no smoking joints in the classrooms, and so on." I fake a laugh to disguise the severity of my acknowledgments.

Cameron laughs at me, then watches my face. My serious face.

He rubs his hand through his hair. "Shit you're serious, aren't you? Kids fucked in your old school, in class?" His eyebrows shoot up in complete surprise.

I laugh a little myself. "Yeah, they did, not in every class, but if they could get away with it, they would. You know, putting on a show for everyone else kind of gave them some weird school cred for their reputation," I explain, lifting my shoulder on a shrug.

Cameron about chokes his words out, "Yeah, there's a name for that, you know."

"Voyeurism," I reply before he can explain.

His eyes widen in shock, and he fidgets. "You into that?" He keeps his voice low for only us to hear.

I laugh. "It's live porn, Cameron. I'm pretty damn sure most of this school is into that."

His excitement at my previous words come out slower, and for some reason, his body is more deflated. "Yeah, I guess you're right." He watches me, analyzing me, before his throat bobs and he looks away.

"So, by next lesson, I will be assessing your speech abilities, please use the audio guides online for reference. Francesca, can you please stay behind, I'd like to speak with you."

My lip curls up in disgust at my full name Mrs. Adams uses.

CAMERON

I had English Literature for my last lesson today, and I was bored out of my fucking head. I was also lost in my head, going over my conversation with Frankie. For some reason, she fucking fascinates me—her body, her tattoos, and her life before coming to Trent Valley. I want to know more, yet I hate myself for wanting it.

I can't believe she can actually speak another language; it doesn't make any sense. When I was in the courtroom, her teacher said she outshone in languages and sciences, perhaps he meant she spoke to them but didn't read or write them, because clearly, she didn't have a clue on paper, that's for sure.

I sit in the car waiting for her so we can go home. Stacey has made a big, long show of saying goodbye, kissing me all over my neck. I'm convinced she was lingering around, hoping to make sure Frankie saw her claiming me.

I watch as the doors open again and out comes Frankie

with Ollie Davies in toe. She smiles at him and waves him off, then walks toward the car.

Getting in and dropping her bag to her feet. "Fucking finally. My feet are killing in these things!"

I can't help but laugh at her, even though I want to maintain a dissatisfied scowl. Her heels are off her feet in no time, then she starts fidgeting in her seat, and I almost crash the fucking car when she shoves her skirt up and proceeds to drag her stockings down her legs. "Fucking Jesus, I'm all for wearing some sexy suspenders and stockings in the bedroom but wearing these things for school? Seriously, this school is governed by some old masochistic pig, isn't it?"

I'm speechless, her bare legs on display as she shuffles the skirt back into place, her snarky, dirty mouth, and her raw sense of humor knock me sideways. She's fucking hot in so many ways, and I'm not even sure she knows it. My dick is harder than it was when Stacey was sucking me off earlier today, how's that right?

"Am I right?" Her words snap me out of my dirty thoughts.

"What?"

"Am I right, a man governs the school board?"

I shrug. "I guess so."

"Knew it!" she cheers triumphantly.

We sit in silence as I try not to think about her comments. *"Sexy suspenders, bedroom."* I rub my hair in frustration. *Jesus, what is she doing to me?*

I clear my throat. "What did Mrs. Adams want to discuss with you?"

She huffs. "She clearly thinks the same as you. That I don't know shit about languages."

"You tell her you can speak French?"

"She heard."

"Yeah, course she did," I agree. Frankie isn't telling me the whole story, and again, I want to know more but decide not to ask. I don't want to appear too interested.

Before I know it, we're home and my body is laced with disappointment.

10

FRANKIE

Today seems to be going better than yesterday, I had Math with Jess. Leo was in my ICT class, although we didn't sit together, and although neither one of those subjects held my attention, it was quite the insight in comparison to my former schooling.

When I make my way to the cafeteria, I feel all eyes on me. I don't let my eyes roam to the table near the entrance. I can already feel his presence and I'm sure as hell not acknowledging it. After leaving his car yesterday, I didn't see Cameron for the rest of the night, and this morning he was waiting in a different car, a top-of the line Suburban, and the music was on today. No doubt as an excuse not to speak, he just mumbled the words, "Three forty" to me as I left the SUV.

Jess has explained to me how the cafeteria works, all main meals and desserts are hand-delivered to your table, via the app, but if you want any side orders, such as breads, fruits, etc., you grab a tray and help yourself to the frequently replenished table at the back of the room.

I glance at the table I sat at yesterday and Jess waves me over. I hold my finger up to indicate I'll be back in a second, and she nods her head with a smile.

I decide to go over to the table, it's manned by a server who offers me a tray, this is like some up-market buffet-style shit, I'm quite impressed. I grab a nice fruit salad.

As I walk back to the table, hushed voices make me aware I'm being spoke about. Looking ahead, I see the fake blonde that was on Cameron's knee yesterday and her little sidekick, the fake redhead, beside her, and they're completely blocking the path in front of me. *Oh goody!*

I fake indifference and continue walking toward them, she stops directly in front of me with her palm held out to stop me, swinging her hair over her shoulder for emphasis. She's loud as she opens her mouth to the audience. "So, bitch, I heard you're some sort of trailer trash whore, a loose slut that stole my boyfriend's car and crashed it in jealous spite!" she spits the words out while sneering down her nose at me.

Sneaking a peak at Cameron, he's sitting back on his chair, watching the show before him, his lips curl into a smug grin. Yes, the fucker is enjoying this. What a bastard.

Well, let's give them a show.

I sigh with annoyance. "Listen, plastic Pammy, I haven't got a problem with you or your pretty little boyfriend over there." I point toward Cameron. "If he's got a problem with me, he needs to grow some balls— preferably with pubes because I can't deal with little boys —and speak to me about it. Now, if you don't mind, shift your fake ass out the way, I'm done with you." I smile condescendingly.

The room is deathly silent. I'm not sure what she expected but her chest is moving up and down a little too fast and her cheeks are reddening in temper, and her fists clench together.

"What did you say? How dare you speak to me like that? You're nothing but scum, you don't belong here!" she screeches as her veins stick out on her throat. *Wow, she looks freaky.*

I laugh and talk slowly to her in a patronizing tone. "Shit, do you have hearing problems? I am sorry, you do realize they can fix that too, right? You know, along with all the other fake shit you've got going on, you might as well have something fixed that can be useful, right?!" I shrug.

An almighty scream erupts, and to be fair, I'd be impressed if I wasn't suffering from ringing in my ears. "Ahhhhh, you bitch! Stay the hell away from me and stay the hell away from my boyfriend!" At that, she pushes her hand under my tray and launches it up into my face, the fruit salad dripping down my shirt, fruit covering me. *No.she.did.fucking.not.just.do.that!*

The whole cafeteria goes from silent to sounds of booming laughter. I stand there dripping with fruit juice.

Glancing over at the pretty boy table, Cameron is holding his fist to his mouth, trying not to laugh, all his friends are smirking and laughing, high-fiving one another, and phones are out, recording, so I decide to give them something to view, again and again . . .

I dramatically and slowly grab the grape on my shoulder and drop it to the floor. "Well, bitch, I hope you've got that surgeon on speed dial because when I'm done with you, you're going to fucking need one ASAP!" I smirk.

Swiftly I bring my knee up to my tray, snapping the tray in two before the bimbo can blink. I smack one part on the top of her head, bringing her to her knees with a howl. The second part of the tray, I swing and smack it as hard as I can against her face like it's a bat hitting a ball, with a satisfying crack, I release the tray. She goes down like a sack of potatoes, her friend screaming and crying beside me—although she hasn't stepped in to help.

I grab hold of the bimbo's hair, wrapping it tightly around my hand, and start to drag her over toward Cameron, she's spluttering and snotting. Blood oozing from her nose, dripping down her chin. Her legs kicking and flailing as I drag her forward.

The room is wild, kids are standing on the tables watching, and cheering, gasping, and hooting fills the room as I march my crazy ass toward the pretty-boy table.

They're all as dumbstruck as each other. Cameron falls over his feet as he gets up from the table to walk before us. I dump the mess that he calls a girlfriend at his feet, and his face is aghast with panic. "Can you please keep your bitchy, little psycho Barbie girlfriend the hell away from me, otherwise she'll need more of that face rearranging by the time I finish with her," I huff out.

Cameron's mouth opens and closes, not knowing what to say.

I turn around and stride back to the table where Jess is sitting, her eyes bugging out of her head, Ollie is wearing an enormous smirk, and Leo is grinning while tapping away on his phone like a man on a mission.

"Holy fucking shit, babe, I take it back, I wanna fuck a white girl!" Leo announces.

We all burst out laughing.

After the little cafeteria drama, Jess offered me a spare shirt, and I took her up on the offer, but unfortunately it's short-sleeved and busting at the tits. I grimace.

I walk into Physics with my head held high. At the back of the room, I notice Cameron, although he averts his eyes straight away. He's sitting next to a good-looking short brown-haired guy with piercing blue eyes. At the next table, I recognize Cameron's friend, the chair beside him empty. I smile inwardly. *Game fucking on boys.*

I strut toward the empty place and sit down next to Cameron's friend; his eyes are wide as he watches me. He glances toward Cameron, whose jaw is ticking.

His friend shuffles uncomfortably in his chair.

"Hey, Cameron's friend, remember me?" I smile innocently while batting my eyelashes at him.

"Fuck yeah." He grins a megawatt smile. Oh my, this boy has dimples. So damn cute. Why the hell I return the megawatt smile, I don't know but he has a likability about him that reminds me of my friend Romeo, so I smile fondly at the thought and feel instantly at ease.

"Name's Joel." He holds his hand out.

Placing my hand in his. "Frankie."

"Yeah, babe, all the fucking school knows who you are, and that was before the whole breaking Stacey's nose thing." He laughs.

I slump. "Shit, I was kinda going for a few broken teeth too, my bad. Maybe next time, hey?!" I laugh, but honestly, I'm not joking. I do feel a little disappointed. *Perhaps the angle wasn't right?*

"You fucking killed it, the whole Bruce Lee shit, snapping the tray and then slamming her head down. Fuck, babe, that shit got me hard!" Yep, he's definitely the Romeo of the group.

I grin back at him. "You remind me of one of my best friends."

"Yeah? You fuck him?"

I choke and look at Joel, his eyebrows are wriggling. "Actually, no, I haven't. I have a friend with benefits but obviously he's there and I'm here." I wave my hand around the room as I feel myself deflate thinking about the boys.

"Well, if ever you need any help with that, I'll be your friend with benefits, how's that?" His cocky smile enhances his dimples.

"Good to know, Joel." I tap his arm in jest.

Looking beside him, I see Cameron's hand tighten on his pen. He's staring down at his workbook with intensity. I'm sure he's heard every word we've spoken, but I don't give a fuck.

"You know, I prefer the short-sleeved top on you as opposed to the long-sleeved one," Joel jokes.

"I know, right, miserable fuckers don't like seeing my ink!"

"Yeah, that and your tits are spilling out!"

I laugh loudly. "Yeah, they are," I agree, gaping down at them.

The teacher makes introductions and sets the work for the class. We're working in pairs, which has delighted Joel, he's certainly the comedian.

"Thank God they put us in pairs, I'm shit at sciences," I declare.

"That's Neo's department." Joel gestures to the guy beside Cameron, and I bend over to see him. He lifts his hand in a wave, and I smile back at him, ignoring pretty cranky pants.

"Who's pissed on Cameron's strawberries?" I ask Joel.

He turns his body toward me and whispers, "He's probably pissed we're getting on."

"Oh. I assumed it was because I'd splattered his girlfriend's face on the cafeteria floor." I grimace and bite my lip playfully.

Joel erupts in laughter. "Nah, babe, Cam won't be bothered about Stacey, it's not like that. She's more of a friend with benefits." He smiles at me knowingly.

I scrunch up my nose. "Let's hope he wasn't relying on her facial expressions to help get him off, then, hey?"

Joel chuckles. "You're fucking crazy, you know that?"

"Absolutely!" I nod.

The lesson is long and boring. I can feel Cameron's and Joel's eyes on me throughout the lesson. Joel shuffles in his seat and then moves a little closer, dipping his head, and he uses his pen to point at my bare arms. "So, what's with the tattoos? I mean, they're cool and all but how'd they come about?"

I move my jaw from side to side, feeling a little uncomfortable, I'm not sure if I want to share myself with Joel, but when I look into his eyes, I don't see malicious intent, only mischievous intrigue. I sigh and relax. "They all mean something to me, either a first memory or like a dare," I answer honestly.

His eyes meet mine, confused. "A dare?"

"Yeah, you know . . . whoever wins gets to choose the tattoo type thing."

Joel nods his head with a cheeky grin and chuckle, then he says, "You lost to some fucker and had to tattoo 'cockblocker' on your arm?"

I laugh. "Exactly, but you should see the state of his arms, he's lost a lot!"

Joel laughs and taps his pen against his lip. "That could be really fucking fun, what tattoo would I get?"

Without thinking, I say the first thing that comes to mind. "Dipshit." We burst out laughing, drawing attention from Cameron, and he scowls in our direction, and I swear to God, he growls. I point my pen in Cameron's direction. "He'd get miserable bastard!" We snicker like a pair of kids.

CAMERON

Seeing Frankie annihilate Stacey in the cafeteria was fucking incredible, like how the fuck did that happen? Where did that fire come from?

Stacey went from verbally slaughtering Frankie to being shredded herself. Frankie can more than hold her own in a heated row but add in the whole physical fight thing, and *wow!* I've never seen anything like it, but the most surprising part? She appeared so fucking controlled. Yet I'd have said Frankie was anything but controlled, she was normally so goddamn reckless.

She disappeared not long after the incident. I'm not sure if she was getting a warning from the principal or if she's run off to hide, realizing she'd gone too far?

Earlier, I got Neo to hack into Frankie's school app, and now I know exactly what classes she has, when and where she is. So, it isn't a surprise when she walks through the door to the Physics class I am in. What does surprise me is her air of confidence. If I thought for one minute the fight at lunch was going to knock her down and deflate her, that went out the window with the look of defiance she swings my way.

I'm beyond pissed that she plonks her sexy ass down beside my best friend when there are other available spaces to sit at, is she doing this just to piss me off? It's working. My jaw is so tight I'm surprised it hasn't fucking locked.

I immediately notice she's changed her shirt. Let's face it, all the fucking class must have noticed. All eyes are on her and her tattoos, not to mention how tight the shirt is. Her tits are full and straining against the buttons. Joel must have a raging boner, at least that gives me something to smile about, how fucking uncomfortable he must be.

Joel, of course, brings out the big guns with his flirty banter, and Frankie is lapping it up.

My body radiates tension. Neo nudges me. "Calm the fuck down, man." I ignore him and move as close to the edge of the table as possible, to listen in on Joel and Frankie's conversations. Joel wastes no time in talking about her tattoos. I'm fucking mortified to think she did those as a dare? A game? She's fucking insane. I was also hoping to ask at some point about the other tattoos she has, at least now I know they all have some sort of meaning, either a dumb game or an important memory to her. I guess they are the same in Frankie's world.

My day seems to go from bad to worse because when the day finally ends and we spill into the corridor, what do I see when glancing at Frankie's locker? I see Chad fucking Wilder leaning against it, chatting to Frankie with a big mother fucking grin on his smug ass face. I can't take it anymore; I've had enough today. I storm over to the locker and push myself between them, knocking Chad away with my shoulder.

"Hurry the fuck up, Frankie, I've got shit to do tonight," I snipe the words out and glare at her with venom.

She fucking huffs and rolls her eyes. "Apologies, Mr. Fucking Happy, I'm done." She slams her locker shut and follows me when I turn on my heels and fast walk over to my car. I'm raging inside, boiling, how fucking dare she enter my life, my house, my school and turn everything upside fucking down.

She slams the car door, making me jump, before letting rip. "What the hell is your problem?"

I'm biting my lip in temper as I speed out the parking lot. "You. You're my fucking problem. Why can't you stay out of my fucking life? Coming in upsetting shit, taking what's not yours!"

She huffs and her veins bulge out the side of her temple. "Are you fucking serious? I upset shit? Your fucking girlfriend attacked me first! And what the fuck are you talking about, taking what's not mine?"

I sag in my seat; she doesn't fucking get it. I'm not about to explain. "Just stay the fuck away from me and my friends, Frankie."

She turns her body away from me and peers out the window. I expect some sort of fight from her. But she doesn't give me one, why the fuck doesn't she fight back? Silence consumes the car as we're almost home.

Sighing with a low, defeated voice she says, "I didn't want to come here, you know. I asked to stay in juvie; I didn't have a choice." She vulnerably fidgets with the hem of her skirt. "James takes what he wants and doesn't give a fuck what anyone else wants. Anyway, I don't want this, same as you. So don't think otherwise." She snaps her mouth shut as we approach the house, and before I get chance to ask her what she means, she jumps out of the car and heads inside, leaving me alone with my thoughts.

Why the hell would she want to stay in juvie? She'd rather be there than here? What's the deal with her and James?

I take the steps up to the house two at a time, lost in my own mind when I enter the front door. I can hear the echoing sound of James's bellowing voice from his office, and I know straight away he's home early because of the incident at school today. And he's going to be pissed about it. I push my hand through my hair with a grumble.

I slow my approach to his office, making sure they don't hear my feet squeak on the marble floor. I listen intently.

"I had to fly home early, Frankie, to deal with this shit! Seriously, you broke her fucking nose, are you insane?" he seethes.

Frankie sighs. "Seriously her nose wasn't all that pretty, someone had to do it for her."

"This isn't a laughing matter, it's your second day! I've had to do some major groveling at that school to keep you there. Stacey's father is a well-respected member of the board, and he's livid!"

Frankie snorts. "Well-respected? Well, he needs to teach his daughter some respect; she's a grade-A bitch."

His voice booms as he stomps his fist down hard on his desk. "Enough! I want no more of this bullshit. I've given you the fucking opportunity of a lifetime, use it!"

His voices softens. "You can accomplish your dreams, Frankie, if you just fit in and do as I ask."

She laughs mockingly. "My dreams? You don't give a shit about my dreams, James; you wouldn't have taken me from my family if you did."

"They're not your fucking family!" he snipes back, his tone laced with venom.

She erupts. "Like hell they're not! You might have forgotten what that means, Uncle Jimmy, but I sure as hell haven't. You can banish your past from your life, but I'm not going to banish them. So you can screw your fucking dreams, they're not mine!"

What the hell is she talking about?

He tries to placate her. "Frankie, I just want you to give this a shot. If after high school you feel the same way, then by all means, go back. But between now and then, I want you to have no contact with the prick that landed you in the shit to begin with, do you hear?"

Silence engulfs the room.

Frankie's voice is so softly spoken I hardly hear her, she sounds wounded, nervous, and vulnerable. "How much do you know?"

"I know everything, Frankie, every fucking little detail. So, I'm warning you now, he's out of the picture, do you understand?" His words are hard and borderline hate filled. I wish I knew what the fuck they were talking about. It's got to be something to do with the crash.

I hear her push her chair away. "Understood, loud and clear."

I move away from the door and into the kitchen.

After doing my homework, I head over to my closet and pull out my old gym bag, searching for answers. I dig out the file I have on Frankie from the bottom of my bag; the one the lawyer I hired put together for me. I flick through the few pages until I reach the sheet I'm looking for. Her rap sheet. A list of offenses and misdemeanors: numerous arrests for stolen vehicles, agg-robbery with deadly weapon, evading arrest, arson, possession of cocaine with intent to supply, possession of a loaded weapon without a license, assault. The list seems endless, and how the fuck James managed to get Frankie off of this is beyond me, it also quickly makes me realize that not only did it not give me a fucking clue as to what was truly going on with her, but she has a lot of fucking secrets. And I want to know them all.

I'm going to watch Frankie Vadetta and figure this shit out.

11

CAMERON

I really didn't want to attend this party, especially with fucking Stacey. *Why the hell I agreed to this, I don't know.*

I'm sure the promise of an abysmal blowjob has something to do with it.

I'm sitting with her cooing in my ear, her whiney voice grating on me. She's done nothing but talk about utter nonsense since we arrived here: the latest clothes, the best plastic surgeon, how expensive her family vacation is turning out to be. Like I give a fuck. She's bitching about everything and everyone, her so-called friends are no exception; her backstabbing has no bounds.

I gaze around the room and see Chad Wilder and Leo talking to someone, and my body tingles, and I know at that moment she's here. I can sense her. Chad laughs at something and throws his head back, and I have an overwhelming need to snap his fucking neck. My fists clench beside me.

He leaves and then I see her. My heart races faster as I take her in; she's fucking stunning in a short red dress and matching red high heels. My cock hardens in appreciation. I'm fucking doomed.

As if sensing my gaze, she stills in conversation with Leo and glances my way. She offers me a small smile, and I scowl at her in return, causing her to roll her eyes and ignore the fuck out of me.

I'm so fucking mixed up where she's concerned.

I down my drink and go to get up only to have Stacey tug me back down. "Sit, I'll get someone to bring us drinks, we are seniors, after all." She laughs as she throws her hair over her shoulder while trailing a hand up my chest. Her sharp nails are digging into my skin, but not in a sensual way, its fucking annoying.

"Oh my God, who the fuck is that?" Taylor's shrill, excitable voice exclaims.

We all stare in her direction. A broad-shouldered guy with an air of danger surrounding him enters the room. He's wearing chunky unlaced boots, black jeans, and black T-shirt that's tight across his muscular chest. A black leather jacket stretches over his shoulders, and he has a cigarette hanging loosely from his mouth. He's clearly out of place here. My first thought is, *shit's about to go down*, but as I work my way up to his face, my stomach fucking sinks. Bale!

All the girls are fucking swooning and the guys are hero worshipping this piece of shit. He gazes around the room clearly searching for something, or should I say someone?

I scrub my hand down my face—you've got to be fucking kidding me.

Her face lights up when she realizes the change in atmosphere is due to the scruffy prick with a shit attitude, and his face breaks out into a tight grin as his arms envelop her into him. She falls into his arms with her hands around his neck as he kisses into her hair.

My fists clench beside me. "Ew, of course he's come from wherever the hell she came from!" Taylor snipes, her attitude soon changed.

"What's he even doing here?" Stacey asks. *Is she talking to me?*

"You want me to ask him to leave?" Seth, one of the quarterbacks, asks me.

I shake my head. If I agree to that, it's going to cause some shit. I couldn't give a shit about his or Frankie's feelings, but I've seen this dude fight, and I'm not giving him the satisfaction. No, I'll sit back and watch this play out.

FRANKIE

I wasn't expecting Bale to come to the party. I only mentioned in text this week that this is where I'd be. He said he had business up north and he might stop by on his way home. I hadn't thought anymore of it, and I certainly didn't expect him to waltz right into a rich-kid party and pull me into his arms.

"You are so fucking hot, Star!" he tells me as he pushes me away, scanning me up and down.

"Why thank you, my little bad boy." I grin up to his dark eyes.

"Miss me?" His cheesy smile spreads up to his eyes.

"Of course! Miss me?" I ask cheerily.

"Nope, not even a little." He laughs.

"Yeah, right. I know you miss me, Bale. Admit it," I tease.

"Yeah, yeah." He pulls me back into a hug before dropping his arm to wrap around my shoulder, he tugs me back into him as he perches his butt on a barstool that's against the wall.

"Do these rich kids know how to party?" he asks with a raised eyebrow.

I scrunch up my nose. "Not even a little!"

He throws his head back, laughing. "You need to loosen up." He digs into his jacket pocket and pulls out a thick joint.

"You miss me or this good stuff?" he asks playfully, his mouth curling into a smirk.

"Both!" I snatch the lit joint from his fingers before taking a long drag, enjoying the taste. *Fuck, that's good.*

"So, how's it going? Honestly, Star." He knows me too well, and my shoulders slacken under his knowing gaze.

I glance down at my hands and then back up to his eyes. He must see the turmoil or unhappiness in them. He moves my hair from around my face and drapes it over my shoulder.

"Hey, look at me, what's wrong?" He uses his hand to raise my chin so I can meet his eyes.

I swallow harshly, my voice full of the sadness I feel. "I want to go home, Bale. I don't fucking belong here." I wave my arms around the room in explanation.

Bale sighs. "You need to pull yourself together, Star; you haven't got long. Think of it as a test. Finish your time here and then you get to come home, where we'll be waiting."

I nod, feeling slightly better. I know he's right, it's just with all the shit at school, fucking Cameron and his hot body, and the strange push and pull we have going on and then living with fucking James, I'm just feeling vulnerable. When I feel like this, I remember the accident, and I can't go back there. I need to stay away from that and the events after it. I need to stay focused.

I nod again, a little harder. "You're right, I need to man the fuck up. I can do this. I've dealt with way worse shit, this is nothing." I talk myself into my own words, feeling more confident as I say them.

Bale laughs. "Exactly, babe. Enjoy this fucking rich-shit lifestyle for a while, it's probably the only time you'll live like this ever again. Back to slumming it before long." He grins.

After taking a few more hits of his joint, Bale gazes over my shoulder. "What's with the bitches over there, anyway? And the guys giving us the evils?"

I glance in their direction and see Cameron with his hand on Stacey's leg. She's draped over his lap and whispering in his ear, but his eyes are trained on me, and they feel like they're penetrating my soul. My heart speeds up at the intense stare.

"Is that . . . that Cameron dude? The guy you're living with?" Bale snaps me out of our stare.

"Yeah, that's him."

He bursts out laughing, making me glare at him in question. "Fuck, babe, he's got it bad for you. He's outright eating you up."

I shake my head. *No, he has it wrong.* "No, he hates me."

"He probably wants to hate-fuck you, babe. Seriously he hasn't taken his eyes off of us."

Bale's face turns playful, and I know his mood is changing. *Oh shit.* His hand slips down to my ass, and he squeezes it, making me jump. "I need to have a little fun with this, babe." He's chuckling to himself as I roll my eyes at his childishness.

He pulls me closer to him. "I say we give him a show." He winks at me.

"Bale . . ." I warn, trying to put on a serious tone but don't stop him. I should stop him. I peek over my shoulder, and Cameron's eyes are transfixed on Bale's hand cupping my ass cheek. Fucking psycho Barbie is nibbling at his ear. Bale moves his hand inside my dress, climbing up my ass. I study Cameron, and his eyes bulge slightly before he meets my eyes with a glare, his lips are tight, and his jaw is taut. His eyes almost warning me. I look back at Bale, who's now decided to move to my neckline, playfully nibbling at my neck. To anyone else, especially behind us, it would seem like he's devouring me.

I hear a commotion behind me and look over my shoulder once again. Only now to see that Cameron has pushed Stacey off of his knee, and she's sitting on the floor in shock. He's leaning forward on his elbows outright staring at us, almost daring us to go further.

Bale pulls back, making me look at him in surprise. "You want to get out of here? Burger, fries?" I nod in response as he takes me by my hand and leads me out the door.

CAMERON

Seeing Bale's paws all over Frankie makes me experience feelings I've never in my life felt before. My heart is pounding uncontrollably out of my chest. She's throwing her head back, laughing at his jokes as they share a joint.

I'm even jealous of the fucking joint they share.

He caresses her face like a lover would, putting her hair behind her shoulder in a sweet gesture that makes my skin crawl.

His hand on her ass nearly tips me over the fucking edge, is she still fucking him? Did she love him? She doesn't seem the least bit uncomfortable, is she encouraging him? Fuck, push him away.

Stacey is constantly trying to touch me. I keep moving her hands away from me, but she starts to get more and more brazen, trying to open my jeans in front of everyone.

Bale's hand moves inside her dress, and fuck, that does it. I push Stacey away and she lands on her ass, hissing curse words at me. But all I can hear is the beating of my pounding chest. I meet her eyes, and she turns, then Bale pulls her away. I slink back into the couch, not hearing anyone or anything. Only white noise.

Pulling into the garage, I take a deep breath and decide to make my next move, telling myself that it's for Frankie's own good as I march into James's office. His head rises sharply from the desk, his eyebrows furrow as he watches me closely. "Problem?"

I brush my hand through my hair, unsure if I'm doing right, then I remember that cocky prick's hands all over her, and I swallow. "Yeah, it's Frankie. She was at a party tonight and one of those guys she hung about with was there."

His spine straightens, alert. "Which one?"

I lie, not wanting to give him too much information, I know she genuinely cares for the guys she calls family. I shrug. "Not sure, they were cozy." I wince at my own wording.

James's eyes narrow on me. "You think it was the boyfriend?"

My stomach plummets, does she have a boyfriend? Is Bale her boyfriend?

"I . . . I don't know, it's just they were very close, and she left with him."

"When?" he snaps and studies at his watch.

"Maybe an hour or so ago?" He starts pacing, and I watch him, he's getting himself worked up. "Why don't you like her hanging with them?" I prompt him.

He stops in his tracks and spins on his heels. "They're in a gang, Cameron, a fucking gang for Christ's sake, guns, drugs. Why the hell would I want that for my niece?" He grimaces.

I almost ask him why he's never bothered before, but he appears beside himself.

"She has a boyfriend?" I ask, trying not to sound too interested.

His tone has a sharp edge to it. "She assured me it's over. Fucking assured me!" His fists are clenched at his side, he's acting a little fucking insane, and I'm starting to second-guess myself, thinking I'm being clever. *Fuck, what have I done?*

I throw myself into his chair. "Maybe I was wrong?" I shrug.

He watches me carefully before shaking his head. "No, no. You did right, Cameron. I need you to watch over her. She's reckless. I realize that, but they won't get to her. I need her, here with me, I mean, as part of our family." He's rambling, and it makes me fucking question him. I'm seeing James in a new light, and I'm not sure what light that is yet.

FRANKIE

FRANKIE

It's almost two in the morning when Bale drops me off at home on his motorcycle. I creep into the house and slip off my heels so I don't make any noise on the marble floor.

There's a glow of light coming off the living area. "Frankie, my office, now!" James snaps out.

I sigh in defeat. *Fuck.*

I walk to the office and through the open door. James is leaning back against his desk with fucking Cameron sitting in his chair appearing mighty proud of himself, a smug smile on his pretty face. *What the fuck is happening? Have I been set up somehow?*

I stare back and forth from Cameron to James, trying to gauge them. "What's going on?" I ask James, my voice uncertain.

"Enjoy the party?" James snipes.

"Not really. I left early, pretty boring actually." I shrug nonchalantly.

"And who did you leave with?" James breathes.

"Bale."

"Bale?" James questions, his eyebrows furrowing, studying my face for answers to unasked questions.

I shake my head. "Not who you think, James."

He rubs his hand through his hair and raises his eyebrow at me. "Sure about that?"

I gasp. "Of course I'm fucking sure! Unlike some, I know who I've been fucking on the regular," I screech a little too loudly.

Cameron's face falls from smug to shocked. He clearly wasn't expecting my reaction. Whatever he was thinking, he thought he'd get one up on me.

"This Bale, who is he?"

"Family!" I snap back harshly.

He shakes his head. "I'm not going to continue repeating myself, Frankie. You will stay the hell away from those boys! Your ex in particular. I know things, Frankie, and if I have to start using the information to get you to comply, then so be it."

My eyes snap up to meet his, my anger boiling over me at his attempts of blackmailing me into compliance. I give him my own sinister tone. "Remember this, Jimmy. I know things too. You try and take them away from me and I will use the information I have to get you to comply!" I snipe back at him before turning on my feet, then I stop and turn to face Cameron. "As for you, you rat, stay the fuck away from me. I can't stand people I don't trust." Cameron's face falls as I march out of the room, seething.

12

FRANKIE

The rest of the school week dragged on. I have the usual pranks done to me, the ones I expected. A locker full of condoms dropping out when I opened the door, my photos pinned up around school with "slut" written across them. All very original, they actually made me smirk at their pathetic attempts to upset me.

Every day after school, I've been greeted by Chad Wilder and his sweet boyish charm. His blond hair is neatly cut, of course. His light blue eyes no doubt make girls throw their panties his way. He has tanned skin, broad shoulders, and obviously he is a jock. He also doesn't appear to be fazed by me knocking him back daily. I explained on day one that I wasn't interested but he tried every day anyway.

By my second week at school, things appeared to be settling down, that is until Chad greets me by my locker at lunch time. He shifts nervously from foot to foot, and I raise an eyebrow at his obvious discomfort. "Hey, something wrong?"

He brushes his hand through his hair, ruffling it from its usual style. "Fuck, listen, I overheard the guys talking about Stacey getting you back for the whole nose thing. The guys were laughing about it during gym class, and everyone is going to have their phones ready. Anyway, I just wanted to give you a heads-up. I'm kinda thinking it might be something around the pool area. I mean, you're in the pool this afternoon, right?" He sighs. "Maybe watch your shit when you change or something? Listen, I honestly don't know what they've got planned but I just wanted to give you a heads-up." His eyes awkwardly meet mine.

Chad looks at me intently and as I smile my thanks, his body relaxes. "Thanks. For the heads-up, I mean."

He nods and turns on his heel. I sigh and rest on the locker. *Fuck. What's the little hoe up to now?*

I straighten myself out, whatever it is, I guess I'm about to find out. *Can't fucking wait.*

English was uneventful. I couldn't shake the nervous feeling in my stomach with Chad's words of advice playing on my mind.

I'm tempted to dodge gym class altogether, but they'd only get me another time, at least I can expect something to happen now.

I get changed in the restroom, and it's clear something is amiss because the mindless giggles and hushed chatter would have given that shit away before the heads-up from Chad. But I'm still trying to figure out their angle.

The doors to the pool swing open and closed multiple

times by the time I pluck up the courage to leave the restroom, my bag casually slung over my shoulder. I locate an empty locker and place my shit in it, tying the key around my wrist. I tug on the long-sleeved swim shirt I've been made to wear to cover all my tattoos.

I feel like a fucking idiot. It's basically a black full-length T-shirt with a high neck and back in lycra swim material. No doubt I'll be the only moron wearing one.

I leave the changing room and enter the pool area to hushed voices, all eyes on me. I feel completely self-conscious and on display.

All the females on one side of the pool and all the males on another, all looking in my direction. I fidget nervously with the tie on my wrist, straighten my shoulders, and give the "I couldn't give a fuck" look at all the minions.

"Wow, have you seen what she's wearing!"

"What the hell?"

"Why's she wearing that?"

"I heard she had scars and they're fucking nasty."

"So fucking embarrassing."

I move to the end of the group. The teacher completely ignores all the comments, and they are really fucking obvious and loud. There's no way she's not heard any —*what a bitch*.

I glance over at the boy's side, each one nudging one another with smirks, whistles, outright leering at me and my tight shirt. *Pervs!* I roll my eyes.

Cameron is standing at the far end of the pool, my eyes briefly flicking over his abs and working their way up to a smart-ass smirk on his face and a forceful, questionable stare not leaving my eyes.

He seems to be loving every minute of my awkward existence.

The teacher tells us to dive into the pool one at a time, followed by laps so she can assess us individually.

At the end of an uneventful lesson, the teacher asks me to stay behind. I wait to speak with her, the pool area now completely empty.

She clears her throat, leaving her head down, studying her clipboard as though she's reading something. Her eyes darting over the sheets but not actually looking at anything in particular. "I just wanted to say you surprised me today, Frankie, you swam very well."

Something didn't seem right, her eyes are still downcast, and she seems uninterested in the conversation. *What the hell is her problem?*

"Thanks, I guess." I watch her carefully, trying to gauge her strange behavior.

"I didn't expect someone from your background to be a competent swimmer." *Ah, so there it is, someone from my background. Wow.*

"Well, I'm pleased I surprised you." I smile smugly.

She nods, and as I start to walk away, she reaches for my wrist to stop me, still her eyes are cast down. *What the fuck's her deal?*

"Is there something else?"

She glances up at the clock. "Yes, I just wanted to say your dives were good too." *Nah, she didn't want to say shit, she wants to keep me here.*

I cross my arms, annoyed, and snipe my words out, "Thanks, now I really have to go because I'm going to be late for Biology, and Mr. Haze is pretty strict."

She laughs uncomfortably and smiles with a nod for

me to leave.

I stalk back to the changing room with my guard up. The room is empty; all the students cleared out.

Sure, I was a little behind them but only by a few minutes. *What the hell is going on?*

I go to my locker and lift my bag out of it, it's lighter than it was when it went in, that's for sure. *Bitches!!!*

My clothes are gone and no towel. *Fuck!*

I slink down to the bench and quickly think. I open the side pocket where I stuffed my underwear as back up, I have my underwear. *Thank fuck!* Relief rolls through me. So, I guess my options are to go out in my underwear or my swimwear. I mean, I have this cover-up, right? And let's face it, they're all going to be out there with their phones.

Nah, screw that! If I'm doing this, I'm doing it in style. I'm done with covering up for this shitshow of a school. Underwear it is. I smirk at myself, proud of my plan.

I praise the gods that actually give a fuck about me, thanking them for at least making sure I chose a matching bra and panties this morning: a bright purple little number. The bra covers my tits well and also enhances them. I smile to myself as I adjust them, the number of boners there's going to be in that corridor in a minute will be insane. More than an archaeological dig, that's for sure.

My panties are a lacy thong, which thankfully haven't traveled all the way up my ass crack but almost. I wrap my ponytail up into a bun to give a full display of my back tattoos. I mean, if they're going to take photos, they might as well see the full package, right?

I spray myself with perfume, add a bit of lipgloss, straighten my shoulders, and I'm good to go.

CAMERON

I've overheard the chatter between the girls and some of the locker room boys about pranking Frankie during gym class. When she came out wearing the black T-shirt to cover the top half of her body, all the girls were snickering and all the guys were hooting. I stare at her; she's completely unfazed by the inappropriate comments she's receiving. As far as I'm concerned, she's a fucking thief and I need to remind myself of that, if that means getting to see the benefits of some idiot's revenge, then so be it. *Do your best, Stacey.*

The whole class is uneventful but rather than linger around the pool area, the guys make quick work of leaving, virtually falling over themselves to get to the locker rooms. My eyes meet Joel's, and he shrugs, unsure, as we follow everyone out.

As we're getting changed, the guys are alive with excitement. Lance, one of the jocks pipes up. "Fuck, did you see those tits, swear to fuck they're real! Make sure your phones are out, ready." He nods in the group's direction. All the guys nod in agreement.

He lifts his chin to Sawyer who nods in return, then looks back down to his phone. I steal a glance at Chad, he's pissed, his eyes meet mine, and I stare through him.

Joel speaks up. "What's got you all fucking hard, then, Lance?"

Lance chuckles. "Hurry the fuck up and get dressed, you're about to see one hell of a show!"

My eyes go to Joel's, and we both know instantly it's to do with Frankie, and my body tenses.

The corridor outside the locker rooms have never been so busy, everyone is milling around, pretending to be doing something, clearly waiting for Frankie to make an entrance. I'm tempted to leave when Neo asks if I really wanted to watch someone being humiliated. But for some reason, I can't do it. *What if she needs something?*

What if things get out of hand? I scrub my hand down my face and wonder what the fuck could be taking her so long.

As if reading my thoughts, the girls' locker room doors swing open and out strides Frankie. My eyes travel up her body.

She's in her high fucking heels, bare legs leading right up to her skimpy panties, a bra barely holding a knockout rack, her head is held high, and if I'm not mistaken, she's taken her hair up. I swallow hard. *She looks fucking stunning!* My body instantly responds to her, my dick hardening in my pants. *She's so fucking sexy.* I lick my lips, imagining running my tongue over her body.

The noise around me is like background noise; I can hear it, but I can't. Her face is rocking a smug smile and her emerald eyes glisten, but I can see behind them, and I can tell she's pissed. The thought sours my mood, she's hurting behind all the bravado.

She walks past us, not acknowledging our existence as she goes past, and the crowd seems to follow her, their phones snapping away. When I see her perfect ass on display, I can see what they're all clicking at. Her back is a full cover of a hawk, the wings travel down her shoulder blades to her ass with the hawk's body down her spine. It's like nothing I've ever seen before.

She stands tall and proud, and she simply looks above us all. Then she does something that makes Joel go from stunned silent to full on hysterics. She holds up both her arms, her fists in the air, and then pulls out the middle finger on both hands, flipping us all the bird.

Before I know what I'm doing, I'm running after her, pushing through the crowd. I grab a hold of her wrist and just as she spins on her heel, I drag her into the nearest empty classroom, slamming the door behind us.

"What the hell are you doing?" Her eyes are wide with annoyance and shock.

I brush my hand through my hair, sighing. I scan her up and down, my mouth is dry, my palms sweaty. The silence is engulfing the room as I take my time to answer her.

My eyes land on a tattoo below her belly button, it's thick in block letters and reads, "Nate."

"I'm saving your ass." I gulp at my own lie. Really, I can't bear the thoughts of anyone else seeing Frankie like that. So sexy. So naked, exposed, and vulnerable.

She throws back her head and laughs. "Saving my ass? Are you serious?" Her jaw tics in annoyance.

I shrug off my blazer and hand it to her. She huffs before reluctantly taking it and pulling it on. I text Joel to tell him of my plan. Frankie's watching me with suspicion in her eyes. I decide to explain my actions. "I'm texting Joel, he's going to make sure the corridors are clear and then I'm taking you home."

Before she can ask anymore, my phone buzzes with a text from Joel. "It's clear."

―――――

Frankie sinks into the car. "Why'd you help me?" She's fidgeting with her hands, it's what she does when she feels vulnerable. I've picked up on that.

I don't answer. I'm not sure why. Not sure why I don't answer and not sure why I helped her.

I hesitate briefly before peeking over at her. "Who's Nate?" I gesture with my hand to her stomach.

Frankie's mouth drops open with shock as she gapes at me in surprise. She waves her hand in front of her. "I deal with all this shit, and you ask me who Nate is?"

I nod and my jaw feels tight with tension. "Yeah."

She huffs out a breath and stares out the window, and I dart my eyes to her, and she briefly meets mine before swallowing thickly, emotion clear in her voice. "He's family."

I nod. "Was he a dare?" I ask, referring to the game her and her so-called family seem to play to get each other to do dumb shit that leads to an even dumber tattoo.

She swallows hard and peers down at her hands. "Nope, not a dare. A memory."

"A memory," I repeat, like a delusional idiot.

"Ex-boyfriend to be precise."

I feel like I've been kicked in the gut. *What the fuck is wrong with me?*

I stifle a choke into an audible laugh as I try to make light of my jealousy. "You know it's a bit dumb tattooing a guy's name on your body, right? I mean, the chances of them being around when you're older are pretty goddamn slim."

She narrows her eyes at me. "Thanks for the advice, but I'm more than happy with carrying his name around with me." *Is she fucking taunting me?*

My hands tighten on the steering wheel, and I splutter, "You're happy to keep your ex-boyfriend's name on your body?"

"Absolutely, he's family. Always will be!" She lifts her chin in defiance.

I pull my hand down my face in frustration. "You never cease to amaze me, Frankie."

She smiles as though I've given her a huge compliment. "Why thank you, Cammy!"

"Ew, fucking don't! I hate that." I scowl.

She laughs loudly, and I follow, shaking my head.

FRANKIE

FRANKIE

The rest of the week is a breeze in comparison to the beginning. Joel tracks down my missing uniform and I have it in time for school the next day.

I'm not surprised when today, being Friday, I find Chad waiting for me. He's slouched against my locker, his tight smile in place, waiting to be knocked back.

I'm also not surprised that Cameron is still in the hallway, lingering about with a group of girls pawing at him.

Since the first day he saw Chad talking to me, he's taken it upon himself to wait in the hallway instead of the car for me. I'm not sure if it's because he's being genuinely concerned or nosy, but what is clear, is Cameron has a hatred for Chad, but Chad doesn't appear to reciprocate it.

"Hey, handsome," I announce, slowing my step as I approach him.

His lazy smile is cute, I'll give him that. "See, you say

shit like that to me and it gets me right here." He places his hand to his heart, making me roll my eyes on a snicker.

I shake my head. "Seriously, are we going to do this every single day, you might as well save both our time. You're cute and all that but it's not going to happen."

Chad sighs. I can't help but like him, he seems so honest, but I know more than anyone, nobody is ever as they seem.

"Okay, so I guess . . . I'm going to be square with you, Frankie, because I get it, you don't want this." He waves his hand between us and lowers his voice. "The guys have been talking, just locker room shit." He seems a little anxious and my curiosity is raised, so I turn and give him my full attention as he continues on, "They have a wager going, five thousand dollars that I can't get a date with you before Saturday."

I suck in a deep breath. *Motherfucker!* He holds his hands up to stop me. "I know, it's shit. And I get you don't like me like that, and honestly, it's not about the money, it's yours, you can have it." He brushes his hand through his hair nervously. "I got into some shit last year and made some bad decisions, the guys, they're still on the fence about whether I deserve another chance or not." His eyes move over his shoulder and as he makes eye contact with Cameron, he fidgets from foot to foot. "I know it's dumb and morally wrong and all that shit. I never wanted the money, it wasn't about that. I thought you were hot, and when I realized it wasn't going to happen, I kinda figured we could be friends and maybe go out for the night as friends?"

I narrow my eyes at him. "Let me get this straight. You're going to pay me five grand to go out on a nondate with you so your locker boys think you won me over and what? Nailed me?"

He chokes. "Fuck no! Not nailed you. Jesus, I'm not that much of an asshole. I can say whatever you want, didn't work out, had a good time. I stay tight lipped, whatever."

"Then what happens after?" I ask with uncertainty. I mean it's five thousand dollars for God's sake.

He nervously brushes his hands through his hair. "I mean, you're kinda cool, so I was hoping we'd be friends. I mean this banter we have going, it's good, right?"

I ponder on my thoughts for all of two minutes, because let's face it, it's five grand. "Okay, pick me up at seven, with my cash!" He nods profusely, seemingly somewhat surprised. As I make my way down the corridor, I turn around. "You know where I live, right?"

He laughs in response with a genuine smile on his face. "Yeah, Frankie, I know exactly where you live."

I slink into Cameron's car, today's ride of choice is a Porsche 911 Turbo S. "What the fuck does Chad Wilder want with you?"

"He wants to fuck me," I respond dryly.

Cameron chokes, his nostrils flare, his grip tightening on the steering wheel. "He's a waste of fucking space, Frankie. Bad news, stay the fuck away from him!"

I watch him, trying to gauge his reaction, he's mad, I get that, but why?

I decide to poke the bear. "Well, Dad, I don't need you telling me what to do, and as I'm sure you've figured out before now, I don't take too well to being told what to do. So, you know what you can do with your advice, right?"

Cameron bristles as he glances at me before he turns

his attitude around, and he smiles in a cunning way that makes me question what he's going to do or say next. "I've seen your rap sheet, Frankie, I know alllll the shit you've done. You're fucking reckless, at best. What you've been involved in, the weapons, the drug charges." He raises an eyebrow at me, shaking his head in disgust, while maintaining eye contact. "You want those charges coming back on you again? Go ahead, hang out with the good boy Chad fucking Wilder, but don't say I didn't warn you." He smiles at me. The prick thinks he's clever.

I slip down into my seat and no doubt he thinks I'm defeated. "You know, not all those charges are true, just because they're on my sheet doesn't mean I did them."

I look to him and his eyebrows furrow before he lets out a patronizing chuckle. "Sure, they're all a load of crap, right?" His eyes are dancing tauntingly.

I stare at him directly in the eye with all seriousness. "I'm many things, Cameron, a thief, maybe an arms dealer, but I'm not a liar. So, no, not all of those charges are exactly correct. Actually, they're all true in a sense, apart from the drug charge. I mean, I guess I'm guilty in the sense I had them in my pocket, but I didn't buy them or intend to sell them." I shrug as I watch his face. He's watching me with curiosity, seemingly unsure of what I'm trying to say. I let out a breath and sigh before going on to explain further. "One of the boys I call family had a lot to lose, a lot more than me, so I took the drugs from him and took the rap; took one for the team so to speak." I shrug and downplay my confession. "He didn't deserve the consequences for his screw up, so I helped him out."

Cameron's back goes from being straight to defeated. "Yeah, I get that." He swallows thickly and says, "You're loyal." His eyes immediately flit back to the road, he's given me a compliment without realizing. Can't have that, can we.

Chad picks me up from the mansion at seven o'clock, and we have an instant connection, but not remotely in a romantic sense. I've always been able to get along with guys easily, probably because I literally grew up in the club with so many around me. There's a brotherhood about the club we're in and even as a "sister" I was never treated any differently.

We drive to a diner on the outskirts of town. Apparently, it's a popular spot for the teenagers around Trent Valley and has the best burgers.

I'm dressed in skinny black jeans and a black vest top, showing way too much cleavage with my red lacey bra poking out at the top. My wavy hair cascades down my back, covering the ink I have there, yet still exposing the ink on my arms. I sure as hell don't fit into the perfect appearance that is reflected in every corner of Trent Valley. Chad hasn't made any lewd comments about my appearance and appears completely comfortable with me, and we bounce off each other with banter. All in all, it's actually quite fun.

Sitting opposite Chad and dunking my fries into the ketchup, I decide to do a little digging. "So, what's the deal with you and Cameron? He clearly hates you with a passion."

Chad fidgets in his seat. "Yeah, that fucking obvious, huh?"

I nod as he brushes his hand through his hair. *Why do men do that and look so hot while they do it?*

"Him and me, we were actually good friends—" He laughs to himself. "Real good friends. We grew up together, like him, me, and Joel." He swallows. "Anyway, at the start of high school, I went down the football route, he went down the basketball route and our friends expanded in opposite directions, but we were still friends, right?" I nod in agreement, and he peers down at his plate and pushes it away. "Last year, I was getting too well acquainted with coke." He shakes his head, at his own shame, I'm guessing.

"There was a bust at a party, my new friends scattered and Cam stuck beside me." He looks me in the eyes and shakes his head, correcting himself. "Nah, he more than stuck beside me, he literally took the fall for me. See, he knew me better than anyone else, he knew my dad had been busting my ass for years, looking for an excuse to send me to military school, and he knew the drugs would be a perfect excuse for him. Cam took the drugs from me and took the fall. Cam never did coke, ever. Yet he did that for me. He got some serious shit from his old man. I mean, he got him off the charges, but I know he's holding them over his head, his trust fund got stopped, and as far as I know, his dad's making all his decisions about his future." He shakes his head. "They're not decisions that Cam would make. So, yeah, he helped me out with my old man so he doesn't kill my future, but he gets his killed in return."

I blow out a breath. "Wow, I was not expecting that!"

Chad laughs nervously. "Yeah, which part?"

I brush my hand through my own hair. "Honestly? That Cameron was such an amazing friend."

Chad stares at me. "Cam's a good guy, I just wish I could return the favor. Make up for the shit I've caused."

I nod solemnly. "Did you apologize?"

Chad stares up at the ceiling, shoulders slumping. "Yeah, I tried, he doesn't want to hear it."

We sit in silence as I dip my fries into my sauce. I swallow hard, pushing the words out. "Sometimes, I think, when things are new, still raw, it's hard to hear sorry. Sometimes it's best to give that person space until they're ready to hear it."

"Are you talking from experience?" he asks me pointedly.

"Yeah, I am," I admit, looking back down at my own plate. I hate feeling vulnerable.

He dips his fries in his ketchup. "Okay, Frankie, so this shit you've got going on with Cam, you apologize to him?" he asks me with a smirk.

I blow out and meet his eyes. "Yeah, I tried once." I shrug. "I guess I could take my own advice and try again." I smile at him broadly, and he nods in agreement and returns the smile.

As he drives me home, I think on our conversation, and I'm beginning to see exactly how I should apologize to Cameron. Sometimes actions speak louder than words. I've been sitting on this for a while, waiting for the right time to return it, perhaps now is as good a time as any.

CAMERON

I've been pissed all evening at home. I beat the crap out of the punching bag and still don't feel any better. Frankie's words echo about in my mind, how she took one for her team—her family.

I don't know whether Frankie amazes me with her loyalty or with her complete reckless way she breezes through life. She openly admits her flaws and makes no excuses for them. *How many other girls can say the same thing?*

After I shower, I ponder what to do next. Normally I'd hang with Joel on a Friday night, but I wasn't feeling it tonight. I wander downstairs to the kitchen. My mom is packing away some groceries. "Hey, honey, how's school been this week?"

"Fine." I open the fridge and help myself to a yogurt, pulling myself up onto the worktop.

"Your dad has asked you to make sure you're around for dinner tomorrow night, he wants to speak to us."

I roll my eyes, no fucking good ever comes out of a family meal. "Sure." I nod in agreement.

"Did you see the fight between Frankie and the girl at school? Your father had some serious explaining to do with the girl's father!" my mom questions with worry in her voice.

"Yeah, I saw. Stacey was being a bitch and went for Frankie first." I'm not sure why I offer up that information, I guess I wanted to make sure it got back to my dad, seeing how he didn't even ask Frankie what had happened. As usual, all he's bothered about is his appearance.

"Where is she, anyway?" I ask my mom nonchalantly.

"Oh, she went out with a friend," she responds with a huge smile. Seemingly pleased with Frankie's friendships.

My face drops, followed by my stomach. *What fucking friend?* Why the hell I'm pissed I'm not sure, maybe it's the shitty week I've had, but I've got a bad feeling about this and I'm not sure why. I drop my spoon in the sink and head up to my room.

I throw myself on my bed and call Neo. He answers on the first ring. "Hey, man, do me a favor and tell me where Frankie is."

"Sure thing, give me a sec and I'll track her phone now." I can hear him clicking away. "Okay, so she's at Wren's Diner." I think for a minute, perhaps she's out with Leo, he has a car. Or maybe Jess? As if hearing my thoughts, Neo offers his own. "You wanna know who else's phone I'm tracking in the same diner?"

I smile inwardly, and this is why this guy is fucking amazeballs. "Go on," I drawl.

"Chad fucking Wilder."

My hand grips my phone with such intensity it's a wonder it doesn't smash. My blood boils and I can't think straight. She completely ignored everything I said to her, all the advice I gave her, she just doesn't fucking care. It's as if she's trying to piss me off on purpose. I should just let her get into shit, let her fuck up with that douche, they fucking deserve one another. And yet the pain in my stomach is there, and what hurts the most, I don't want it to be there, it's as though I'm worrying for her and yet, why the fuck should I care?!

After pacing my room for what feels like an eternity, I decide to go another round in the gym, anything to take my mind off them both.

I go to pick my car keys up twice, planning to drive over there and see what is happening.

I call Joel to rant, and he just tells me I need to get laid.

I've even contemplated going to Stacey, but honestly, she would just piss me off more.

Completely spent, I leave the gym and head through the kitchen to go up to my room.

The kitchen's dark but slightly illuminated with the cabinet lights, and I see Frankie sitting on a barstool scrolling through her phone. I take her in, studying her, scanning her for what . . . I'm not sure myself. Her long hair is in waves, hanging down to her tits, which are busting out of her fucking top, and my jaw tics in annoyance. She's clearly dressed to impress him. I squeeze my water bottle in frustration.

Her eyes shoot up and meet mine. "Oh, hey, I didn't realize you were in. I thought you'd gone out." Her voice is soft and her expression I can't read, she almost appears vulnerable as though something has happened. She's playing with her fingers nervously.

My eyes knit together while trying to decide what her game is. "Where else would I fucking be? Out with coke-heads? Not my style, sweetheart," I spit.

Her face is shocked at my words, then she works quickly to mask it, biting the inside of her mouth as if trying not to respond.

"You don't always have to be such an ass, you know. Chad actually said you were a decent guy."

I laugh mockingly. "Sure he did. He's a little prick that only looks out for himself. But you'd know all about that, right? Looking out for yourself, fucking over undeserving people to get what you want. I mean, what did you have to do for the five grand Chad offered you?" I wave my hand up and down her body. "I mean, you got the dressing like a slut down to a tee, so did you get your knees dirty? Or are you a filthy little cum bucket like your whore of a mother?"

My head is pounding as I spit the vile words out. Her face is indifferent. If I wanted a reaction, I sure as hell wasn't going to get one. I might as well go in for the kill. "At least psycho Barbie has something you'll never have, some fucking class!"

She sucks in a breath and gulps slowly, darting her eyes away from mine.

I turn on my heel and walk away, leaving her in the darkness.

Taking the stairs, I speed up to my room. *Fuck.*

Stepping in my room, I shut the door and push myself against it. *Fuck!* I hit my head against it. *What a fucking asshole. Jesus, what the hell is wrong with me?*

I walk over to my mirror above my desk and stare at the prick in front of me, a complete dickhead that tore a girl down because of what? *Is this fucking jealousy?* Because it's gone beyond me hating her now.

I glance down at my desk and there, right there on my desk, is my father's St. Christopher Chain; the only thing I had left of my father when he died. The last time I saw it, I was tucking it into the glovebox of my Bugatti, not trusting it wouldn't get damaged at the fight. I'd paid the recovery team extra to double check the crash site and the vehicle before they destroyed my hopes of recovering it from the wreckage. Obviously, I assumed the assailant had stolen it and sold it off.

And now here it is, returned. The person might have taken it, but they hadn't stolen it. In fact, she'd kept it pretty damn safe, considering she's been uprooted, been in juvie and rehomed. No she hadn't stolen it, she'd clearly saved it.

I grip the chain in my hands and bring it to my lips, my filthy fucking lips that just tore her down. I crumple to the floor. I don't deserve this chain, and she didn't deserve my anger.

I spend most of Saturday avoiding Frankie. Joel has come over to cheer me up. I briefly explained what I'd said and then how I returned to my room to find my father's chain there.

He knew I was having a pity party and came over to help me out of this funk.

After going head-to-head on the Xbox multiple times, he suggests going around the pool.

We breeze through the kitchen area, grabbing a couple of beers from the fridge. We lay out our towels and just as

I'm about to lie back, Joel scares the shit out of me. "Holy fucking shit, she's in the pool, dude!"

I dart up on the lounger, Frankie is doing laps in the pool, and all I can see is her hair covering her back and her orange swim shorts which are so small they're tucked up her ass.

I suck in a breath. "Fuck!"

"I know, right? Fuck, man, how the hell does your dick cope? I mean, seriously, is it raw from all the jerking?"

I laugh at Joel and his serious tone. "Something like that," I admit while clenching my jaw.

"Shit, she's getting out!" Joel all but panics.

We both sit back on our loungers, trying to act unfazed, and I scroll through my phone but keep a watchful eye on her. She wraps a towel around her middle, and I see the minute she realizes we're here. Her eyes dart away from us, and she plays with her fingers. Fuck, I'm such a prick.

Frankie almost shakes herself up and walks toward us to go into the kitchen. "Hey, Joel," she greets.

Joel offers her a super cheesy smile as I try not to even peek at her. His eyes roam blatantly up and down her, stilling on her chest. I could kick him for the shit he comes out with. "Fuck, Frankie, are your tits pierced?"

Frankie laughs and then stares down at said tits, making my eyes dart there too. *Fucking sweet Jesus.* I brush my hand through my hair and avert my gaze, licking my lips in the process. My dick throbs against my shorts.

"Yep, they were the last time I checked." She winks.

"That's so fucking hot!" Joel glares, his eyes fucking stuck on her tits.

Frankie raises her eyebrows to him, and he either doesn't realize what he's doing or simply doesn't give a fuck. She looks to me and her eyes are blank; there's no humor in them, no spark she normally holds. "Well, with me being a slut, a whore, and without class, I figured I might as well live up to that and put them back in, right?" She shrugs and throws me a look of disgust before stalking off into the kitchen.

Joel wastes no time in rolling his head in my direction. "Fuck, man, she's pissed at you!"

I feel like I'm fucking shrinking. I've felt like shit all day, but seeing Frankie without the fire in her eyes, yeah, that's giving me a numb feeling I can't fucking stand.

"Yeah, she fucking hates me," I admit. I know I deserve it too.

"I know but imagine the hate sex you could have. Apparently, it's the best, you know hate make-up sex." Joel shrugs and wriggles his eyebrows. "Not something I know about, I mean, girls just don't hate me, and I never do anything to warrant make-up sex, but from what I'm told, when you finally get it on, you're in for a real fucking good time!"

Yeah, somehow, I can't see that happening.

Me and Joel are lounging in the cinema room when I hear Grant call for James, saying there's a visitor at the door for Frankie. My ears prick up on the conversation. Looking over at Joel, he smirks at me and nods to my phone, where I can bring up the mansion's cameras to view what's happening. Joel scoots closer to me on the couch, and I put one ear pod in and hand the other to Joel.

We watch as Frankie comes into the lobby and is

directed into James's office. "Ah, here you are, your teacher from Hawks View has stopped by to see how you're getting along, Frankie. I'll leave you two to it." James nods to the guy standing in his office.

I stare closer at the screen, and sure enough, it's the teacher from her trial. The one the guys called teach.

Frankie's demeanor is out of character for her, and I wonder what it is that she's hiding. He's taller than me, maybe just over six foot two? He's in gray dress pants, a white shirt with his sleeves rolled up and his buttons open at the top. His shirt tight across his shoulders tells me he works out, he has smart brown shoes on and appears every bit the professional that he is. His hair's the same, light brown short at the sides but longer on top, it's smart-looking. But I remember he had the star tattoo behind his ear, and I can't decide how that fits in with this guy.

"What are you doing here?" Her tone is clipped.

He sighs and stares down; he's got something in his hands he's fidgeting with. "I erm." His eyes dart around the room as he spins on his heels, gazing around the room. He stops and stares directly into the camera in the corner, the one that isn't visible to the naked eye but clearly this guy knows his stuff, and judging by his spine straightening, he's well aware there's eyes on him. Frankie has also just realized this, probably as a reflection of his body language, and she nods at him as though letting him know she understands. They can obviously communicate without words, and that's something I don't like.

He clears his throat. "I, erm, I'm leaving for a while"—he peers down at his hands—"to sort things out." His head snaps up and his eyes meet Frankie's, she nods.

He tips his head back and stares up at the ceiling, his

hands on his hips. He's obviously struggling with the conversation. Frankie is watching him closely but doesn't move. I think it's calculated, she's not giving anything away.

"I'm selling my house." He watches her, and as he says that, her back goes ramrod straight. "I have everything planned but there's a box there, if you could keep it safe for me?"

Her voice comes out as low, emotional on a delicate whisper. "Okay."

He nods and walks toward her, and she holds out her hand, and he drops the keys into them before walking to the door.

As he's about to go through it, she turns and says, "Hey, teach." His body stops but he doesn't turn around to face her. "You're doing the right thing." He nods once and walks out the door.

Frankie sighs dramatically and then looks up at the camera, as though she knows we're watching, before turning on her heel and leaving the room.

13

CAMERON

Before I know it, it's evening and the ominous family dinner. Somehow, I manage to rope Joel into staying for dinner. I kind of need a wingman through this.

We're sitting in the usual uncomfortable silence before James decides to open his inappropriate trap. "I had my PI look into your mother's death, Frankie. It appears they found the remains of her body years ago, and she's currently listed as a Jane Doe." He pauses briefly. "I'll see to the paperwork for that to be changed." He nods to her with a small gracious smile, as if he's done her a massive favor and not just brought her dead mother up at a family meal with Joel sitting beside me.

I watch Joel, and his face pales. He stares at me, then Frankie and then back at me as if needing confirmation my father is serious. I eyeball him, and he ducks his head back down to his meal, cutting into the potatoes.

"You didn't need to go to all that trouble, James. As you're aware, Jodie had addictions and very loose morals that were bound to catch up with her, a nasty combination." Frankie speaks firmly, almost sticking James's lack of empathy up his ass. I inwardly smile.

"Would you like a service for her? A headstone, perhaps?" Jesus, he makes it sound like he's offering her something off of a dessert menu.

"Nah, I'm good. I'd appreciate you putting that generous and caring hand in your pocket and paying for my dad's headstone though. It's shit seeing the little cross the guys made for me instead of the real thing," she says in a sweet condescending tone.

I glare toward James. *Is he fucking serious? He hasn't made sure she had a headstone for her father? His brother? What the fuck is going on?*

My mom's fork clatters to her plate, and I study Frankie in question, whose eyes are transfixed with hatred on James. Joel's head is still ducked down. *Jesus, this is fucked up.*

James fidgets uncomfortably, the nerve in his temple ticking, his fist is clenched by his side. He's pissed she pulled him up on it. *What a prick.* He nods his head and puts on a fake smile. "Of course."

The meal continues in utter silence, the atmosphere resembles something of a wake. James clears his throat. "Did you manage to get your father's possessions, Frankie? When he passed away."

She looks at him blankly before breaking the gaze. "No, I didn't, James, I was given a few photographs, all the rest were seized." She pushes her plate away. "Thanks for the meal, I'm out."

"Where do you think you're going?" His tone is severe and pissed.

"Out with friends."

"I'd prefer it if you stayed in tonight, Frankie. After the week you've had again. I think that's for the best." He's punishing her, being a complete and utter dick. He knows full well she went out last night.

"I can go out with her, me and Joel, make sure she doesn't get into shit?" Why the fuck I volunteer that, I don't know. My voice sounds hopeful. *What a fucking sap.*

I spare a glance at Frankie. She appears confused. I guess I would be too after being torn down and hated on.

James's spine straightens and he looks from me to Frankie, a sly smirk spreads out on his face, he palms his hands together. "Excellent idea." He beams with a reassuring nod.

Frankie pushes her chair back, and just as I think she's going to protest, she shocks me. "I just have to go change." She points toward the door.

Me and Joel are waiting at the bottom of the stairs when Frankie appears, bouncing down the stairs with a spring in her step, her wavy hair bouncing in a high ponytail. Carrying a hoodie in one hand, she's in barely there shorts, a cropped top exposing her stomach and too much cleavage, and combat boots. I can practically hear Joel swoon.

I drop my head and go to open the door when James's voice stops me dead in my tracks. "Absolutely no way in hell are you going out dressed like that!"

Frankie's body tenses, she spins on her heels. "I

thought you liked this look, James?" she asks mockingly, making me and Joel eye one another in question. My mom sure has hell doesn't dress this way.

"Upstairs and change, now, otherwise, don't bother leaving this house!"

Frankie smiles at us both and shrugs. "Back in a minute, boys." She happily hops up the stairs, leaving me and Joel checking out her ass cheeks as she moves.

A few minutes later, Frankie bounces back down the stairs with her hands held out. "Happy?" She twirls on the spot. Her shorts are replaced with a tight pair of jeans, and she wears a loose hanging white T-shirt.

James assesses her outfit, his eyes are sharp and pissed. "Fine," he snaps the word out.

"Oh goody, have a wonderful evening, James!" Frankie calls out as we exit the house. She exhales deeply as she shuts the door, her bravado clear.

"We need to take the Suburban," she says, while glancing at me briefly. I nod in confirmation.

———

Frankie has typed the zip code into the GPS, and after driving for over an hour and a half listening to Joel's chat-up lines and easy banter, I decide to question where we're actually going.

"Where are we going, Frankie?"

"A club."

I look to her. Nah, she's not going to make this easy for me. I raise my eyebrows. "A club?"

"Yeah, it's called Con & Doms; we're about fifteen minutes out."

I gaze around at the area we're in. It's on the outskirts of Hawks Town, its run-down and sketchy; it should be fucking condemned. Basically, a fucking shithole.

"Is it even fucking safe?" Joel asks, mirroring my own thoughts.

Frankie lets out a small laugh. "Contrary to popular belief, Joel, I'm not a complete raving bitch. If I wanted you dead, I'd do it myself. It's safe."

I'm reeling from her words, and Joel sits forward in his seat. "Are there any hot chicks?"

Frankie turns in her seat to face him, her eyes alight with encouragement. "Joel, there will be every chick you can imagine, every origin, every shape, size, nationality, chicks with dicks, whatever your sweet little cock fancies." Her voice is full of playfulness.

"My cock ain't little. Although I've heard it's sweet! Fancy giving it a try?" He wriggles his eyebrows as we both laugh at his stupid humor.

Frankie bends down to her boot and pulls out something shiny; she flicks a button and out pops a knife. I swerve and nearly crash the goddamn car. "What the hell, Frankie?"

"Calm your tits, I'm just re-adjusting this fucking outfit!" She grimaces.

She starts ripping holes in her jeans with the knife, then proceeds to whip her T-shirt over her head to reveal her crop top. My eyes dip to her tits, making me bite my fucking lip. "I can't go in there looking like a fucking nun, can I?" *A nun? Is she serious? A T-shirt and jeans make her look like a nun?* I brush my hand down my face. *What the hell has she got us into?*

As we approach the location, Frankie directs me to

some large metal gates with barbed wire on the top, she winds down her window and a guy in baggy clothes and a beanie approaches the car with a fucking AK-47 slung over his shoulder. I glance through my mirror at Joel in the back seat, he's shrinking into it. *Yeah, me too.*

She puts her fist out for a bump. "Cuanto tiempo sin verte, Micah." *Long time no see Micah.*

"Ah, Star, where've you been hiding your sweet ass?"

"Rich Valley," she muses.

"No shit, you want a brother?" He laughs.

"Nah, sorry man, got two here." She motions at us both. I give him a chin lift, because what the fuck else am I meant to do?

"Bale's not here, there's a fight up north," he adds.

"Yeah, I know. I'm here to see Vaughn."

"He's inside, babe, have fun!" He waves us in.

Frankie directs me to park the car, the huge warehouse in front of us coming into sight. The place seems derelict, and if it wasn't for the raging music and lights glowing from the broken windows, I'd have said it was abandoned.

"Micah will watch the car," Frankie confirms before I have a chance to ask her.

"You speak Spanish?"

"Yeah, I do." She rolls her head to my direction and adds, "Although, being uneducated and dumb, I only speak it. Not read or write it." She winks at me and moves to get out the car. But not before I see her remove a thick brown envelope from her hoodie on her knee.

I grab her wrist to stop her. "What the fuck is that, Frankie?" My tone is serious.

She must see the panic on my face. "It's why we're here."

I'm annoyed she isn't giving me more of an explanation. After driving all this way, I deserve to know what we're fucking doing here.

"That's not good enough, explain!" I snap.

She sighs and moves some hair from her face. "It's money, Cameron. Nothing illegal, don't panic."

My shoulders sag in relief and I nod. "Okay, I'm trusting you."

We follow her out of the SUV, and as we're about to move, Joel nervously announces, "Hey, Frankie, erm, do you think we, well, do you think we look okay, to be going in there?" He points to the club. Fuck, he's got a good point. We look like a pair of rich-kid frat boys.

Frankie's eyes bug out as if only just thinking of that. "Shit, come here." She proceeds to whip her knife out and approaches my jeans.

I put my hand out to stop her. "Whoa, hold the fuck on, these are two-thousand-dollar jeans!"

"Yeah, well I'm sure Daddy will buy you a new pair!" she quips with a small smile gracing her lips. She tears rips into both mine and Joel's jeans. "Pull out your shirts, mess your hair, and leave your rich-boy watches in the car."

After following Frankie's instructions to "de-rich" us we make our way through the dirt-filled parking lot to the club entrance.

"Anything we should know?" I ask, feeling apprehensive.

Frankie stops in her tracks. "Yeah, if you fuck a slut, wear a Johnny, and don't forget to give them a tip." I watch her, unsure if she's kidding. I move my eyes to Joel's, whose eyes are popping out of his head and his mouth gaping open.

"Where'd it get its name from?" Joel asks, beaming up at the club's sign.

"The guys that own it, they're called Connor and Dominic. So they called it Con & Doms, witty, eh?" She smiles a broad smile before going on to explain further, "Con is our leader and Dom has his own teams."

The entrance to the club is manned by three huge security men. I sag when I see the queues to get in. But obviously, I should have known better. Frankie marches up to the entrance with me and Joel in tow. She greets one of the guys who makes a fuss of "Star," then leads us inside.

Holy. Fucking. Shitballs. My eyes are fucking burning! No word of a lie. The smoke is melting my eyes. A mixture of fog machines and smoke from drugs is in the air, even the smell of fucking sex. *What the hell is this place?*

A bar lines the left-hand side of the entrance length ways. Waitresses walk around either in something resembling a bra or completely topless. The club's atmosphere is electric, the floor beneath us is booming with vibrations from the music. There's a balcony above us overlooking this main area, a huge crowd gathered at the right-hand side of the club with spotlights lighting up that area. There are exotic dancers on poles and on crates between the two areas, almost dividing the club in half from the dark dance area to the spot-lit crowded area. To my right is a bar that runs the width of the warehouse. Directly above where the left bar is are windows overlooking the whole club, clearly that's where the owners are. Strobe lights flash in all directions.

I turn and smile at Joel. He's in absolute awe, his eyes darting in every direction, excitement racing through him.

I look back at Frankie and she offers me a small smile. She's fucking beautiful. "You okay?" I ask her.

She breathes in, her chest inflating with comfort and confidence as she gazes around and nods at me. "Yeah, I'm good." She's clearly happy to be back here, and I'm pretty damn pleased for her too.

She nods toward the bar. "You want a beer?"

I nod. "Yeah."

We walk over to the bar, and Frankie hugs a waitress en route. Joel nearly falls over his feet staring at the poor girl's ass cheeks hanging from her shorts. I push his shoulder. "Stop fucking drooling, you'll embarrass us!" I joke.

"Fuck, dude, I can't breathe. I'm so goddamn excited, and horny, I'm horny too! This, this is fucking insane." He waves his hand about while bouncing on the balls of his feet like an excited child.

"I know, right?" I throw my head back and laugh at him.

When we reach the bar, Frankie whistles to get the attention of a bartender. He scowls in our direction before his face breaks out in a wide smile, then he bypasses all the other customers and comes to us. Virtually throwing himself over the bar, he lunges at Frankie and pulls her in for a hug. He whispers in her ear, and she nods, she talks back to him, and I wish I knew what the fuck they were saying. He motions with his head to the back of the room, and I take in the stairs leading up to the balcony. The bartender turns and unscrews the caps off the bottles of three beers before placing them in front of us. I go to get my wallet from my back pocket, but the guy holds his hands up. "Drinks on the house for entertainment." He motions his head in the direction of Frankie, making my eyebrows furrow in question. Before I get chance to ask her anymore, she grabs her beer and gestures us to follow her up the stairs.

At the top of the stairs, there's a large serious-looking guy with an earpiece in, the clear bulge in his jacket exposing a gun. I scrub a hand down my face. *Jesus, Frankie what have you gotten us into?*

The guy breaks out into a sly grin and fist bumps Frankie. "Star," he says with a nod in her direction.

"You good?"

"Am now I've seen you, babe. Sorry about all the shit that went down for you."

She lowers her head vulnerably and licks her lips. "Yeah, thanks for that, appreciate it."

"These with you?" His eyebrow raises.

"Yeah, they're good."

The guy gestures for us to go ahead with a wave of his hand.

We walk into the open-plan loft where there's a balcony to the right. The room has multiple couches with various people lounging in a state of undress.

At the back of the room, a guy that screams importance about him is seated in the center with half naked chicks sitting on either side of him. He has a military-style haircut, white wifebeater, and chains hanging from his tattoo-covered neck. His arms are draped over the back of the couch, and he has full sleeves of tattoos covering them. He screams danger.

He whistles low as we approach. "Well, well, well, look who we have here."

My eyes dart to Frankie to make sure this guy isn't a

danger. She smiles playfully at the guy, my heart rate can fucking slow down now.

"Present!" Frankie announces, holding up the envelope before throwing it onto the table.

The guy eyes Frankie inquisitively. "Five grand," she responds.

He laughs at Frankie. "Thought you said it was going to take you a couple of weeks, Star. Wasn't expecting it to be a couple of days."

"Yeah, well I saw an opportunity and I took it." She's referring to Chad, so this is what she used the money for, even though I still haven't a fucking clue what it's actually for.

Frankie breaks my thoughts. "How's he doing?"

The guy looks down at the table and huffs out. "This will help, babe, no doubt about it."

Frankie nods solemnly. "Don't tell Bale I brought you this. He's still having his fucking tantrum." She sighs.

The guy laughs, then looks pointedly at Frankie and presses his finger to his nose, tapping it.

"Heard you're staying in Rich Valley, that where these pretty boys are from?" My spine straightens, and I bristle at his words.

Frankie laughs it off. "Yeah, they are. Figured I'd show them a good time."

"Little bird tells me there's a bitch you're searching for there, she's hiding out up there too, got herself a sugar daddy." He eyes her pointedly.

Frankie's face pales, and her hand grips my arm. "You're shitting me!" Shock laces her voice, and I watch her in question, but her eyes are transfixed on this dude.

The guy shakes his head. "Shit you not, Star, have my

boys looking into it. Keep your eyes and phone line open. I'll let you know when I have more intel." She swallows hard and nods.

Bending over the table, the guy digs his hand into a bowl of condoms on the table and stuffs them in Frankie's hand. "They're on me, for your boys." He eyes me and Joel, then nods toward the women on a couch. Frankie grins, her eyes lighting up in mischief. "Some good shit in the joints too, help yourselves," he adds.

"I'll see you around, Vaughn. Hopefully have another five in a couple of weeks."

We turn to follow Frankie. "I appreciate this, Frankie; won't forget it," the guy shouts back, and her lips quirk up in a smile.

Following Frankie, we go over to the balcony. "What the fuck was all that about?" I ask, my eyes frantically searching hers for some clue as to what the hell is happening.

"Which part?" she asks innocently, making me pissed.

"Well, I wanna know why he gave you a hand full of condoms, babe, because I'm pretty fucking sure those hotties over there are waiting for us, am I right?" Joel is practically bouncing and salivating on the spot, eyes darting to the near naked girls on the couch.

I look to Frankie. "Yep, they're waiting for you both. Tell them what you want, and you have it. Here . . ." She holds the condoms out for us to take.

Joel wastes no time in snapping her hand off to grab the condoms, and I shake my head. "Not interested." Her eyes narrow on me, surveying my response.

———

Joel has fucking disappeared to the couches and is currently being eaten alive by two topless women who are openly fondling him and kissing up his neck.

I take this opportunity to look down at the club setup. I can see it all from up here, the area that was lit up by a spotlight is a familiar fighting ring, currently empty. To the left of the ring, two double doors from outside open and in walk two guys and a young chick probably around our age, only they have an air of danger about them. They're wearing Kevlar vests. The guy in front is older-looking. The blond guy behind him has a psychotic look about him with sharp features, and they both seem pissed off. The girl following behind reminds me of Frankie, small with dark wavy hair, she's ripping her vest off as she walks behind them, and as they disappear through another door, I turn to Frankie and point in the direction they left. "Who were they?"

"Girl at the back is called Mayhem, the guys are hers."

"Her crew?" I question, raising an eyebrow.

"Well, I meant her guys, literally. But yeah, they're a crew too. A high-up crew."

I stare at her in question, and she clarifies without asking. "She's fucking them both, Cameron."

I choke. "They know that?" I gape.

"Yep, know it and love it, apparently." She grins.

I pull a hand down my face and take a swig of the beer, it's like another fucking world. "You into that shit?" I ask, a little unsure. Hoping to fuck she isn't.

"You?" she quips back, not answering.

I meet her eyes, because it's as close we've ever come to openly discussing ourselves with one another. "Never had a girlfriend, and I wouldn't fucking share her if I did."

"What's Stacey, then, if not a girlfriend?" She drinks her beer while watching me closely.

I laugh. "I think you best described her as a psycho Barbie? That gives shit head."

She splutters her beer with laughter. "I've heard they're pretty good." She nods toward Joel and his little harem.

"Nah, I'm good." She raises her eyebrow at me but drops the subject as she turns to watch over the balcony.

We stand watching in silence as I contemplate how to say the words, tugging at the label on my beer bottle I suck it up and say them. "About the other night, Frankie, I'm so fucking sorry, I was out of line, and I shouldn't have said what I said. Then I found the chain in my room and . . ." I scrub my hand through my hair and blow out before continuing, "I fucked up, major fucked up, I'm sorry. I know the shit I've said is fucking unforgivable. But I'm sorry."

She shrugs. "Don't worry about it."

I look to her and she's still facing the club. She's pissed, I get it. Before I can try again, she turns. "Seriously, Cam, I'm not into holding grudges with people I like. You fucked up, apologized. I'm over it." She shrugs.

Just like that? That fucking easy. Who is this girl?

I scrutinize her face, for what, I'm unsure. So shaking my thoughts aside, I ask, "You like me?" I grin.

She chuckles. "Yeah, for some stupid reason, you and your dumb friend over there," she says, darting her eyes to Joel.

We stand in comfortable silence for a while.

"So, truthfully, Frankie, what was all this about tonight?" I gesture to where Vaughn is sitting.

Her jaw is ticing, and her tongue pushes against her

cheek, unsure whether to trust in me or not. "I was helping a friend out who made a mistake." She swallows deeply with emotion.

"Same friend you took the rap with the drugs for?"

She laughs and glances up at the ceiling. "Yeah, that one."

"Bale, he's the guy I fought, right?"

"Yeah."

"Why don't you want him to know you're helping your friend out?"

"He's pissed about the shit he got into; he'll come around eventually."

"What makes you so sure?"

"We're family, they always stick together." She's so fucking trusting, it both astounds and annoys me.

"Even when they hurt other people? People who trust them?"

"I guess it depends on their intentions." She shrugs. "His intentions weren't to hurt us."

I empty my bottle. Leaning over the balcony so I'm level with Frankie, I ask her, "Why'd you give me the chain back?"

She meets my eyes. "I never intended on keeping it, I was waiting for the right time. I wasn't sure when that would be. I thought, fuck it, you might as well have it, I might be waiting a while for the right time," she jokes.

I smile at her softly, and clearing my throat, I decide to explain myself. "It was my dad's, it's the only thing I have of him. It means a lot to me, so thank you," I admit honestly.

I'm fidgeting nervously with the bottle label. I feel like I'm opening myself up and it's not something I ever do.

"I figured it was something like that. The night of the crash . . ." She shakes her head in memory. "I saw it in the glove box. I ran from the car and all I could think about was it had to be something important for you to leave it in there. I mean, you had a watch and shit on, but you left that. Anyway, when my dad died, they couldn't find his dog tags, and it ripped me apart. They meant something to him, you know? So, yeah, I couldn't leave them in the car; the car was on its way over a cliff for fuck's sake." She laughs nervously, watching me.

"Was your dad in the same branch as James?"

Her eyebrows furrow in confusion. "No way. James wasn't in the Army, too much of a wuss to be in the service." My gaze narrows on her, because I'm pretty fucking sure James has some dog tags in his safe.

"You're sure about that? James not being in the Army, I mean."

"Positive. Listen, I may not know the James you guys know, but I know the Jimmy before the James and he definitely wasn't in the service, what makes you think he was?"

"No reason, I guess I assumed." I shrug.

Before she can question me further, the spotlight highlights the fighting ring and an announcement is made that Rivers will fight Tonks. I move my eyes to Frankie. "Mayhem's guy, Rivers, the blond dude, will kick his ass," she explains in an excitable and confident voice, her head gesturing toward the ring.

"You know this Tonks?"

"Nope but Bale trained Rivers, and he's an expert in combat."

"Bale trained him?"

She nods. I brush my hair with my hand. "Fuck, I didn't stand a chance, did I?"

She laughs to herself. "Afraid not. I heard you fought well, though." She's smiling at me, causing me to roll my eyes. "I'm going to take you to Bale's gym. You'd fucking love it there."

"Yeah, that's probably not the best idea." I wince at the thought of meeting Bale again.

"Bale's cool; you'd actually like him, he can teach you, Cam. Don't close that idea down just yet." She smiles confidently.

I watch intently as the guy I now know as Rivers approaches the ring. Watching from the side is the other guy with Mayhem sitting on his knee, his hand palmed over her stomach in a possessive manner. Rivers is ripped; his lean physique highlights his muscles, he's a serious-looking guy, his hands are wrapped and shards of glass sparkle from them. "His hands?"

"It's like dirty boxing, with glass" she winks.

"This is fucked up."

"You haven't seen anything yet!" She smirks at me.

Rivers comes closer to our side with his back to us, his spine on show, displaying the same tattoo as Frankie. "You all got that tattoo?"

"Only people in the crew officially."

"How do they feel about you not being in the crew now?"

"I'll always be in the crew. I guess I'm on vacation." She smiles at me, her face lit up and her eyes shine with pride.

We watch the match, and Frankie was right, Rivers is like a machine, the other guy didn't stand a chance. By the time the whistle is blown, the poor guy is a crumpled bloody heap and three men have restrained Rivers. Mayhem greeted him, holding his face in both palms, putting kisses to his face and cheeks, almost childlike.

I glance over at Joel, his head is lolling from side to side, courtesy of the joints he's spent the last half hour puffing on. His jeans are open at the waist, making me laugh. "I think Joel's had enough." I nod in his direction.

"Yeah, come on, let's get him out of here."

As we head over to Joel, a young-looking dude approaches Frankie. "Hey, Star. I've been sent to give you a hand with your boy here." He points to Joel. Frankie nods.

Me and the kid drape Joel's arms over our shoulders. He's a dead fucking weight, his head drops backward, and he's mumbling his words. "Best fucking night of my life, man. I'm in fucking love, I swear, I'm in love. I gave her my number. She fucking sucked my balls dry. I told her I was a whore virgin. She fucking went to town on me. She popped my whore cherry, fucking amazing. The girl with the white hair, I'm in love with her. Seriously, she's beautiful, I came, imagining it was her sucking me off." He grins in awe. "I love Frankie too, where the fuck is she? Frankie, I fucking love you, best night of my life."

FRANKIE

After strapping Joel in the car, we make our journey back home and he's out for the count. We decide to take Joel home with us, it'll be easier to explain rather than him going back to his house.

I'm going over the night's events in my head. I shared a lot with Cameron tonight, more than I intended, but it felt good. I enjoyed talking to him, and as the night went on, he relaxed more and more.

His interest in the fights was genuine, and he was intrigued. I'm hoping he opens himself up to learning from Bale. I'm not sure why, but I can't help but feel like he'd be an asset to our crew and that's something I want to explore. I just hope I'm not blinded by my attraction to him.

I know he feels some attraction to me, I can sense it. And I'm pretty damn sure he's been getting jealous. Every time a guy came near me tonight, Cameron moved a little close and his hands twitched as though he wasn't sure whether to grab me or punch them. Being close to him was hard fucking work. I mean he smells gorgeous, his tanned skin glistens, and his pissy attitude actually turns me on. When he smiles, I feel like I've won the lottery. *How fucking sad is that?* He doesn't smile often but when he does, it's as though someone has taken you from the dark and given you light. My body swells and not just with lust.

I was surprised he wasn't up to Vaughn's freebies. It never crossed my mind that a guy our age, and a single guy at that, would turn that offer down. Jesus, I expected him to take the offer, even when I thought he was with psycho Barbie, so to discover they genuinely aren't a thing, and still not take the freebie. Mind. Fucking. Blown.

We manage to get Joel into the spare room beside Cameron's, where Cameron drops Joel to the bed. "Should I undress him?" I ask.

Cameron's head spins toward me. "No, don't fucking touch him!" His tone makes me jump. "Fuck, I'm sorry, I didn't mean to sound like such an ass. I just don't like the thoughts of you touching him," he admits meekly.

I gape at him, is that meant to make me feel better? He must have read my face. "Shit, fuck. I'm screwing this up." He brushes his hand through his hair and takes a step toward me, his voice low and soft, almost vulnerable. "I don't like the thoughts of your hands on him, touching him when they shouldn't be."

"What's it matter to you?" I ask, both confused and hopeful. I nibble my lower lip in anticipation.

My heart is thumping hard against my chest as he moves closer. So close I have to crane my neck to look up to him. "You're so fucking beautiful, Frankie. I don't think you're even aware how beautiful you are." His thumb grazes my bottom lip. I dart my tongue out to catch his thumb, he stills it on the end of my tongue and gently pushes it into my mouth—*fuck, that's hot*. I suck his thumb as his left hand rests on my hip, pulling me flush with his body. He slowly and seductively moves his thumb in and out of my mouth, each time grazing my lip, causing tingles to break out over my body.

He swallows thickly before he removes his thumb and uses his hand to cup my jaw, almost painfully. He grips me, pulling my mouth up to his lips, and his tongue enters my mouth, sweeping in, causing wetness to pool between my legs. *Fuck, he's hot.* He kisses me delicately, his tongue gently swooping in and out of my mouth, coaxing my response.

Abruptly he stops and pulls away, he glances at a moaning Joel in the bed, and I'm reminded that we're not alone. Before I can think, he takes my hand and pulls me out the door into his room. My head quite literally spinning as I stumble over my feet, he gives no time for me to think through what is happening.

He shuts the door and locks it before practically pouncing on me, his soft kisses have been replaced by his frantic and passionate mouth. His hands tug at my top, encouraging me to lift my arms while pulling me back toward the bed. His legs hit the bed first, forcing him to sit, he opens his legs for me to stand between while he rids me of my top. He sucks in a breath, watching me, eyes heavy with lust as I unstrap my bra. His eyes are filled with passion, his mouth slightly open and his lips slightly swollen from our kiss. In other words, he looks fucking hot!

I drop my bra to the floor. His tone comes out clipped. "Untie your hair." I do as he asks as he sits back on his elbows to watch me. "Drop your jeans." I shimmy them down my legs, maintaining eye contact. I'm so fucking aroused, desperate for his commanding voice and possessive eyes.

Cameron lifts his own T-shirt over his head and there on his chest is his father's chain. I move as close to the bed as I can and he sits forward, his hands work from my hips up to my tits. He watches me closely as if checking I'm okay with his movements.

When he gets to my breasts, they sit in his palms heavily, and he brushes my nipples with his thumbs. The action makes me moan, particularly my left one which is pierced with a barbell. "Your tits are incredible, Frankie." He licks his lips.

He moves his head to my pierced nipple and licks it gently. "Are you okay with me sucking it?" I nod in agreement, too lost in being turned on to talk. His lips gently tease my nipple, and it's so erotic, I can feel my panties getting wetter. I hold his head as he suckles gently onto my nipple. I stroke my hand through his brown waves.

I cry out when he latches onto the piercing and gently tugs on it with his mouth. "Fuck, that's good, Cam," I gasp and swallow harshly.

Cam releases a soft moan of his own, the vibration hitting the piercing. His other hand is kneading my breast roughly, the nipple hardened. He pushes his face harder into me, his mouth opening wider, his teeth grazing over my sensitive flesh, he changes to kisses. Frantic and desperate kisses to my breast, his hands have gone to my ass and he's squeezing my cheeks, rocking me backward and forward rubbing me against him.

His mouth has latched onto my skin and he's sucking at my breast to leave a mark. "Ah, fuck, Cam that's good."

He stops and stares at me, his eyes heavy with lust as he pulls me into his lap, his mouth meets mine, and his hands tugs on my hair. I rock gently in his lap, straddling him. I can feel his hardness in his jeans, the thought of his length makes me clench myself together.

I hold his face as I kiss him, and I suck at his tongue, encouraged by the moans from his mouth.

He pulls away, panting. "Take my cock out, Frankie. Fucking feel what you do to me!" I move back slightly on my knees to make room to open his jeans, and he shuffles them down a little. I move my hand inside his waistband, and he sucks in a breath as I make contact with his cock, closing his eyes to the sensation of my hand. I brush my thumb over the head, causing him to hiss. I wipe away the pre-cum and bring my thumb back to my mouth, sucking on it. He groans. "Fuck, that's good. You like sucking cock, Frankie?"

I can barely respond but manage a "Fuck, yes" before my mouth is back on his.

My hand slides up and down the length of his cock, and Cameron emits moans of encouragement. I stop and watch him, our eyes making contact, and I shift my body forward so my pussy is lined up onto his cock, my panties covering his access.

"I can't have sex with you, Cameron. I'm not ready for that, that's not what I do," I pant out through my own arousal.

I expect him to be shocked or annoyed, but if he is, he doesn't show it. Instead, he cups my jaw in one hand. "I'll take whatever you're prepared to give me."

His words encourage me as I surge forward and attack his mouth with mine. I pump my tongue into his mouth with the same motion my body is doing. Rubbing myself onto his cock, he falls backward onto the bed as I fully straddle him, his cock between us.

"Fuck, Frankie, you're so fucking hot, I need to see you come, baby, come on my cock, my dirty girl." His grip on my ass is painful but in a good way.

"Fuck yes." My own moans are getting louder.

"Fuck, Cameron there, right there." His hips jerking faster against me, his cock rubbing between my panties and his stomach. "I'm almost there, Cameron!" My voice is pained.

"Fuck yes, give it to me, Frankie, fucking come!" he spits through gritted teeth.

My mouth drops open as I scream his name, and Cameron jerks and grabs my hips tighter. Ropes of sticky, warm cum spill from him, his eyes on me as my chest heaves.

"So fucking beautiful, Frankie," he says as he reaches up to kiss me again, this time slow and passionate.

I lower my body onto his, not caring about the state we are in.

He wraps his arm around me gently. "Stay the night in here with me?" His voice is gentle and not remotely like the Cameron I've come to realize he portrays, almost vulnerable. I nod in response, barely able to do anything more. His arms stay tight around me, as if to reassure himself I really am staying.

14

CAMERON

Last night with Frankie was incredible. We didn't even have sex and it was the most erotic and intense sexual experiences of my life. I know whatever it is that we have together has changed me. There is no way I'm going to lose her, lose what we have.

She'd woken in the night with soft whimpers, clearly some sort of nightmare. I held her tighter and stroked her hair as she settled down. I gently kissed her shoulders and neck, unsure if I was comforting and reassuring her or me.

I decide to leave her sleeping in bed this morning. As I pull on my gym clothes, I glance at her, she's lying on her back with her naked body exposed, apart from her panties. My eyes dart to her stomach, and in particular the tattoo with the name Nate. It leaves a bitterness inside me when I see it. I clench my fists at my sides in frustration.

Was she still in contact with him? How could she be happy to have his name tattooed on her, for all to see? Did she still love him? I shake off the thoughts and decide to unleash all the uncertainty and insecurity in the gym.

My mom is in the kitchen as I approach. Soon I realize she isn't alone, she's blending a smoothie with a very hungover Joel draped over the worktop, barely propped up on the barstool. I inwardly chuckle to myself.

"Good morning, Joel!" I singsong.

Joel's head slowly rises, and he throws me a death glare. "Why the hell are you so happy?"

I grin back at him, no doubt looking like a complete loon. "Guess I didn't have as much to drink as you, huh?" I shrug.

My mom breaks off our conversation. "I'm out today, shopping and then dinner with the Harrises. Your father has asked for you to keep an eye on Frankie." She looks at me pointedly.

I can't hide my smile. "No problem, Mom." I nod like the good boy.

As she leaves the kitchen and her heels click away, Joel watches me with intensity. He groans. "Oh my fucking God, you fucked her, didn't you?" His eyes are wide with intrigue.

I can't help but laugh. "Actually, no, I didn't." I smother a smile.

His eyes narrow on me as he tries to figure out what has gone down between us.

"She blow you?"

I grin and shake my head at him. "Nope."

"Then what the fuck she do?" His eyes bore into mine, desperation in his voice for the juicy gossip.

I shrug, not prepared to give anything away. Probably for the first time in my life I want to remain private and not share what I have with anyone else. She's mine, and I'm not about to fuck that up.

I grab a shake and move down the hall to the gym, with Joel hot on my heels.

"You're really not going to tell me anything?"

"Nope!"

"Fuck, man, that's so fucked up. I need to live through you if I'm not going to get some from her."

I spin around on him, my body tense, anger radiating from me. My words come sharp as a knife. "You won't be getting any and you won't be getting anything from me, understand?"

Joel huffs childishly. "What the fuck ever, you spent five fucking minutes in there happy and now you have to go and ruin it, dick," he grunts and rolls his eyes as he pushes past me to go in the gym.

FRANKIE

I wake slowly, stretching and taking in my surroundings. *Yep, definitely not my room.* I smile to myself as I remember what went down between Cameron and me last night. I half expected him to want me gone, out of his room. But he surprised me when he clung to me and asked me to stay, almost scared of me leaving. I like this vulnerable side to him; I'm convinced he doesn't just show anyone this part of him.

I could feel him cuddling and kissing me in the night, and I must admit I loved it. I'm not someone who feels needy and needs to be cherished, but last night that's exactly how he made me feel. For the first time in my life, I knew that's what I wanted. I felt warm and wanted, needed.

When me and Nate were together, we spent so long trying we never just got to simply enjoy one another. We literally needed each other but being treasured was not something I was used to, it's not something any of us in Hawks knew anything about, but fuck, did it feel good.

I pull on one of Cam's T-shirts and check the hallway before making my way to my room with my clothes bundled in my arms. I decide to shower before going in search of Cameron.

I chew on my lip with uncertainty. I just hold out hope in my heart that he isn't regretting last night, I couldn't bear the thoughts of giving myself to someone for them to destroy me, not after what I've been through, I couldn't take any more heartache or trauma.

After a long shower and a lot of courage, I dress in yoga pants and a gym top and make my way downstairs to the kitchen. I grab an apple and a bottle of water for breakfast and then make my way to the gym.

I walk in and to my utter delight, I find Cameron in shorts and topless. He's pummeling the punching bag with a hungover Joel lying on the floor, eating a bag of chips.

"Morning," I say cheerily, hoping to gauge their responses, completely faking my confidence.

Cameron's head whips around, his hair a little unruly and sweat glistening on his golden chest. His eyes lock with mine, and I swear he can read my sexual thoughts. His mouth quirks up knowingly at the side in a small cocky grin. I give him a flirty smile back and raise an eyebrow.

He takes a sip of his water, and I watch his Adam's apple bob as he swallows, and I have to clench my legs together in anticipation. Fuck, I want him bad.

Joel starts chuckling. "Fuck, babe, you want him as bad as he wants you!" Cameron's eyes meet mine and they seem both relieved and humored. He smiles to himself, then lowers his head and shakes it. I've a feeling he's just as relieved as me at our interaction.

"Good to know," I tease back to Joel.

I decide to break the tension. "So, what are you working on?"

"Snap kick," Cameron responds.

I nod and go to sit next to Joel, deciding I'd sooner watch Cameron than actually workout myself. As I saunter over to Joel with a flirty swagger, Cameron chuckles to himself and then turns his body and begins practicing the various roundhouse kicks.

"You need to remember to chamber your leg when you land," I quip at Cameron after he performs another impressive move.

His head shoots around, and his eyes narrow on me. I hold my hands up in defense and joke as I explain my observations. "I've been around enough gyms and fights to pick shit up." I shrug. Okay, so I could be a little more truthful, but he'll find out soon enough. I'm sure.

We've been sitting here a while, watching Cameron. Joel has now taken it upon himself to lay his head in my lap, and I hadn't realized I was sitting there stroking his hair—much like I do with Aiden—until Cameron stops what he's doing and peers down at us. He eyes Joel and then eyes me in question. I peek down at Joel who is barely awake and hold my finger up to my mouth. "He's tired," I say in explanation. Cameron rolls his eyes.

He walks over to us and pushes Joel with his foot. "Yo, motherfucker. Get up and fuck off home to bed."

My eyes dart up to Cameron in shock, but the big grin on his face makes me stop and soften. They are just like the boys back home with the banter.

CAMERON

Not going to lie, seeing Frankie walk into the gym this morning with her hot little yoga pants and gym top on is such a fucking relief.

I expected her to pretend nothing has happened between us and us going back to the whole we hate each other bullshit but seeing her smile and check me out was fucking amazing. I am done with pushing her away, although I am also aware of not coming on too strong. I don't want to scare her off, but at the same time, I have an overwhelming, possessive urge to declare she's mine.

She clearly trusts few people, and I want to build myself into her circle; I want to prove myself to her.

The tips she gave me while watching me train were spot on, she knows her stuff and that in itself is fucking hot. How many girls do I know that know any of that or are even interested in my training? Not a single fucking one. Not until her; no fucking way am I letting her go.

I turn and look down to see fucking Joel virtually passed out in my girl's lap. I had a crazy urge to rip him apart but then I studied Frankie and saw a softness in her I hadn't seen before, she was stroking his hair like you would a child, and in that moment, I saw another part of her that she didn't let many people see. Love, softness, and compassion.

Once Joel goes home, I quickly shower. I was at a loose end and basically wanted to go to Frankie's room and fuck her senseless. Clearly that isn't an option, so how can I see her without coming across as too fucking desperate?

I start pacing the floor and then I'm stopped in my tracks by a soft knock at my door. "Yeah?"

The door creeps open, and Frankie pokes her head inside, she is a little downcast and has her vulnerable face on. The one that makes me want to protect her. "Hey, I wondered if you could do me a favor?"

"Sure," I reply a little too fast and desperate, making her laugh as her eyes meet mine.

She smiles an adorable smile. "You going to ask what the favor is first?"

"Nah, I'm good." I shrug, because, let's face it, I'd have done any fucking thing.

"Okay, well I need to visit a friend's house and collect something. I need a lift." Her shoulders straighten as she talks to me, as if trying to be confident in herself.

I nod. "From the teacher's house?"

Her eyes bug out and dart to mine, narrowing slightly as I give her a knowing smirk. Just to let her know I don't miss a fucking thing. "Yeah, his," she admits while glancing away.

"Sure." I smile back and grab my keys for the SUV.

We pull up to a small colonial-style house on the outskirts of Hawks Town. If it wasn't for the overgrown grass on the front, the house would have actually been pretty damn nice for the area, not what I was expecting, that's for sure.

A small porch is wrapped around the house, with pots of flowers on the steps leading to the door.

Frankie turns to me with a small smile as if reading my thoughts. "His brother Ryan brought him up, it's their family home." She sighs as if not sure whether to say more before continuing, "He was a police officer and died in the line of duty." I nod my head in understanding, the teacher was brought up in a decent area by a man of decent caliber.

Frankie opens the door and walks inside, seemingly knowing full well where she's going. "You spend much time here?" I ask as I walk through the virtually empty rooms, odd bits of furniture and dusty boxes lay scattered about.

"Yeah, we all did. He's family." There's that word again. And honestly? I'm jealous as fuck. I want to be her family. I scrub my hand down my face.

See, this is what I struggle with, I expect a bunch of fighters, gangs, whatever you want to call them, to be in a crew but teachers? Police officers? I guess it's something I don't understand.

"Was the brother in your crew too?"

Frankie laughs from the kitchen area. "Once upon a time, I guess." She pauses. "He chose the legal route."

Okay, so I guess he wasn't a part of the crew, after all. I wondered how this all worked, the good guys on the same side as the bad?

I'm lost in my thoughts when Frankie appears at the

door to the living room, carrying a big brown box. I approach her to take it from her, and as I look down, I see the big blue star on the top, no name, no other clue but it is clearly for Frankie.

After loading the box into the trunk, I get into the car. Frankie is lost in her thoughts, staring out of the window toward the house solemnly. I wish I could take her obvious pain away. She's struggling, that's for sure, the place must have held so many memories for her and her family. I take her hand in mine and squeeze it gently, then she turns to me and smiles softly and I know we're good.

About an hour into the drive, I figure, fuck it. Why keep trying to work shit out when I could simply just ask her? "So, what's with the star?" I point to her tattoo.

She laughs low and pulls her lip between her teeth in a playful way before meeting my eyes. "Oh, well that was a dare!"

I laugh because that is so fucking typical of Frankie. I'm here thinking it was a crew thing and all along it was a game they played. "It was my first tattoo. I was dared to steal a police car while the cop ate doughnuts on a park bench." I look at her in shock and she giggles at me. "I left it two blocks away, don't worry. Jeez, the poor guy needed the exercise, believe me." She shakes her head. "Anyway, I did it and the guys had to get a tattoo of my choice. I chose a blue star and when they had it done, I felt a little bit annoyed that I didn't have one as well. So yeah, I got that." She points to it.

"That's where your nickname comes from, I assume?"

"Yep, everyone back home knows me as Star. My mother gave me Starlight as a middle name." She rolls her eyes in jest while shaking her head in mock disgust.

"They didn't find out you took the car?"

She glances at me, cringing. "Let's just say there was one police officer who was very pissed for a while, and luckily for me, we were considered family, so it kinda got swept under the carpet. Along with a few other little things throughout the years." Her admission makes perfect sense to me now. I guess even having professionals on the wrong side of the tracks is helpful.

15

FRANKIE

Cameron asked me earlier if I'd like to go to a party with him and Joel tonight. I wasn't actually keen on the idea, a bunch of rich kids measuring dicks at a prissy pompous fuck-fest, but I got the feeling he was trying to distract me, so I decided to go along with it.

Okay, so after spending more time than I ever have done before getting ready, I actually was quite impressed with myself. My hair is in thick dark waves down my back, and I have a tight little black dress on and black combat boots. I feel both glamorous and comfortable. I feel like me.

Cameron and Joel haven't left my side, almost sensing my anxiety at being here, and I'm grateful for their silent support.

Cameron's hand keeps grazing mine and it sends tingles down my arms. We haven't discussed the night we spent together any more but the underlying sexual tension and feelings are evident.

I can feel Cameron's heated eyes on me throughout the night, and I feel like the night is building into something more between us, and I cannot fucking wait.

Leo comes bouncing over with extra drinks and informs us that Ollie is outside setting up various party games. Joel is quick to want to join in, practically bouncing out the doors, making me glance to Cameron, who gives me a little side smirk at Joel's excitability. We follow behind onto a huge deck where various games are taking place around the pool.

We go over to Leo, who is now straddling a chair, along with other furniture scattered around in a circle. We all take seats on the comfy lounge furniture as more join us to play a game of Never Have I Ever—*oh, fucking goody*. I groan internally.

Cameron's eyes dance with a mixture of flirtatiousness and humor; he's going to enjoy this, that's for sure.

I suck in a breath when Stacey and Taylor plonk themselves on the couch either side of Cameron directly opposite me. Cameron's eyes narrow on me as if questioning my reaction, and I quickly scull my emotions away. I'm not going to be jealous of those fucking bimbos. *Fuck, why the hell am I so annoyed?* It's not like we're official.

Joel takes the chair next to me, the one sat between the

couches. He glances at me and winks. I get the feeling he is sitting next to me for moral support.

There's now about ten people in the circle, all of us in some of the same classes at school. Cups are filled and joints are being smoked. Stacey and Taylor are both trying to flirt with Cameron whose eyes are solely on me, almost gauging my reactions. *Yeah, not giving you a fucking thing, buddy.*

"Okay, so everyone knows how it goes," Leo starts.

"I'll go first!" Stacey declares. Of fucking course she would. I roll my eyes. "So never have I ever had an STD?"

She giggles and stares directly at me. She's being a complete bitch, of course. I groan back my irritation and don't take a drink because contrary to what she thinks of me, I'm not a dirty hoe bag.

However, she picks up a cup, along with another guy and Joel, and tips it back, giggling to herself as though it's something to be proud of. I gaze at Cameron whose face appears completely mortified! *Yeah, you've been there, buddy.*

Cameron is next, he seems deep in thought before looking at me, a small smile gracing his lips before he shifts his eyes away. "Fucked more than five people?"

Everyone, and I mean everyone, picks the cups up and drinks; everyone apart from me, of course. Stunned expressions cross everyone's faces.

Taylor declares, "No fucking way! If you're playing, you have to be truthful!" she spits out, with accusing eyes.

My head snaps in her direction. "I'm a lot of things. But I'm not a fucking liar, and I have fucking standards about who I let in my pussy. I don't give it up for just anyone!" I snap back. My nails digging into my palms, trying to keep my cool.

Between the stunned silences there are laughs and ooohs. I chance a look at Cameron, he won't meet my eye and his jaw is tight with a tic in it.

What the fuck's his problem?

Stacey puts her hand on his knee, and he doesn't move it. *What the fuck?*

My eyes meet Joel's who has a sneer of disgust aimed Cameron's way. He sighs and then shrugs at me, as if to say, *Whatever.* The game continues on with Taylor next.

"Ever thought of someone else while messing around with someone?" *What the hell?* Everyone apart from me takes a drink. My eyes practically bug out.

I draw my gaze up to Cameron and he is looking directly at me, he shoots me a cheeky wink. *What the fuck was all that about?* My heart thumps in my chest. *Is he fucking with me right now?*

A few more questions are asked, to which we all take drinks.

When it comes around to my turn, I can't decide whether to go with something dirty or sensible. Mmm, I mean, I don't want to disappoint, do I? I guess I should live up to my reputation, right?

"Ever been fucked in the ass while pleasuring someone else?"

All eyes turn to me. I wait . . . then I do it. I lean forward, take the cup, and raise it with a cheers salute. "Just me, then?" I down the fucker. Eyes wide at me, mouths drop open. Yeah, just the reaction I was going for.

Cameron takes an intake of breath. I gaze around at everyone and can't help the smile on my face.

Joel cracks up laughing. "That's so fucking hot, you do realize that's the fantasy I'm jacking off to tonight, right?"

I rub his arm in an almost condescending gesture but completely playful. "I'm sure it will be a great dream too, Joel. You enjoy!" I wink at him.

I can feel Cameron's eyes boring into me, venom oozing my way. But I don't give him the satisfaction of looking at him. He's pissing me off. Stacey's hand has been rubbing his thigh, and Taylor has her whole body turned in toward him, yet he makes no move to discourage them. *What. The. Fuck. Ever!*

Joel's turn doesn't surprise me in the least. "Licked cum up after someone shot their load." To my surprise, Stacey doesn't drink, obviously I do, but what surprised me more was Joel does too?! Didn't see that one coming.

Stacey's turn again doesn't surprise me. "Been with someone black," she spits it out like it's a bad thing. I glance toward Leo, the only black guy at the party. *What the fuck is wrong with her?* She's watching me with a raised eyebrow. She's not questioning if I've been with Leo. No, she's questioning where I'm from and what color the guys I've previously slept with have been, like it fucking matters.

Everyone watches me. "Define 'been with,'" I add.

She rolls her eyes. "Okay, well." She shuffles from side to side. "Been sexual with someone black."

I pick up my cup and down it, throwing her a patronizing smile before glancing at Leo and winking at him. Apart from Leo, I'm the only one to take a drink, what a shocker.

Cameron watches me carefully as the words slip from his mouth. "Been sexual with someone and then regretted it?" A shiver runs up my spine, his eyes drilling into me. *What the hell? Is he telling me he regrets it? Because he said sexual and not sex, right? Is this why he's off with me? He regrets it?*

Well, I fucking don't! I don't do anything with my body that makes me regret it after, that's for fucking sure! I don't move, but he does. Oh yes, he fucking does, he watches me, just me and then downs his fucking drink.

Taylor is next. "Had period sex?" Oh my God, if I wasn't so open, I'd die right now. These people. Fuck it, I pick up my cup and down it. Because, let's face it, if you're in a long-term relationship and your horny around the time of the month, you couldn't give a shit, you jump on it.

Fuck the mess, right? Cameron doesn't move, nor does Joel, or either of the plastic bitches, okay, just me and one other.

When it gets around to my turn, we're all well on our way to being very, very drunk.

I ask the lame one, the one that makes everyone's eyes roll and moan at. "Ever been in love?"

I watch Cameron, his head is down and he's concentrating on a spot on the floor, his back is rigid. Slowly, almost as if time has stood still, he laughs a little at himself as though disbelieving what he's thinking, then he picks the cup up and downs it. Everyone apart from Joel and Leo down their drinks.

Joel's turn. "Ever been with someone with their cock pierced?" His eyebrows wriggle at me in jest. *No way?!*

"You've got a pierced cock?" I gasp out in astonishment. "Joel, you've been holding out on me! I need to see." I playfully go to grab him, and he shakes my hands away, we're giggling like a pair of children.

"Well?" Cameron's voice snaps loud above our playful banter. Captain Serious is at it again.

I miss who had a drink and who didn't. But I shake my head to inform them I haven't. "Not yet!" I grin happily.

I add my comment with a wink in Joel's direction. Cameron's eyes are like lasers burning into me, they're dark and cold. His body radiating tension, his shoulders straight and jaw tense. His fists clenching at his side. Fuck. He flicks a switch and he's suddenly someone else, it's hard fucking work with him sometimes.

After another round of everyone's sexy secrets exposed, Stacey announces we need more tequila. "Come with me, Cammy, come and help me find the tequila!" she purrs while shoving her tits in his face. I eye Cameron. He doesn't even look at me now. No, he's now taken to completely ignoring me. *What a fucking dick.*

Joel affectionately squeezes my knee. "You good?"

I turn and smile up at him, he's wasted. His eyes are glazed, and his mouth is open more than necessary. "Yeah, I'm good, Joel." I grin back at him.

Stacey wobbles onto her feet and holds her hand out for Cameron. He takes it without hesitation and pulls himself up. Without giving me a second glance, he tugs her into him, and they head off into the house. I can't help the disappointment I feel inside. *Why the fuck do I do this? Why do I let myself start to feel something for someone, yet they make me feel like shit?* I sigh heavily, bringing myself to Joel's attention. "Come here, hot lips." He sits forward to grab me into his lap, only he hasn't realized he's still holding his cup of beer and I'm holding mine. They both smack into his chest at the same time, and poor Joel is drenched. His shirt soaked through. I can't help but laugh, he's such an idiot.

"Shit! I need to strip now, don't I?" He wiggles his eyebrows as he stands.

My hand goes to my mouth as he proceeds to pull his sodden shirt over his head. "Oh my God, Joel, stop!" His hand is on his belt as though he's getting ready to strip those off too. Christ, his jeans aren't even wet. *What the hell is he thinking?*

There are chants of "Take them off" going around the circle. Any other time, I'd probably join in, but Joel is trashed. His body is sagging, his head lolling, his eyes virtually closed. I jump up. "Nope, mister, not going to happen."

He pouts at me, literally pouts. His belt and jeans are open. "Leo, can you give me a hand?" I gesture to Joel and his loose jeans with a grimace.

Leo pushes past the chairs and drapes Joel's arm over him as I trail behind.

"Where are we taking him?"

"Erm, bathroom to tidy him up and then bedroom, maybe? I need to find Cameron." I exhale a breath.

Leo chuckles and shakes his head as Joel drags his feet. While making our way through the house, he proceeds to tell everyone how amazing they are. How hot they are and how he's not drunk. Yep, completely deluded. He even tells multiple guys he's fucked a whore's mouth and she was the best! Oh, and he's in love with a snow angel. I stifle a chuckle at his drunken state as we make our way toward the staircase.

"We best try and get him upstairs, most of the

bedrooms have an adjoining bathroom." I nod, agreeing with Leo.

The stairs are tricky, and Joel keeps stopping and leaning backward to talk to me, making it harder for Leo to hold him. "Frankie, are we sleeping here tonight?" he asks softly.

"No, Joel. We're just going to clean you up and put you down on a bed to relax until I find Cameron."

"If you fuck Cam, can I watch?"

I huff. "I'm not going to fuck Cameron, just keep walking, Joel, nearly there."

"Dude, stop talking and move your legs, not your mouth!" Leos grunts, clearly getting pissed with Joel's heavy body.

We walk down a corridor and Leo pushes open the first door we come to, and he nods toward the room. "Here, this will do."

"Let's get you into the bathroom, Joel. You're all sticky. Come on, let's get you cleaned up, buddy." It's like talking to a child, but I can't help but treat Joel like he's Aiden or Romeo. I like looking after them.

Leo turns on the bathroom light, then his eyes dart from me to Joel. "Am I done here?"

"Yeah, leave us alone. We'll be okay, wont we, Frankie?" Joel's head lolls to the side, trying to look at me, his body struggling to stay upright.

I laugh as Joel attempts to wriggle his eyebrows and push his jeans down. *Oh my God!* "No, don't leave us alone, Leo, for fuck's sake!"

Leo's laughing harder as I try and wrestle Joel's jeans back up. His hand is swatting mine away as he tuts at me with his puckered lips.

I wet a towel and start wiping his chest. "That feels go good, Frankie, fuck you're making me hard!"

I gasp. "Oh my God, Joel, you better not."

He's laughing to himself. "Do you still want to see my pierced dick?"

I steal a glance at Leo who's leaning back against the sink counter watching with his arms crossed, grinning at the scene in front of him.

I can feel my cheeks redden. "No, Joel, I don't want to see your pierced dick! Come on, let's get you on the bed."

He shuffles forward, moving some hair from out of my face. "You're so beautiful, Frankie, you'd love my pierced dick."

"I'm sure I would. Come on, let's go, stud!"

I push him toward the bed, he throws himself down and then rolls onto his back, his eyes barely open.

"Leo, I'm going to go search for Cameron."

"Okay, I'm going to take a piss, be down in a minute," he calls back from the bathroom. I glance at a semi-conscious Joel. Surely, he'll be okay for five, right? Making my mind up, I head toward the door, and just as I'm about to go through it, I walk smack bang into a hard chest. A heaving familiar chest. I stare up straight into those hazel eyes, only they're almost black, and cold, so cold. He's sneering down at me with a look of almost . . . hate?

I shift my eyes away from the intensity, and Joel breaks the tension. "Frankie, where'd you go? Hey, man, she wanted to see my pierced cock!"

CAMERON

Since beginning the game, I knew it would be a bad idea. But I just can't help myself, I'd get to learn more about Frankie and her life. I can rely on others asking the questions I'm desperate to know about her.

For some reason, I assumed Frankie would have a ton of sexual partners, so to learn she'd had less than five is a shock. I sit there mulling over her words. *"I have standards who I let in my pussy." Did she mean me? Is that why she didn't want to fuck me? But she fucked others from where she lived, but not me? She didn't think I was good enough? What the hell was all that about?*

"Ever thought of someone else while messing around with someone?" Sure, I have, all the fucking time. Like when I fucked Stacey's mouth but thought of all the things I wanted to do to Frankie.

But not Frankie. No, she's clearly all in when she fucks someone. *Why the fuck did I not like that?*

Just when I start thinking that Frankie's sexual liaisons might be a little more clean cut than the rest of us, therefore, completely misunderstanding her altogether, she drops the bombshell question, "Ever been fucked in the ass while pleasuring someone else?" *What the actual fuck?!*

All the fucking group goes silent. She just shut us all the fuck up! And then she drinks! *What. The. Hell.* I have a deep-seated feeling inside of me, I feel sick. Not because I was disgusted, because I was fucking jealous. Jealous of whoever has fucked her ass. Jealous of her sucking someone's cock. Jealous of her doing those things with someone else, experiencing those things without me. How many fucking times I've wanted to do those things but haven't found anyone willing. Sure, I could offer something for Stacey or Taylor to do it, like a handbag or a date somewhere, but I want someone to want that, not have to fucking bribe them.

Yet, here in front of me, the girl I'm fucking lusting after, the girl who doesn't want to fuck me, has done all those things and wants to do those things, just not with me. My heart plummets at the realization that I'm not what she wants.

I watch her being playful with Joel, wishing it was me. He asks, "Licked cum up after someone shot their load?" Of course she's done that, no fucking problem. I groan inside, so fucking gutted.

Am I seriously not good enough? Am I not her thing? I watch her closely. She's watching Stacey intently, and my eyebrows furrow in confusion. *Is she jealous?* I'm not sure. I realize then that both Stacey and Taylor have their hands on my thighs. Yeah, not something they'd do sober, and probably not something they'd do if Frankie wasn't sitting opposite me either. I scrub a hand through my hair, completely uncomfortable. I just need to know how she feels.

I take a gulp of my beer and watch her closely. "Been sexual with someone and then regretted it?" Her eyes narrow on me, as if assessing me as much as I'm assessing her.

I've been with multiple girls, and I often wonder after if I made a mistake. Up until that night with Frankie, I hadn't realized how much I regret the others. Mainly because they aren't her, they mean nothing, they didn't feel right, and they didn't make me feel what I do when I'm with her. With Frankie it is incredible, but with them it was what it was, quick, easy, boring. I never feel fully satisfied. I always want something more, to release something inside me I am desperate to release, without complaint or judgment. To go fast, hard, intense. Fuck, I was getting hard just sitting here thinking about what I really want. With Frankie.

I take the drink and watch Frankie carefully; she is schooling her emotions well. I can't read a fucking thing on her face, but she has told me she didn't regret us. Thank fuck for that.

Taylor asks another question. "Had period sex?" *Who the fuck does that?* It's not something guys think of. But then again, periods aren't something we think of.

Of course Frankie takes a fucking drink! And suddenly, I want fucking period sex. *Jesus, I'm screwed. What the hell?*

It's true what I said to her, I'd take whatever she would give me. Any. Fucking. Thing!

Frankie watches me when she asks her question. "Ever been in love?" That's the first question I have to think about for real. Why I'm even pausing for this, I'm not sure, but I glance down at my feet while I think and then it hits me in the chest. The jealousy, possessiveness, the need to know everything about her, be around her, wanting to protect her, make her mine. I'm pretty fucking sure this is love. The realization hits me like a truck to my chest, making me laugh to myself. *How fucking stupid have I been?*

I'm in love with a foulmouthed, tattooed, reckless little sexpot. My very own dirty girl.

I pick up a drink and down it.

Mine!

Joel's turn. "Ever been with someone with their cock pierced?" Frankie all but squeals in excitement.

Yeah, something else I haven't got to offer her. I sag inside. Let's face it, she's into the whole rough and rugged thing, reckless like her. She sure as fuck isn't into the clean-cut fucking good-boy image I portray. I scrub my hand down my face. I knew this would be a disaster; I never should have played.

I watch her and Joel, she's playing around with him, and I'm sitting here with the realization that I'll never be enough for her.

I help an overly flirtatious Stacey with the bottles of tequila, the salt pot, fresh cups, and a dish full of limes. Yeah, we're about to play Naked Tequila. We make our way back outside, and she exaggerates her strut to make her ass shimmy from side to side. I think she's trying to flirt, but it isn't fucking happening. I shake my head at the thought.

We approach the table to find a missing Frankie and

Joel. "Where the fuck is Joel?" I ask, not wanting to let them know I'm asking where Frankie is.

Taylor throws her hair over her shoulder and pouts. "Frankie and Joel were playing a game of strip"—she points to Joel's T-shirt on the floor—"and they got a little carried away. So, they've gone inside for some alone time." She flicks her gaze to Stacey and smiles.

My heart fucking sinks, anger builds up inside me. *Fucking stripping? Fucking alone time? What the fuck?* I feel fucking betrayed. Betrayed! *How the fuck can I feel that when me and Frankie never even agreed to anything? How could she do this with my best friend? Who fucking does that?* Frankie, that's who.

I dump the tequila and cups. "Where are you going?" snaps Stacey.

"Going to find Joel," I shout back at her as I storm toward the house.

"Bring him back to play!" *Yeah, like fuck I will!*

I make my way inside and gaze around the crowd. I pull Dane, a guy from school, away from some chick. "You see Joel?"

"Frankie was dragging him upstairs. Think they're getting their kink on, she was tugging at his jeans. He had his belt open, ready to go!" He laughs, slapping me on the back.

Dread pools inside me. I look back at the pool area. *Do I go back out and forget about them, or do I track them both down?* My teeth clench in anger. *Fuck!*

I practically run upstairs, shoving past people. I push open the doors one by one. Not in there, nor the second one I try, not in there either.

I turn and go left, almost running into someone coming

out of a door. I know it's her instantly; she's so much smaller in her boots than her heels, yet just as sexy. Her scent hits me.

I gaze down at her, and she appears sheepish. Then I glance past her shoulder toward the door. The door she's trying to discreetly shut. Joel is lying on the bed with his jeans pulled down to expose his boxers. "Frankie, where'd you go? Hey, man, she wanted to see my pierced cock!" I stumble backward slightly, because seeing something is completely different to hearing it. My chest tightens and it fucking hurts.

I quickly try and mask my feelings. I won't give her the satisfaction of her knowing how I feel, that the pain in my chest that's making me wince is for her.

"What the fuck are you doing?" I practically spit out, curling my lip in disgust.

She blinks at me in shock. "I was helping Joel," she replies, her voice gentle.

"Helping him?" I laugh, a patronizing laugh. "Is that what you call it in that shithole you're from?"

Frankie's eyes narrow on me, and her spine straightens, and her tone changes. "What the hell's your problem, Cameron?"

"You. You're my fucking problem! Taking advantage of my fucking friends, you really are a piece of work, aren't you?"

Her face falls. "You can't be serious?"

"I'm deadly fucking serious! What did that bartender call you? Entertainment, right? Is that what this is? Are you entertaining Joel?" I shake my head, laughing at my words. "Fuck, I hope he wore a rubber, what was it you said? Leave a tip? Well here, take this fucking dollar and leave my friends alone!" I shove the dollar at her, it drops to the floor, her eyes blink, and I'm pretty fucking sure I see tears.

She's not going to draw me in though; she isn't going to make me feel bad for her being a whore. I lower my face to her ear and whisper-yell the words, "Like mother like daughter, right? Perhaps you should fuck off back to where you came from." Her gasp is audible.

Her shoulders straighten. I hit a nerve, that's for sure. She swallows thickly. "Yeah, you're right." She pushes past me and runs down the corridor toward the stairs. My own shoulders sag instantly at her exit.

The bedroom door flies open, and a fist connects with my face before I can register who hit me. I stumble backward against the wall as Leo charges at me again. He's pummeling me with blow after blow, but I've got technique on my side. I use my left foot to swipe his feet from under him before I launch myself on top of him. "What the fuck is your problem?" I practically spit.

His dark eyes bore into me, he's seething. "I heard the shit you said to Frankie, you fucking asshole!"

I throw my head back laughing. "You too, huh?"

"What the fuck are you talking about?" His eyes narrow in confusion.

My eyes meet his, and I sharpen them as reality hits him of what I'm accusing him of, his mouth drops open. "Shit, you think I fucked her?" I don't speak, Leo laughs slightly to himself and shakes his head. "You've got it all wrong. So wrong, you fucking idiot!"

I eye him, confused, so he goes on to explain. "Me and Frankie were stopping Joel from stripping his clothes off. The idiot is off his face, he spilled beer all over himself, and every-fucking-where. We had to practically drag him upstairs to the bathroom. Frankie dumped his ass on the bed, she was coming to find you to take them home!" I relax my hold on him. *Oh shit, what have I done?* Sickness consumes me.

My face must show my panic. "You need to find her, man, you need to apologize." He shakes his head slightly. "The things you said, Cameron, they were fucking awful."

I let him go just as the bedroom door swings open to a naked Joel. His pierced cock swinging in the air, his boxer shorts around his ankles. "Have you seen Frankie? I wanted to show her my pierced cock. Oh, fuck, I think I'm going to be sick!" His face blanches as he releases a stomach full of alcohol, all over said fucking pierced cock! *Jesus.*

16

CAMERON

I was tempted to go after Frankie last night but by the time I'd gotten Joel showered and home, I thought it was best to give her the break she no doubt needs.

First thing this morning I'm up and showered. I had Neo track her down and now I'm sitting in the Suburban outside of a run-down two-story house in Hawks Town at 10 a.m. I glance around the surrounding area; they're all shitholes. The street is littered with garbage and toys, kids are playing in the street, and adults sit on their doorsteps smoking. Random cars on driveways, they seem abandoned but I've a feeling they're their actual cars.

There are beer bottles heaped on gardens, lawns are overgrown. Yeah, a fucking shithole, the whole street goddamn street.

This house appears a little better kept than the rest, but there's a bunch of broken toys on the front overgrown garden. I take a deep breath and make my way to the front door. One window is bordered up, the front door is wooden and so badly damaged, I'm surprised it can shut fully. I can hear kids from behind the door, squealing and chaos. I blow out a breath and knock loudly, then quickly panic that I nearly break the fucking door.

It swings open a moment later to the tall blond guy from the court. He's wearing basketball shorts and a baggy white T-shirt. His long blond hair is to his shoulders, his features are sharp, his eyes a little wild. He stares at me, studying me as much as I am him. Then he glances over my shoulder to my car as if to see if there's anyone else there.

"Hey, I was looking for Frankie." I tug on my hair, uncomfortable as fuck.

He stands there watching me, his legs are parted, and his arms are crossed over his chest, then he smiles, it lights up his face. He then holds his hand out to me, completely shocking me. His tattooed fingers meet mine, shaking them heavily. I take notice of the word cocksucker on them, making me laugh. "Aiden," he says with a smile.

"Cameron." I nod back with my own smile. My body relaxing instantly.

"I know who you are, Cameron Donovan." His eyes dance with jest.

I roll my eyes. "Of course you do." Yeah, because the fuckers set me up.

He opens the door wider. "Come on in."

He swings his arm to gesture me in, and when I stride into the house, I see it's littered with toys. A staircase to my right, to the left is a small living area, with two kids watching cartoons, and straight ahead, I can see a kitchen, a small, stocky lady with hair pulled back into a bun is busying herself.

"Come on, follow me." We walk toward the kitchen but turn right before getting to it, there's a small corridor with two doors. Aiden opens the left one and walks in, I follow. I take in the room, to the left is a bunk bed followed by another where that one finishes, then a small window, then another bunk bed going horizontally across the wall. To my right is a broken dresser with clothes hanging out. A small television sitting on top. The room has clothes and shoes strewn around, along with toys, it's a mess.

I glance back to the left bunkbed and Frankie throws her feet out of the bed, shocking me. Her legs are bare, but she wears a long baggy white T-shirt. No prizes for guessing where the fuck that came from.

Her eyes take me in but don't meet mine. Yeah, I fucked up big time. My heart pounds in my chest at the thought of losing her completely.

"Frankie, Cameron is here!" Aiden declares.

She laughs slightly. "Yeah, I can see that Aid." She huffs.

I fidget uncomfortably, from one foot to the other. "Can we talk?"

"Lucas, get your ass out of bed, man. Mama is making us pancakes!" Aiden practically screams.

A head pops up over the bunk above Frankie. "Fuck yeah. With blueberries?"

"Only if you hurry!" Aiden tells the kid.

The kid all but leaps down, he's a scrawny little thing, maybe about eleven or twelve? "Hey, Frankie, I didn't realize it was you there last night, why were you crying?" Of all the things he could have said, and he said that. *Fuck, I'm a bastard.*

I watch her, but she doesn't look at me, she's fiddling with the T-shirt, then wrings her hands in her lap vulnerably.

"Make it right," Aiden whispers into my ear. I nod back as he leaves the room, pushing the kid with him.

I clear my throat. "I fucked up!"

She nods back at me but refuses to look in my direction. "Yeah."

I gulp, she still won't look at me. "I'm sorry." I hope she hears the desperation in my voice.

She shakes her head slightly, she isn't going to forgive me, I know it. I'm going to make her, I can't lose her. I need her. I just didn't realize how much.

"I don't know how to explain things, Frankie." She doesn't respond. I sigh. "I've never felt like this. I know you have and that makes me feel worse, about myself, I mean." I bite my lip in frustration.

"I don't understand." Her voice is quiet.

I tug on my hair and study her, still no eye contact. I swallow hard. I'm about to talk about fucking feelings for God's sake! "I hurt you because I thought you'd hurt me. I purposely wanted to make you feel bad, because when I thought you were with Joel, doing shit, I felt sick because it wasn't with me."

"Doing shit?"

I breathe out and tug on my hair in annoyance with myself. "Having sex, Frankie, I thought you were having sex."

"Right, because I'm a whore like my mother, right?"

I wince at my own words. I sigh, she isn't going to forgive me. "I don't know what came over me. What I feel, I've never felt before. I didn't even realize these feelings existed, Frankie."

She shakes her head. "You're going to have to explain those, Cameron, because you pretty much acted like you hated me, and you've just admitted you wanted to hurt me."

"I . . . I . . . fuck, I'm jealous. I've never been jealous before, I want you. All the fucking time, and not even just for sex. I want you to laugh with me like you do Joel. I want you to care about me like you do your crew. I just want you to want me like I want you, Frankie, but I'm prepared to take anything you can offer. I just can't lose you, please. Tell me I haven't lost you," I practically beg.

She looks up at me, her eyes are rimmed red. I did that, I hurt her. I swallow the sickening emotion down. I don't fucking deserve her.

"You can't keep lashing out at me, Cameron. You didn't even ask, you just lash out!"

"I know. I won't. I'm sorry!" I swallow thickly. "I'm sorry, Frankie, and desperate for your forgiveness." So, fucking desperate. I watch her with hopeful eyes.

"I didn't like Stacey and Taylor touching you," she admits. My eyes meet hers, and I feel a small bit of relief, she was jealous too. "I'm a lot of things but I'm not a whore, Cameron."

"Fuck, I know that, Frankie." I tug my hair and try to control my breathing. I can't bear her saying it, let alone thinking that.

She shakes her head slightly. "I've slept with two people . . ."

I stop her, holding my hand up. "You don't have to explain, Frankie."

"Yes, I do. You see, you've got it in your head I'm something I'm not. While you don't know things about me, you're going to wonder and question things. Probably make things up in your head. So we need to be honest with one another and open with things we have or haven't done, with questions we have for one another." I nod, because what she's saying makes sense, perfect fucking sense. And Frankie's slept with two people. *Jesus, I'm such a dick.*

"When I heard the things you'd done when we were playing the game—" I swallow hard. "I was jealous, so fucking jealous. I was mad too, because I haven't done that stuff, but mostly because you did it without me. It wasn't with me," I admit.

Her face softens on me, her eyes show understanding. "If it makes you feel any better, I don't like the thoughts of you being with other girls before me." She smiles softly.

"Yeah?"

She nods and bites her lip. "I was in a relationship a long time, Cameron. We've pretty much done everything. That's what happens in a relationship, you experiment together." I nod in understanding. Still, I don't fucking like it.

"I've never been in a relationship, Frankie; I've had quick fucks. I don't know how to deal with the whole feelings bit. As you can see, I'm shit at it!"

She laughs softly. "Yeah, you are."

I walk over to her and hold out my hand, she takes it and I pull her up. I tilt her chin up to me, making her look me in the eye, hoping she can see and hear the honesty of my words. "I am really sorry."

She lifts up on her tiptoes. "I believe you." Her lips touch mine quickly and gently.

The door flies open. "Mama says you gotta come have pancakes, Frankie." Aiden smirks.

Frankie grabs my hand and pulls me out the door to the kitchen.

A small wooden table sits with four chairs. Aiden plonks himself down on one. "Lily, grab me your hairbrush, sweetie." The little girl, Lily, grabs a hairbrush, sits on Aiden's knee, and he proceeds to brush her hair with a small, graceful, childlike smile on his face. Lily sits cutting into pancakes.

"Mama, this is Cameron," Frankie introduces me.

She wipes her hands on her apron, gracing me with a big smile. "Hello, Cameron. It's lovely to meet you. I've heard a lot about you."

I hold out my hand. "Nice to meet you, ma'am."

She throws her head back laughing. "Aren't you the little charmer? You can call me Mable, sweetie." She smiles, shaking my hand. "What would you like on your pancakes?" She gestures to the table.

"Oh, I'm good, thank you."

"Nonsense. Frankie, get Cameron a plate please. There's plenty."

"Mama's pancakes are the best, Cameron. You need to try them! Homemade too," Aiden explains while shoveling a mountain of pancakes into his mouth. The little girl, now adjusting a dolls outfit, stands with perfect pig tails courtesy of Aiden.

Frankie hands me a plate of pancakes and tips her head toward the table. I smile and accept the plate.

The front door flies open, and from where I'm sitting, I can see the Latino from the courtroom waltz in. He's in a wifebeater, showing off his muscular physique and arms covered in tattoos.

"Is that Romeo?" Frankie asks no one in particular.

Aiden nods, pancakes hanging from his mouth. Frankie quite literally squeals, and she jumps from her chair and rushes to the hallway, almost barreling Romeo down. He lifts her so her legs wrap around his waist as he marches toward us in the kitchen.

"Miss me, Star?"

"A little!" She smiles widely at him.

I watch on while eating the pancakes, trying to disguise my intrigue in their relationship.

He drops her to her feet and walks over to Mable, and he slinks his arm around her. "Mama, baby. I hope you saved me some pancakes." Romeo coos.

Mable laughs, she clearly loves the hustle and bustle of the house. She whips her towel at his arm. "You, Jerome Leon Jenkins, are a charmer! Sit your charming body down!" She thrusts a plate into his waiting hands.

He grins back at her. "I'm a charmer, Frankie!" He winks. Frankie rolls her eyes.

"Romeo, this is Cameron," Frankie introduces us.

"Hey, man, nice to officially meet you," he says while stealing the blueberries from the bowl on the table.

"Yeah. You, too." I nod back.

"Well, whatever bullshit Frankie told you, it's probably true, apart from the small-dick thing!" He makes us all laugh, his overly charming personality reminds me of Joel, this guy loves himself too.

I eye his tattooed arms, and the words cocksucker, muff diver, frigid-fucker, and limp dick all mar his skin. I choke on the pancake, causing Romeo to laugh knowingly when he sees where my eyes are staring.

We all sit making idle chit chat until Romeo clears his throat. "So, has anyone heard from Nate?" There's silence. I watch the interaction. Aiden's eyes dart to Frankie who gives a subtle head shake before they go to his pancakes, effectively stuffing his mouth so he can't speak while shaking his head.

Frankie speaks up. "No, why?"

Romeo's eyes watch Frankie for sincerity. "Bale asked me to find out. Nate's been quiet lately, that's all."

"Didn't think Bale had welcomed him back?" Frankie asks sharply.

"Never said he did, just saying he's been quiet." Romeo shrugs.

"Why wouldn't he be quiet?" Fuck, even I want to tell Frankie to shut up. She clearly knows something.

Romeo brushes his hand over his head and hold his hands up. "Not saying he should be quiet, not saying he shouldn't. Just saying Bale asked me to ask you both. So have you heard from him?" He sits back in his chair and exhales deeply.

"No!" she snaps.

Aiden shakes his head, his mouth full of pancakes. "Nope," he mumbles.

"I'm going to get some clothes and take Cameron over to The Bar, you guys coming?" she asks as she stands, effectively cutting off the conversation.

Aiden nods. "When I've finished here." He points at his plate with his fork.

Romeo grins. "I'll see you over there later. I've got an errand to run."

"What sort of errand?" Frankie narrows her eyes at Romeo.

"He means he's got to go fuck Latesha Simmons to keep her sweet." Aiden laughs.

Frankie scrunches her nose up. "Really? I thought you were screwing her mom?" My eyes bug out at that. *Jesus, he's worse than Joel.*

Romeo laughs. "Yeah, I am on weekends when the hubby is working away!" He grins.

"Be careful!" Frankie kisses the top of Romeo's head and pulls me up from my seat. We make our way back to the bedroom.

"You sleep in there last night?" I ask pointing to the bottom bunk.

"Yes. With Aiden, if that's what you're getting at. But no, we didn't have sex. Nor have we ever had sex, messed around, or even contemplated it. I've known him almost my whole life and he's like my brother." I nod. "I'd rather you ask me things than assume or get angry with me, Cameron."

"I'll work on that." I smile, pulling her into me. I bend my head and pull her lips to mine, it's slow and sensual. Her soft lips open, allowing me to push my tongue into her mouth, and I sweep it around, drawing a moan from her.

We hear kids outside the door, so I immediately step back and adjust myself. Stealing a glance at Frankie, she raises her eyebrow to me with a smirk. I narrow my eyes at her and shake my head with a smile. *Fuck, she's hot.*

Aiden comes barreling into the room; the guy is like a fucking tornado. "I can't deal with him asking me questions, Frankie!" The poor guy seems flustered and panicked. He throws himself on the bed before sitting up to look at us.

"It's fine, Aid, just change the subject. He won't ask anymore. I pissed him off enough." She grins.

"All right for you to say, you're not here!" His face is red with tension.

She walks over to him, moving his hair to behind his ear. "Hey, it won't be long, I told you last night, as soon as school has finished, I'll be here. Everything's going to be okay, I promise."

He peers up to her like a child, vulnerability showing in his eyes. "You promise?" *Fuck, this guy has clearly got some issues.*

"Yes, Aiden, I promise. We'll look after each other, okay?"

He nods his head repetitively. "Okay!"

"Now, where did you put my spare bag of clothes?" Frankie searches around the room and proceeds to check under the beds.

"Mama, Mama!" Aiden shouts.

In marches Mable with her hands on her hips and eyebrows raised. "Frankie left a bag of spare clothes, where are they?"

Mable huffs. "Check my bedroom closet, then come and do these dishes, Aiden." Her tone tells me she's pissed he shouted her into the room.

Aiden grumbles and throws himself back on the bed. "Elle me fait travailler comme un chien!" *She makes me work like a dog.*

"Vous etes dramatique!" *You're being dramatic!* Frankie quips back, laughing.

He drags himself up off the bed and out the door, presumably to Mable's closet.

"Do you all know French?" I ask Frankie with a curious smile at their interaction.

She laughs a little. "No, just me and Aiden."

My face must change to confusion, and she explains further. Lowering her voice, she says, "His family were rich and prestigious; they insisted on him speaking French, so he taught me."

"Were?"

Frankie's voice lowers further. She almost mumbles the words, "They died." I nod in understanding, no wonder Aiden is a fucking mess. Speak of the devil, in he comes, stomping with a rucksack and launches it at Frankie.

She digs around in the bag, pulling out a vest and jeans, then proceeds to strip the T-shirt off in front of Aiden who is now sat on his bed rolling joints. Frankie's bra-clad chest fully exposed, I stand as a shield effectively blocking Aiden's view, although he hasn't so much as raised his head in her direction.

She makes quick work of the jeans while I stand with my back to her, watching Aiden roll his joints. "I'm just going to freshen up in the bathroom!" she declares. *Why the fuck wouldn't she get dressed in there too?*

"You can borrow my toothbrush, it's the red one!" Aiden shouts.

"It's green, and I'm good. I've got one, thank you!"

Aiden chuckles to himself. "Apparently I'm color blind!"

I smirk at him.

"You hurt her." He stares at me in the eye.

I swallow and nod at him. "I know, it's not going to happen again."

He nods. "Good. She was broken after Nate. We can't go through that again." I nod, agreeing with him but haven't got a fucking clue what happened. God, do I fucking want to.

"Don't hurt her, please." He eyes me, almost pleadingly.

"I'll make sure I don't."

He nods his head and smiles. "Can't believe you live with fucking Jimmy. And he adopted you?"

"Yeah, I was probably about eleven when he adopted me. Did you know him?"

Aiden's eyes narrow at me, seemingly confused. "Frankie didn't tell you?"

"No, she doesn't mention him much; she barely manages to speak to him."

"Yeah, she's probably still salty. He was fucking her mama and then he disappeared and left them in the trailer while he lives the high life." He's laughing to himself.

But I'm not. I'm digesting the fact that James was fucking Frankie's mom. Frankie's mom, who was a whore, who died, and he didn't know or care. Meanwhile, leaving them in a shitty trailer while he lives a high life as a millionaire. Yeah, I'm fucking pissed for her. No wonder

Frankie can't stand him. *But why the fuck wouldn't she tell me this?*

The door opens and in walks Frankie, tight vest and all. "Ready?" she asks.

I nod my head with a smile and try and disperse the questions swirling around inside me.

17

FRANKIE

Cameron's quiet as we drive toward The Bar. I put the address into the GPS.

To say I was relieved when he tracked me down this morning was an understatement. I purposely took my phone with me, knowing he'd be able to find where I was.

I've never felt so desperate to keep a connection with someone as I do with Cameron, anyone else I would have probably taken their eyes out but with Cameron, I seem to have a deep-seated need to have his approval and be wanted by him. *Fucking desperate much?*

"You okay?" I ask meekly.

He glances toward me and smiles. "Yeah, you?"

"Yeah, you're just a little quiet."

"Who was the other guy?"

"What?"

"You said you fucked two guys; who was the other?"

I internally groan, chewing my bottom lip, this isn't going to go down well. I take a deep breathe. "Bale."

I watch him; his chest sags, and his head goes back against the headrest, and he groans. "Fuck, I really didn't want you to say that." He rolls his head toward me, meeting my eyes, and his appear pained. Yeah, its official, Cameron Donovan has it bad for me.

"It's been a while, if it makes you feel any better?"

He scoffs and asks with a defeated voice, "How long ago?"

I smile at him. "Over a year."

He perks up a little at that. "Yeah?"

"Yeah, I told you. I don't sleep with just anyone, Cameron. I'm quite determined not to become my mother!"

His face turns serious before morphing into disappointment at my words. "You're not your mother, Frankie. I know I said that shit, and I said it to hurt you, it won't happen again. I could have lost you last night. That's not going to happen again either." He takes my hand and brings it to his lips, gently kissing it before placing it on his thigh. It's a really sweet gesture, and I feel all warm inside; a completely foreign feeling to me.

"So, how come you and Aiden don't want to tell Romeo where Nate is?" he asks, quirking an eyebrow at me with a cocky grin on his face.

Mm, he clearly doesn't miss much!

I sigh, defeated. I don't want to go into everything with Cameron, but I don't want to lie to him either, so I decide to go with basic knowledge.

"Long story short, if we tell Romeo, he'll tell Bale, and Bale will throw a bitch fit and hate Nate even more for contacting us. So we don't tell Romeo, and he won't tell Bale."

"Why, would Bale throw a bitch fit?" He smiles at my choice of words.

"He's still upset at how things went down between us. Nate betrayed me—us, he betrayed us—and Bale's ordered him to stay away from us."

Cameron's eyebrows narrow, deep in thought. "He cheat on you?"

"No."

"What did he do?"

I grumble, my heart beating faster. "Do we have to do this?"

He watches me closely, his eyes bore into mine, he nods. *Great.* "Nate has addiction problems; he was doing really well, then one night he screwed up and did some coke. It had a knock-on effect to events that happened after. Bale basically blames Nate for it all. For taking the coke again."

Cameron squeezes my hand. I'm shaking with trying to keep my emotions in check. He brings it to his mouth again. "Thank you for telling me." I smile softly at him in response.

"Frankie, where the fuck are we?" His sharp tone snaps me out of the moment.

I glance up and laugh, we're pulled into our destination at a garage. A bunch of guys surround the car at every angle. Luckily, I know them all. I roll down the window as Pauly, a big, burly black guy, recognizes me, and he puts his gun back into the back of his jeans. "Jesus," Cameron grumbles under his breath.

"Hey, Star, didn't know it was you! Is this a new one

for us?" He gestures to the car, causing Cameron's eyes to bug out.

I laugh a little at Cameron's reaction. "No, we're just parking. We're going to The Bar."

They all back away from the SUV, and Cameron visibly relaxes. "Is this where you planned on bringing my Bugatti?" he asks, swiveling his head toward me accusingly.

"Maybe," I reply a little coy.

"Good thing I fucking like you, Frankie!"

"Yeah, why's that, Cameron?" I flirt.

"Because you're making me more turned on than angry right now. He kisses my hand again."

"I guess that's good, then?" I smile.

"It is." He releases my hand and proceeds to adjust himself, making sure I can see exactly what I do to him.

18

CAMERON

We enter the dive they call The Bar. It's a big dated open-plan room with a small bar as you first walk in. Multiple worn-out couches are scattered around, a big screen TV in the far-right corner and multiple pool tables and arcade machines.

Only a few customers are in, the bartender greets Frankie like another long-lost friend. The guy is older than us, maybe in his forties? Frankie explains he knew her dad well.

Frankie walks us over to a couch at the back of the room with two beers in her hand. I sit next to her and drape my arm over the back of the couch behind her head with a cocky smirk. I start to play with the loose tendrils of hair that have fallen from the knotted bun on top of her head. She turns her head to me, her green eyes sparkle with mischief. "How do you like The Bar?" She tilts her head in the direction of the room.

"It's different . . ." I reply with a wince, leaving the answer open.

"You fancy a game of pool?" She smiles teasingly.

I lift my lip into a cocky side grin, knowing I'm pretty fucking good at pool. "Sure."

Three games in and I'm toast. Turns out, Frankie is pretty fucking good at pool too. Apparently, her dad taught her how to play, and he's done a pretty damn good job. Like, really fucking good.

The music is pumping through The Bar, giving the atmosphere a relaxed vibe, and we're enjoying some playful, flirty banter when Aiden comes in like a fucking hurricane. He swaggers over to us in his tight denim jeans and his signature long baggy T-shirt, hair up in one of those man buns with a bottle of beer in his hands. "Miss me?" I'm not sure who he's even asking, but his eyes dance with playfulness with a hint of vulnerability. He grabs a pool cue and joins us.

"You do realize we saw you just this morning right, Aid?" Frankie eyes him with a light banter to her voice.

He nods his head frantically, not making eye contact with either of us. "Sure." I watch him closely. He has a nervous energy about him, it's clear the guy has some serious issues.

A noise from the front of the room near the bar grabs our attention as a group of five guys come inside. They're overly loud at ordering their drinks, each turning around to scan the room, eyes landing directly on us.

Frankie's and Aiden's demeanor change in an instant. Their backs are straighter and their faces serious. "Everything okay?" I ask, completely unsure of what's happening. *Are these guys a threat?* The air surrounding us certainly points me in that direction.

Frankie meets my eyes with a soft smile. "Everything's fine." I smile back and tilt my head toward the pool table, encouraging them to continue the game.

Aiden is standing with his arms crossed over his chest, blatantly staring at the group in an antagonizing way. Fuck, he's going to cause some shit if he doesn't cool it. He needs to chill the fuck out.

I break his gaze. "Aid, your shot." I nod toward the table in hopes of distracting him.

He huffs a little, then relaxes. As he starts to lower himself to take the shot, the group approaches the table.

I glance around and notice the bartender is on his phone, watching us from the corner of his eye. Hopefully he's letting someone know we're out-fucking-numbered.

The broadest of the group stands tall in the middle of his crew, stopping at the end of the table. "Star, haven't seen you around for a while." It's not a question, it's a firm observation.

Frankie smiles, too sweetly. "Miss me?" she taunts.

He laughs to himself. "Something like that; you've not been entertaining at The Vault either."

Again, an observation. The Vault is the warehouse where I had the fight the night Frankie stole my car. Entertaining? There's that word again. *What the fuck does Frankie do?* A sickening feeling begins to churn in my stomach. I shake my head to try and rid myself of the doubts surrounding Frankie.

She sighs heavily, acting bored of the conversation. "And?"

"And Nate's been MIA. I assumed you two worked shit out. Fucked off together."

My heart stops as I wait for Frankie to respond. She's taking her time, walking slowly around the table, before stopping and rubbing the chalk onto the end of her cue slowly.

"Nope, you assumed wrong. Now, if you'd kindly fuck off. We're trying to play some pool and your ugly-as-fuck face is putting me off!" Oh my fucking God. She did not just say that. I brush a hand through my hair. Jesus fucking Christ, she's reckless. I watch carefully, expecting some shit to happen. I glance at Aiden and he's standing tall with a grin on his face, not a care in the fucking world. He almost seems like he's enjoying this and welcomes the aggression.

The guy, the leader, chuckles to himself, but the laugh is fake, and his smile doesn't reach his eyes. He taps his fingers on the pool table, and his voice turns dark, threatening. "Your crew is getting smaller, Star, clocks a ticking, tick tock," he mocks, tilting his head from side to side, before turning his back, and his guys follow suit. I blow out a breath of air in relief.

As they make their way over to a corner near the front of the bar, my eyes shoot up and meet Romeo's. He's sauntering in, relief washing over me. He looks freshly showered and has changed his clothes.

"Get your dick wet?" Frankie asks playfully. Her grin lighting up those green eyes.

He scrubs a hand down his big-as-fuck smile. "Slight problem."

Aiden stands still and tall, watching him closely, his

eyes narrowing on Romeo. Romeo's words don't match his body language; he's grinning like a Cheshire cat.

He laughs his words out in what sounds like disbelief. "Something's wrong with my cock!"

I choke on my beer. Frankie watches me with mirth in her eyes, she's laughing at me and Romeo. Aiden's eyes sharpen. "Explain!"

Romeo proceeds to start opening his belt. My eyes widen, they dart to Frankie in question, she shrugs back with a wide smile.

"It's fucked up, Aid," he explains.

"Explain fucked up," Aiden asks with all seriousness, and he watches the scene unfold before him with an analyzing face.

Romeo is taking his jeans down and starts to pull his boxers down, right out in the fucking open for anyone to see. These guys are off-the-charts crazy.

He pulls his dick out, an angry-looking thing. A dick that's absolutely red fucking raw. I scowl at the raw dick. Offended it's flapping about for us all to see.

Frankie moves closer to him to stare at his fucking dick. "Jesus, Rome, you need to get something for that, it looks like it's been tucked raw!" She gasps in shock as she lowers herself onto her knees for a closer inspection. My fists clench as I have to restrain myself to not pull her away from someone else's fucking cock.

Romeo gulps. "I know, right! I think Latesha's mama gave me something nasty." He grimaces.

"You should always wrap it, Rome. Always!" Frankie mocks, pointing her finger at him and the raw dick.

"I do! Fuck, I do! I don't know what's happened."

"Latesha's mama has an acid pussy and it's burned through the rubber, looking at that fucker!" Aiden jokes.

"Yeah, at least I'm getting some pussy," he quips back at Aiden.

Aiden's face turns serious. "I'd rather use my hand than end up with my dick dropping off!"

Romeo's face pales as his eyes dart to Frankie. "Your dick won't drop off, Rome, you just need to get to a clinic and sort it," she placates him. I've quickly come to learn that the guys look at Frankie as a mother figure and she sure as shit lets them, it's actually quite endearing to watch. Romeo is still standing with his dick hanging out, staring at it as though it's dying on him, he sighs and zips himself back up.

After a round of pool, we take to the couch and laze around chatting. The group from the corner is watching us closely, but I follow Frankie's lead and ignore them.

We're mid-conversation when Bale appears from nowhere; he throws his leather jacket off and plonks himself beside Frankie. My posture straightens in defense, and I don't think it goes unnoticed. Frankie squeezes my knee and leaves her hand there, and I instantly relax because she's making a point in front of her friends.

"So, Cameron, I hear you've made a name for yourself up north," he directs at me.

I snort. "Something like that," I reply curtly, not wanting to continue the conversation.

"You were trying to branch out the night you came to The Vault," he tells me knowingly.

I sigh in response, that's exactly what I was trying to do. "Yeah, something like that," I reply shortly again.

I can't get past the night we fought, and I got fucked

over. I sure as hell can't get past the fact that he's screwed Frankie. I don't want to make conversation with him, that's for sure. The atmosphere is tense, Bale sighs, then leans back on the couch at an angle to face me. "You should come to my gym. I could give you some pointers, or one of my trainers, if you prefer?" He's offering me a lifeline, an olive branch, and seeing him with Frankie, I can tell he's doing it for her. Frankie lifts her head to meet his eyes and smiles softly at him, and he smiles back, there's nothing sexual there.

My shoulders relax, and I choose to give in, if he can try for Frankie, then so can I. "Thanks, that would be great." I nod in approval and decide to be the bigger person too. "I watched a fight at Con & Doms, and the guy fighting had some sort of MMA training? He was amazing, so yeah, any additional training would be great. Thanks."

Frankie's spine straightens. *Shit, I've said something I shouldn't have.* Bale's eyes watch her closely, assessing. Before he glances away, he asks, "Rivers?"

"Yeah, I wanted to show Cameron the different fighting styles," she lies. No, what she was doing was handing money over for someone I'm quickly starting to realize is Nate. Bale accepts the lie and conversation is once again back to jovial stories of Romeo and his red dick.

"Do you get along with Jimmy, Cameron?" Bale asks out of the blue, stopping the conversations short.

"Bale, stop it!" Frankie warns, her teeth grinding together.

"Just a question," he defends back on a one shouldered shrug.

"It's okay," I tell Frankie. "I didn't like James when my mom first met him, no. I thought he had an ulterior motive in her. But as time went on, I realized he cared for her, so I went along with things for her sake. I want her to be happy."

"Not what I asked, Cameron," Bale quips back. He's intense, bordering on being an ass, but I think this is just his personality. He's straight to the point.

I think for a minute, and he's right, it's not what he asked. His dark eyes watch me closely, he's extreme, that's for sure.

"I can't say I dislike him, he's treated me and my mom very well. However, that's not to say I don't think there's more to him. I don't appreciate how he's treated Frankie; it makes me wonder what I'm missing," I reply honestly.

Bale throws his head back laughing. Aiden sits with a dark glare on his face, assessing, and Romeo rubs his chin in thought. Frankie is tense beside me. She's clearly uncomfortable with the conversation, and I'm not sure if it's James on the whole or the fact that Bale is questioning me.

"Tell me, Star, what does Cameron know about our guy, Jimmy?"

Frankie's hand tightens on my knee, her head spins around so fast it's a wonder she still has it left on her neck. "Stop it, Bale!" she spits.

He chuckles. "Fuccckkkk, he's done a number on you, huh? What's up with not being allowed to talk about his past?"

Her shoulders drop a little and she blinks slowly as if trying to think what to say next, he beats her to it. "He's blackmailing you I take it?" He nods to himself curtly, seemingly impressed with James.

Romeo's lips tighten and his eyes anger. "What's he have?"

Frankie's demeanor deflates. "Every. Fucking. Thing!" She sighs and her body drops back into the couch.

"Nate?" he asks softly. Frankie nods. She's vulnerable in this moment, her hands wringing between her knees. I feel a deep need to pull her into me and protect her.

Whatever the fuck James has on her, on them, it makes me want to kill him. I pull her to me, and she falls willingly into my chest. I stroke my hand on her hip, and she pushes her head into my neck. *Fuck, I could get used to this.*

The three of them watch us closely, Bale's eyes dart to Aiden's, who's grinning at mine and Frankie's exchange.

"You hurt our girl and we'll kill you, Cameron." Bale's deep, venomous voice penetrates the air cutting through our tender moment.

I meet his eyes with the same intensity. "You don't have to worry about that," I remark back. He nods, pleased with my response, and continues to light a joint.

We sit and watch Aiden and Romeo playing another game of pool before they come back over for another round of drinks. I've taken to drinking water now, trying to be cautious of driving home.

I'm getting along well with the guys, and at some point, Bale lightened up toward me, although he's still very intense; he's actually got quite the personality. He likes to sit back and watch people, whereas Romeo is clearly the joker, and Aiden the odd one of the bunch. Frankie is the mother hen. It makes me wonder what this Nate guy was like. *Was he in the position I'm in? Sitting with Frankie? Will he come back into the crew? Where will that leave me?*

The bartender walks over with another tray of beers for us, speaking directly to Bale in a low voice. "Another guy just came in."

Bale nods in understanding, then the bartender walks away. As I watch, the group has now become six.

Bale turns his attention to me. "So, Cameron, out of us"—he waves his hand around our small group—"who do you think is the most psychotic?"

I sit forward and gaze round the group, they're sitting watching me assess them all individually. I look back to Bale with his dark, fierce eyes. He's fucking cold, yeah, he's definitely a psycho.

I smile and point my bottle of water at him. "You."

They all crack up laughing. Bale's dark chuckle standing out. "Nope!" He grins, his eyes lighting up in jest.

I eye the group again, watching them closely. Aiden's eyebrows start doing a little dance and he's got a megawatt, proud grin on his face. "That would be me!" he announces proudly.

"He's about to show you how psycho he can be, aren't you Aid?" Bale tells him while pointing his beer bottle in Aiden's direction.

"Oh goody, playtime!" Aiden rubs his hands together and glances back at the group of six in the corner, whom are watching us intently.

"How about it, Cameron? You up for helping Aid out?" Bale asks.

I glance to Frankie, and a small smile curves her lips. *Why do I get the feeling this feels like an initiation of some type?*

I look at Bale and shrug, not about to chicken out. "Sure." Not really all that sure what I'm agreeing to.

Flicking my eyes back to Aiden, he's now taken off his T-shirt and he's wrapping it around his head into a bandanna. His chest is absolutely chiseled, peering above his jeans is a tattoo of a hawk's head, he pulls his jeans down, kicking them off, the wings of the bird flow down his thighs, the body somewhere between.

I lower my lips to whisper in Frankie's ear, "What's he doing?"

"He's turning psycho." She grins back up to me. *What the fuck?*

"I'm like the fucking karate kid, whoa, motherfucker!" Aiden excitedly declares, throwing his arms out in front of him in some sort of karate pose.

Romeo approaches us, throwing a pool cue at Aid who proceeds to jump up on the couch in just boxer shorts, completely barefoot. He catches the cue, then snaps it in half on his knee, much like Frankie did the day in the cafeteria with her lunch tray. He studies me and flicks his head in the direction of the group of guys who have now started to make their way over to us.

Romeo throws me a cue. "You take the left two and I'll take the others," Aid instructs. My eyes bug out. *He's taking four?!* I glance back at Frankie, and she nods her head and smiles as though enjoying the entertainment.

Aid runs to the pool table, jumps up on it and stands, doing another crazy fucking karate pose with his pool cue in pieces, one in each hand. He turns his back to me, and I quickly see why his tattoo isn't on his back, it's completely scarred, torn to shreds. It looks like someone has lashed him over and over a thousand times. The scars appear old but there's not a single part of it untouched. My heart sinks for him. *What the fuck happened?*

I'm quickly broken back into the insane moment now upon us as a fist flies toward me. I swing my body to the left and he completely misses. I swipe my foot low, taking him down as his friend comes behind me with his arms around my neck. I hold him and throw him over my head. My cue smashes into his face before he can raise his head from the floor.

I throw my eyes over to Aiden to watch him, and he's an absolute warrior, it's nothing but pure talent and energy. His body moves swiftly and strategically. His four men are down on the ground before I can register what he's even done. His face is lit up, he's in his element.

Bale saunters over with his beer. His voice is eerily calm as he says, "Come into our turf again and I will let Aiden fuck you up. Understand?" He pours the beer over the ringleader who is struggling to stand.

Aiden grabs my cue and swipes it under a stool leg, bringing it up to his hands in a swift, graceful movement. He takes the stool and throws it onto one of the guy's backs, forcing him back down onto the floor. "Understand?" he grins menacingly. "Tick tock, motherfucker!" Aid cackles.

The ringleader is choking. "Yeah, yeah, we understand."

"Good, now, get the fuck out!" Bale tells them while turning his back and slapping me on the shoulder. "That was pretty easy for you, Cam! Fighting turns Star on, am I right, Star?" My eyes narrow on him. *What the fuck is he talking about?*

I eye Frankie, her eyes are hooded and she's smiling seductively at me. *Fuck, she's hot.*

"The back room's free, Frankie." Bale smirks.

Before I can register what's happening, Frankie has me dragged down a fucking dark corridor and into a spare room that only houses a couch. I try not to think what the fuck this room is used for as Frankie pushes me down on the couch. I grip her thighs, pulling her between my legs. I stare up at her, she's stunning.

"I'm going to suck that cock of yours dry, Cameron." Her eyes haven't left mine, and the heat between us is boiling. My heart is pounding out of my chest as she drops to her knees, and I lean forward and grab her head, pulling her hair from her bun for it to flow down her back.

She smiles softly at me, and I realize I like her hair down. "You're so fucking beautiful, Frankie." It's true, every word.

She nibbles her bottom lip almost innocently. "Tell me what you want, Cameron."

I swallow because I've literally dreamed of this with Frankie. Do I be honest with her? What if I scare her away? I swallow deeply. "I like it rough," I admit with a hint of vulnerability in my tone.

She must see something she likes because her eyes sparkle. "Perfect, I'm going to submit to you, Cameron and you're going to tell me exactly what you want. You're going to own me."

Jesus. Fuck! My cock twitches and weeps at her filthy words. *Fucking submit?! Jesus!* I groan and shift uncomfortably while my cock leaks into my jeans. Every cell in my body is alive at her words, desperate for me to release myself on her.

My hands tighten on her hair. "Pull my cock out, Frankie," I demand.

She fumbles with my belt and jean buttons. Then I

shimmy them down a little, for her to pull my cock free from my boxers. The instant her hand touches my cock, I jerk, thrusting into her palm harder. "Fuck, yes!"

She glances up at me with those sparkling green eyes. I lick my lips in anticipation. "Lose the top, Frankie. I want to see those pretty fucking tits."

She obliges, without question, losing her bra too. So fucking obliging my cock is dripping, "Lick it!" I demand. She smirks at me.

Dipping her head, not losing eye contact, she flattens her tongue and licks the head of my cock, spreading the pre-cum around the tip before pulling it into her mouth with a seductive moan. *Fuck, this is insane.* My heart is pounding in my chest, my veins boiling with the sexual heat.

My chest is heaving with eagerness. "Lick my cock, Frankie, use your mouth and fuck it!" She moans but surges her wet tongue forward.

Her hand goes to gently squeeze my balls as she licks from the bottom of my cock to the top before covering her mouth fully around the head. Her soft lips tighten before going farther and farther down her throat. Then retracting and licking it from root to tip and doing the motion again, farther and farther toward the back of her throat.

My breath hisses from me as I clench my balls, trying to ward off coming so soon. My fist tightens. "Fuck, that's good," I chant through clenched teeth. "Are you wet, Frankie?" I pant out.

She nods and moans. "You can touch yourself," I tell her.

Fuck, do I want to see that. She releases the gentle hold of my balls and fucking starts unbuttoning her jeans, this is insane and now the most erotic fucking experience. "Don't stop sucking my cock, Frankie," I spit, even though she hasn't, I just want to remind her who's in charge.

"Ah, ah." Her soft voice vibrates over my cock as her hand works faster. Fuck, I wish I could see it. "I'm close, Cam!" Her seductive voice vibrates through my veins.

"Fucking greedy girl, aren't you. So fucking wet already. Fucking suck my cock down, don't fucking stop!" I spit the words out aggressively.

Her tongue works my tip over and over, her greedy mouth thrusting down toward my balls, all the way to the back of her throat. In-fucking-credible! "Don't stop, Frankie! Fuck, don't stop!" I chant as my hips lift up toward her mouth.

My hands tighten roughly into her hair as her noises and moans encourage me on.

I start to let loose and really fuck her mouth, something I've always wanted to do, but worried it was going too far. Only, with the noises coming from Frankie, I know she's loving it, she's fucking perfect.

My balls tighten, and I still my movements just as Frankie's movements stutter and she screams around my cock as I also tip over the edge. I groan as I release ropes and ropes of cum into her mouth, her greedy mouth. The pulsing of my cock hitting her tongue.

I watch her slowly come down from her orgasm. Her eyes meet mine with my cock still in her mouth, cum dripping from the sides of her lips; her intense stare is intoxicating. She's waiting for a reaction from me. I nod at her and smirk. "Fucking lick it clean." Her lips curl up. Frankie licks my cock to the tip and continues to lick around the head of it, making me twitch with the sensitivity. I release her with a pop as she pushes the remains of the cum into her mouth from her lips.

I take her hand. "Come here."

I pull her onto my lap. She straddles me, her tits almost to my face, and I bring her lips to mine. "You're so fucking perfect." She smiles at me as I kiss her lips gently.

Going to be honest, I don't particularly enjoy the taste of my cum on her lips, but whatever.

She giggles at me. "You're scrunching your nose up!"

"Yeah, I'm not like Joel. I don't enjoy tasting my own cum," I admit on a wince.

She licks her lips suggestively, moving in to kiss me again gently. "Lucky for you, I love the taste of your cum."

"Was I too rough with you?" I ask her, a little concerned but also full of hope.

Her eyebrows furrow in confusion. "No, I liked it."

I drop my shoulders in relief. Moving my hand to her breasts, I stroke and squeeze them. "Your tits are amazing; they're making me hard again," I tell her as I brush my thumb over her nipples, and she pushes them into me.

I dip my head to them and suck the skin into my mouth, pulling it tight to leave a mark. I have the sudden urge, the desperate need to make them mine, I need to mark them as mine.

I throw her onto the couch on her back. I make quick work of thrusting my hand into her panties, reveling in the wetness as I lean one leg into her groin and the other straddling her torso.

My cock hanging loose as I squeeze her tits with my free hand. "Ride my fingers, Frankie, rub yourself off on my leg and hand. Come on me, beautiful. I'm going to make your tits mine!" She gasps and moans at my finger's intrusion, thrusting two of them roughly into her tight hole. I rub my leg in her groin, encouraging her to ride it as I suck her breast into my mouth, leaving numerous marks on her. One of her hands is in my hair while the other starts tightly jerking my cock. "I'm going to come on these tits, Frankie!"

"Ah, fuck. Yes, come on my tits, Cameron. Come all over them, please!" she begs as her movements become more and more rapid; our pants escalate as our bodies ride the high. "I'm close," she pants. "So close."

I sit up on my knees, and she releases my cock to me. I continue rubbing her clit, her body tightening as my cum pulses out of my cock all over Frankie's tits. I aim it at her nipples, and her face is contorted with pleasure as she lets out a cry as the warm cum hits her. "Yessss!!!"

I gaze down at my handiwork, she's marked. I've marked her as mine and I've never seen anything so damn beautiful. I'm never letting her go. Never.

19

FRANKIE

The day spent with Cameron over in Hawks Town was one of the best days I've had in a long time. Probably for as long as I can remember.

Just having all the guys together, and Cameron with us, was completely satisfying and comfortable. The guys welcomed Cameron to the group like another brother.

When I watched Cameron fight without so much as breaking a sweat, I was ready there and then to rip his clothes off and show him how much I wanted him.

The blowjob and orgasms were some of the hottest I'd ever experienced. I loved the fact that Cameron was domineering. I always felt Nate held back on that. But being in the crew and having a badass persona, I was more than willing to be dominated in the bedroom, where I could finally let my defenses down.

With Nate, our relationship was based around the need we felt for one another; we had always been drawn together and supported one another through obstacles in our life. Sex was something we just experienced together. Nate had always had issues with addiction and abandonment, my issues were the need to be wanted and loved. We threw ourselves together and satisfied one another, not wanting anyone else, and we used sex to help keep us together.

The love we shared was unlike something you'd probably find in any relationship, we were just naturally drawn together, therefore naturally loved one another.

With Cameron, my feelings are completely different. I want him desperately. I'm keeping my heart guarded because I can't bear the thoughts of being lost, or abandoned again but physically? I'm all in.

———

It's Thanksgiving break this weekend, and Cameron has asked me to attend a fight with him and Joel tonight at an arena on the outskirts of Trent Valley. I haven't been here before, but I know Bale has taken fighters there, so I was intrigued to see the difference in fights and the premises on a whole.

James has been away on business again all week and isn't due back until midweek. Josie has kept to herself and spent time outside of the house, at friends'. We are basically a house cohabiting together; we sure as hell were not a family.

Still, it gives me the freedom I was used to and the fact I now live in luxury is certainly no hardship. Josie explained she would be away this weekend at a spa retreat; she sure knows how to pamper herself. It is obvious we aren't having a traditional Thanksgiving of any kind.

Arriving at the venue, even from the outside it's clear there is a huge difference in wealth. For starters, the venue is a nightclub, a very up-market nightclub.

Cameron explained we were to go in the side door, he's fought here multiple times and the confidence is oozing from him. Joel is bouncing on his feet, reminding me very much of my excitable Aiden.

"You want a drink?" Cameron breaks my thoughts.

"Sure, a beer." I smile back at him. *Fuck, he's gorgeous.*

His eyes light up when I smile at him. His bronzed pecs are showcased in a tight white T-shirt, his hair is styled with his brown waves pushed back off his face. He catches me checking him out, his smug smirk adorning his chiseled face. He moves his mouth to my ear, while his hand grips my hip tightly. "You're licking your lips, Frankie. It reminds me of when you sucked my cock dry." He flicks his tongue seductively over my neck before pulling back with a smirk.

I moan. I hadn't realized I was licking my lips, but I sure as fuck am now. "Maybe it's an incentive for you to win?"

He chuckles. "I can do that!" His eyes zoning in on my lips and tongue. I clench my thighs together.

Joel thrusts a beer into my hand. "Will you both stop with the eye-fucking? It's making me hard!" We break apart, laughing.

I gaze around, taking in the room. The vibe is certainly more extravagant and screams wealth. Women are dressed up in tight designer clothes, every enhancement possible, they have it. Boobs, nose, hips, ass, lips. Every-fucking-thing.

My eyes catch on a broad figure from the balcony above. His arms stretched over the balcony; fists tight on the banister. He watches like he's surveying his kingdom, dressed in a gray suit with a white dress shirt on, his top buttons open exposing his tight chest, his cropped hair and rugged features seem familiar.

I narrow my eyes in, scrutinizing him. "His name's Mika, Russian Mafia. In other words, stay the fuck away!" Cameron fills me in with a laugh.

I smirk back at him, causing his body to become tense. "I mean it, Frankie. These people don't mess around. They aren't some crew from the backs of fucking beyond, they eat that shit for breakfast." I roll my eyes at his defeatist attitude.

I raise up to my tiptoes and kiss his cheek mockingly. "I understand, I'll behave!" His eyes are narrowed on me, causing him to push a worrying hand through his wavy hair.

"Listen, I have to go get ready, are you going to be okay here?" He glances at me nervously.

I smile back at him, waving my hand to shoo them away. "Of course, go get ready. I'll behave and wait right here!" I point to the spot I'm standing on. Joel throws his head back laughing at my childishness.

As soon as the guys' backs are turned, I return my attention to Mika on the balcony. Because sure enough, I do know him.

I stop on the top step and give my name to the security man on the door. I'm starting to second-guess my intentions, let's face it, Bale is going to blow a fucking gasket.

After the guy confirms my identity, I'm waved into the open-top balcony. Mika greets me with a wide grin, his skin pulled tight against the scar down the side of his face, courtesy of a gang war when he was a teenager.

"Ah, welcome, Star, it's good to see you!" His Russian accent is thick as he pulls me against his chest for a hug.

"Great to see you again, Mika, I wasn't aware you worked in this area."

He rubs his chin in thought. "This is where the money is, Star. I tried telling Bale that, but as you know, he's loyal to his roots."

I nod in confirmation. "He is, yes."

"So, moy dorogoy, what are you doing here?"

"I was wondering if there are any available fights on tonight?"

His eyebrows rise. "Bale know about this?"

I grin widely. "Nope, and he's not here tonight. Is he?"

Mika blows out a harsh laugh, throwing his head back. "Fuck, moy dorogoy. You're going to get me killed." He wags his finger at me mockingly.

He turns his back and pulls out his phone. I turn and watch the arena lighting up, a fight is going to begin.

I watch as Cameron enters the ring, his chiseled bronzed body free of tattoos jumps from side to side, warming up. My heart thumps quicker.

The opponent is taller and broader than Cameron, older too. I nibble my thumb, nerves racking through me, no doubt this guy has a lot more experience.

The bell sounds. Before I can guess who is going to make the first move, Cameron speeds forward and his fist connects with the dude's jaw, snapping his head swiftly backward. Cameron doesn't give him chance to respond, he sweeps his feet from under him and throws his elbow into the dude's chest. Cameron won this round without breaking a sweat and without it eating into the five minutes.

Round two, Cameron waits for the guy to attack. I have a feeling he's doing it to make sure it looks like the guy has a chance. The dude clocks Cameron in the face before Cameron strikes with a low kick and a simultaneous cross to the face, making the dude stumble backward. Before he can attempt a move, Cameron makes a spinning backfist move, causing the guy to fall to the floor with a heavy thump.

The third round, Cameron doesn't hold back. He completely dominates it once again, giving a sequence of crosses to the face and swiftly following them up with a perfect snap kick to his face, I'm elated! He performed it perfectly. My heart swells with pride.

The referee holds Cameron's hand up as the winner. He turns him around to face me, sweat dripping from his gorgeous face, his eyes scan the crowd, then, as if sensing me, his head lifts to me. His face turns into a smirk with a cheeky wink, in return I give him a gigantic smile and two thumbs up, he shakes his head at me and raises his eyebrows with a nod indicating Mika beside me. I roll my eyes back at him.

20

CAMERON

I pull myself under the ropes of the ring and grab the bottle of water from Joel. "I found Frankie," I snap at him.

His head swivels around, searching for her. "You won't find her down here, try up there." I gesture with my hand to the balcony. Joel's eyes widened in panic. "Needless to say, I'll wait for a shower, I need to go get her."

I push past the crowds and make my way to the staircase. I was about to ascend the stairs but come to an abrupt stop with an arm stretched out in front of me. "No access!" the gruff voice spits.

"I have to get up there. My girlfriend's up there." I brush my hand through my hair with frustration, pissed at Frankie for not staying put like I asked.

When Joel joined me without her beside the ring, I was tempted not to fight and go help him find her.

"Who's the chick?" he sneers.

Fuck, I want to lay him out, if it wasn't for the bulge in his jacket I would. My patience is wearing thin. "Frankie."

He shakes his fat bald head. "Never heard of her!"

My eyebrows knit together in confusion because she's definitely up there. Then it comes to me. "You might know her as Star? She was just up there chatting to Mika!"

Recognition hits his dumb face. "Ah, Star, yeah she's one of the entertainers." He laughs, waving his hand for us to go upstairs. *Entertainers? What the fuck?* My heart sinks. *What the fuck is she doing?*

Entering the room, I glance around. There are only a few people here, and Frankie isn't one of them. Mika approaches, and I gulp as he comes closer. He's watching me like a fucking lion. I'm standing here, barefoot with just gym shorts on for Christ's sake. I stand broader, feigning confidence.

"Ah, Cameron, mal'chik, welcome!" I gape at him. *Is he expecting me?*

He laughs, a deep bellied laugh. "You're searching for Star, yes?"

I nod while looking around. *What the fuck has she got herself into? Where the fuck is she?* "Come, she is entertaining tonight!" His face alight with excitement. Dread flows through me, and I spare a glance at Joel, his face pale, riddled with panic.

We follow Mika to the balcony and watch the scene below unfold. The referee speaks through the microphone. "Ladies and gentlemen, we have an unexpected performance for you tonight, please welcome our Kali fighters! Preach." The light flicks onto a man standing still with his head down in a bow stance. "Our opponent from Hawks Town, Star!"

I'm sorry, what the fuck did he just say? My stomach plunges, I look to Joel who is standing wide-mouthed, gawking down at the image of Star. She's kneeling with her back crouched, displaying her tattoo in her pantie shorts and her fucking bra. Anger bubbles inside me until I see the fucking knives in both of her palms. Panic, no other word than utter fucking panic!

"You need to stop the fight!" I spurt out to Mika.

He chuckles, fucking chuckles, at me. His thick accent is booming. "You need to watch your woman! She will win this! She is an enigma!" He slaps me on the back and points to Frankie.

The bell rings, signaling the first of three rounds. I swallow thickly, unsure if I even want to watch, while Joel's hands tighten on the railing. I bite the inside of my mouth to stop myself from screaming for someone to end this before it even starts.

Star jumps up to her feet, her movements fluid. She spins a knife in her right hand before thrusting it up and forward, slashing into Preach's upper arm. Blood instantly spurts from the incision. Preach runs forward, and my heart plummets, but Star dodges his swipes. She hooks her foot around his ankle, toppling him over. She strategically throws herself on top of him, holding the knife to his throat. The bell rings, signaling her a point above him.

My heart is pounding against my chest as they move back into position. Star is walking up and down with the knives in each hand; she's pacing, assessing her opponent, as he stands stoically still, watching her.

She briskly moves forward on one foot before swiftly moving back. He takes the bate and rushes forward, she lowers her body and slides across the floor, slashing his leg en route.

The crowd goes wild.

Joel is panting hard beside me, anxiety rolling off us both equally.

Preach turns and grabs Star from behind, tackling her into a headlock. She swiftly drops her body, making it go lax. Then proceeds to throw her head harshly against his chest and flip him over her shoulders. Preach doesn't let go, and he's somehow slashed the insides of her thighs, and she doesn't so much as grimace!

She's now in control, with Preach on the floor and her straddling his chest, again with the knife to his throat. The bell rings, Star has won yet another round.

The third round starts off with Preach dominating, but some of the moves that Star is making are antagonizing and naïve, which leads me to believe she's in complete control of the fight and is baiting him. She's clearly very experienced. I don't know whether to be pissed or impressed.

"She's making sure I get my money's worth with the entertainment, yes?" Mika chimes in, "I told her to drag it out." He laughs while lighting a cigarette, completely transfixed on the scene below us.

Joel huffs a laugh out. "Un-fucking-believable!"

This is what everyone has been referring to. Entertainment. I had a deep-seated feeling of dread when the word was mentioned. But, to be fair, I was thinking more like she was using her body sexually for entertainment not for fighting.

I watch Star go into full-blown combat mode. She roundhouse kicks Preach and follows it up with several small cuts to his torso. It's clear she could do more damage but that is not how she works. She's absolutely phenomenal! I can't believe she's managed to hide this from us. I shake my head at the realization.

Deep down, I'm a mixture between being torn with pride or anger. Because, right now, all I want to do is rip the remaining scraps of clothes from her and remind her and everyone watching her who the fuck she belongs to.

The fight finishes as Mika predicted, Frankie wiping the floor with Preach. The poor guy is torn to fucking shreds. Frankie turns around to face us, and she gazes up to the balcony. My breath hitches and I gasp as our eyes meet, my heart pounding in response. Sweat dripping from her beautiful face and chest, she winks at me and smirks the same way as I did to her after I won. She's so fucking stunning, she takes my breath away.

21

FRANKIE

I sit on the bench in the changing rooms, internally grinning and high-fiving myself that I just won ten thousand fucking dollars! Sure, Bale is going to lose his shit, but it's so worth it.

The door to the changing room slams open and in storms Cameron. His bare chest heaving in temper, and behind him is a sniggering Joel. "Get the fuck out and leave us alone a minute!" he bellows, making me wince at his spiteful tone.

I glance up at him from below my lashes. *My God, he's fucking hot.*

Sweat glistens on his bronzed skin, the urge to lick it off is overwhelming. I lick my lips in anticipation. His glare at me is ferocious, making my heart pound at how pissed off at me he truly is. He turns his back, and my stomach plummets with dread that he's turning away from me, shutting me out.

The lock clicks on the door, making me raise my head. Cameron struts across the tiled floor with his bare feet exposed. "I'm so pissed off at you right now, Frankie." His chest heaves at his admission.

"I know," I agree meekly.

He lowers in front of me, crouching so we're eye level. "You scared the shit out of me." His face bared for me, his pain seeping through his expression. "So fucking scared," he admits vulnerably. His hazel eyes bore into me with the truth of his words. He cares.

I drag my finger gently over his cut eyelid. "I'm fine." I smile confidently, hoping he can feel how I mean my words.

His head drops forward, almost in defeat. Then his spine suddenly straightens as if he's seen or sensed something. His fingers gently trail the small cuts on my thighs as he sucks in his breath. "He fucking hurt you, Frankie." His eyes meet mine before ducking back down to my thighs.

His body moves lower so that he's sat back on his legs. Lowering his head, he kisses alongside the cuts before grazing his tongue lightly over them. They're no longer bleeding but I'm sure he can taste the copper in his mouth. The sensual act makes me suck in my breath, my body coming back to life with his movements. He doesn't miss my reaction, his head darting up to watch me, a small, sexy smirk gracing his face.

Cameron's hands move tighter on my thighs, moving up toward my pussy. He grips the sides of my lace panties and pulls animalistically at them, shredding them between both fists. I'm completely bared to him.

Before I can contemplate his next move, he pulls me

closer and licks straight up from my opening to my clit, making me gasp with desire and opening my thighs wider. His palms clasped on my thighs; he buries his face deeper into me. I move my hand to his wavy hair, encouraging him.

His tongue wildly whips out, relentlessly lapping up my juices as I fist his hair tightly in my fingers, my moans echoing off the walls. "Fuck, Cam, I need more!" He chuckles at my confession but doesn't stop.

He draws his right hand away from my thigh, traveling it up tightly to my apex. He brutally shoves two fingers inside of me, taking my breath away. I release a moan and throw my head back and tighten my fists.

I can feel his smile against my pussy as he continues to push his fingers in and out of my opening while sucking on my clit. My ass rising off the bench to meet his force. I'm becoming frantic, and desperate for my release, I continually clench, and Cameron knows it's coming. "Don't stop, don't you dare fucking stop!" I beg through clenched teeth.

Cameron pulls away from me, causing me to exhale loudly. Pissed, I yell, "What the fuck, Cameron!"

He laughs as he casually turns his back and moves toward a locker, my chest rising and falling in both anticipation and anger.

He pulls a bag out of the locker and rummages through it. Turning around, I see him rip a condom open with his teeth.

His eyes drill into mine, lust taken over. "I don't care what you want anymore, Frankie. I fucking need this right now!" I study him, his eyes wild with a combination of passion and anger. I nod and offer him a smile while removing my bra. "Fuck!" he hisses out as my tits release with a bounce.

I stand up and he rushes me. Lifting my thighs around his waist, I notice he's dropped the shorts and sheathed himself before plunging into me.

He stills for a moment, searching my eyes. "I'm sorry," he says. His eyes appearing vulnerable as he glances away from me. I catch his jaw between my hand and pull him back to look at me, my eyes narrowing in confusion. "I wanted it to be more, for you." He nods down at himself as I realize he means our first time. He wanted it to be different for us, not as quick, brutal, and laced in anger.

I bite my lip and smile at his words. "What I really want right now, Cameron, is for my man to fuck me senseless."

His eyes flare at my words as his mouth ravages mine, my body held tightly between himself and the lockers. He starts to fuck me hard! His hands grip my hips, bruising me.

I tighten my hold around his neck and squeeze his cock with my pussy as he pounds into me. His tongue exploring mine, fucking my mouth with his own. The taste of me on his tongue sends me into overdrive. "You like that? My dirty, dangerous girl?" he pants and pushes the words out with the same force he fucks me.

I mumble incoherent words back to him, desperate for him.

He's fucking me like an animal, it's brutal and harsh, fast and wild as his thrusts hammer into me harder. I release his mouth, struggling to breathe. The sweat on his neck glistens. "Fuck, Frankie, I'm close, fuck, baby. I'm sorry, I'm fucking close," he grits.

I sink my teeth into his neck and tug the skin between my lips as I feel him thicken inside me. "Ah, fuck yeah. Fuuuckk."

The swell of his cock makes me come. "Oh god, Cameron, oh fuck."

Cameron's pace doesn't stop, my hips jerk with his movements. The lockers rock as he continues his thrusts, not stilling or stopping. Not until my orgasm has ended. My body going limp in his arms as I feel his final spurt.

His forehead rests on mine, breathing each other in. Both our chests rise and fall in unison. He smirks at me. "That was fucking hot!"

I smile back. "Yeah, it was." I bring my lips to his, the gentle touch melting me inside. Cameron pushes his tongue slowly in and out of my mouth. It's sensual and loving, the perfect end to the perfect fucking.

We start to dress in silence but it's not awkward; we're both just content and a little shell-shocked.

A pounding on the door brings us out of our lust-filled daze. "Otkryt!" *Open up!* Mika bellows from the other side.

"Odna minuta!" *One minute!* I shout back.

Cameron's head darts around, and his eyes search mine. "You speak Russian?"

I nod and smile. "Yes, this little uneducated, dumb girl can speak Russian." I mock him, but his face falls.

"Frankie, fuck. I was a dick. I shouldn't have said any of that shit!" He walks toward me, gripping my hip tightly. "You know I don't mean that, right?" His eyes search mine for confirmation.

I smile up at his desperate face. "Cameron, it's fine, I was joking. I forgive you, okay?"

He nods and ducks down to my lips for a swift, gentle kiss.

The fist pounds the door again. "Open the fuck up, Frankie!" Mika's thick accent bellows.

"You know him?" Cameron quizzes.

"Yeah, I know him. He's a pussy cat!" I giggle at Cameron's horror-stricken face as I make my way toward the door and switch the lock.

As I step away, Mika pushes past, followed by a very sullen-looking Joel. He's a combination of embarrassed and scared shitless. God knows what Mika's been saying or doing.

"Frankie, I got Bale on the phone!" Mika puffs out, spinning on his heels and glaring at me. *Shit, I knew he'd find out*. But I didn't expect it to be so sudden.

"Put him on speaker." I nod toward the phone and watch Mika as he strokes the scruff on his face anxiously.

Bale's angry voice fills the room. "What the fuck Frankie? Did I tell you that you could fight? Did I? And Kali fighting? Seriously? What the fuck were you thinking? How the fuck did you know who you would fight, huh? Do you realize how long it takes for the preparations to go in place for a fight? Do you even fucking care? Have you got a fucking death wish?" I roll my eyes at his extended verbal battering. "You haven't even been fucking training! Are you even ready for it physically? After everything that's happened?"

My spine straightens as he gets dangerously close to some home truths. I snap, "Bale, calm the fuck down! I'm fine. And you're on fucking speaker phone, so watch what you say!"

He takes a deep breath, and silence consumes the room. Choosing his words wisely before speaking. "Is Cameron there?"

"Yeah," Cameron speaks up.

"Good, good. Is your house free tonight?"

Cameron's eyes dart to mine for clarification. I shrug back at him. "Yeah, it's free."

"Good, cut the cameras. Me and the guys are having a sleep over." *Wow, I was not expecting that.* I can't help the excitement building up inside of me, and my grin widens as the line goes dead.

Mika's eyes flit to mine. "Fucking told you, Frankie!" His finger wags at me. "Next time, Bale approves it!" He throws the brown envelope of cash at me before slapping Cameron on the shoulder and leaving the room.

22

CAMERON

'm still reeling from discovering what a badass my girl is, she truly is magnificent! And she's fucking mine.

After showering and changing into lounge clothes, we've been watching the *Fast and Furious* movies since returning from the fight. Frankie's boys joined us half an hour later.

Aiden was like an excitable puppy, running around and searching the house. He's even been for a swim in the pool, naked. Romeo is a lot more subtle with his excitement but went straight outside to the garages, checking the cars out. Bale hit the gym and sent me a text with a list I needed to get for equipment upgrades. I'm not sure if the guy was trying to help or having a dig at my equipment. Either way, I take it on the chin and add the stuff to my credit card.

Joel has been the tour guide and he's clearly been

buzzing off the guys' excitement. It's been amazing to have us all here together. Frankie hasn't stopped smiling either, which makes it all worthwhile in itself.

Romeo and Joel have spent the past half hour outside comparing joints and sharing them, no doubt. Aiden rests his head on Frankie's lap as she tenderly strokes his hair. I get up to go to the kitchen, aware that Bale has followed me.

"Frankie ever say anything to you about Nate?" he asks quietly.

I watch him and offer him a water bottle. "Not really, she's guarded. I sense she doesn't like talking about it, and I don't want to push her," I admit.

He nods. "That trust will come, Cameron." He brushes his hand through his hair awkwardly. "She's been through a lot, and I don't like seeing her hurt." I stare at him, unsure if he's asking me not to hurt her or if it was more of a statement. "When I heard Jimmy was bringing her here, I thought it was a good idea, to give her a break."

"From Nate?" I question, watching him closely, trying to gauge a reaction and gain some insight.

His head is ducked low, but he brings his eyes up to meet mine. "From the situation they were in." I feel like he's trying to tell me something but I'm not sure what. *Is it the drugs?* "She deserves better." He throws in.

"I wouldn't hurt her," I tell him, "I care for her." I need him to see that. I need his approval, as screwed up as that sounds.

He rolls his lips. "Yeah, I can see that. What about Jimmy?"

I narrow my eyes at him, my stomach sinking. "I'm not giving her up, if that's what you're asking," I spit out, because no fucking way! I've never felt like this before, she makes me feel complete. Alive.

He laughs at my response before turning serious. He shakes his head. "Jimmy might be a problem, Cameron. But if you need us, if Frankie needs us, we're here for you both." His words confuse me. Sure, James might be pissed but I really don't think he would be a problem. I mean, he hasn't had anything to do with Frankie for years, and as long as we're both happy, what the fuck does it matter?

"You don't hold James in high regard, do you?" I laugh, trying to keep the conversation friendly.

"No, I don't. Nor should you. He's blackmailing Frankie to not expose his past to you and your mom at the risk of upsetting all this." He waves his hand around the kitchen. "What he knows about Frankie, and us, would hurt her deeply if he was to use the information. Tell me what sort of person would do that? A loving uncle?" I shake my head as my chest tightens at the thought of anyone hurting Frankie, my substitute father only emphasizes the pain.

Bitterness and a fierce need to protect her engulf me. "I'd kill him before he hurts her." I make sure Bale can see the truth in my eyes. The words seep from my lips with venom.

He nods in agreement. "Well, that's good because Jimmy fights dirty, and I wouldn't be surprised if it doesn't come to that. He has secrets, Cameron, and I think he'd do anything to keep them hidden. This good-guy act he's got going, it's a fucking front."

I think on Bale's words and everything I know about James. I've since learned he's used Frankie's mom as a prostitute, and knowingly left Frankie in a trailer surrounded by drugs and sex. He's far from the loving and caring uncle, father, and husband he would lead us to believe, and I don't doubt for one minute the truth behind Bale's words.

"What do you suggest we do?"

"I don't know if you should expose your relationship yet, Cameron, maybe keep it under wraps until we can figure out if he's going to be a problem?" He shrugs at his suggestion, watching me closely. I can tell by the seriousness in his eyes and tone that it's not a suggestion, it's a command.

I nod my head and swallow thickly. "Yeah, I agree. We'll keep it under wraps until we know more."

He nods his head sharply in approval, his body exhales the tension before smiling at me. "So, tell me, what do you think of Star?"

I chuckle back at him. "She's fucking incredible!" I grin, my girl can sure fight. Hot and a fighter, not to mention goddamn beautiful. And she's mine.

"Yeah, she is." He beams with pride as we make our way back to the living area.

FRANKIE

Joel moved himself off into the spare room upstairs while we left the guys downstairs to sleep in the living room. I gave them all extra blankets and pillows.

I pull Cameron upstairs and into my room, making sure he knows where he's sleeping tonight.

He laughs into my ear, nipping on it playfully. "You want me to sleep in here with you, beautiful?"

I spin around to face him. "You know I do!" I tug my teeth on my bottom lip, acting coy.

Cameron lifts his eyebrows before picking up my hips and throwing me effortlessly onto my bed. "Strip!"

I beam up at him, and his smile greets mine as we both lift our tops over our heads.

He strips down his joggers first, his raging hard-on springing free, the sticky cum leaking from the tip. His eyes meet mine and he nods at my shorts, I pull them down, baring myself to him.

His eyes grow heavy with lust as he tugs his cock a few

times. Letting out a hiss, he utters, "Fuck!" I crawl toward him as he holds his cock in his hands.

I move forward and open my mouth as he directs himself into me. I swipe my tongue over the engorged head. "Fuck, that's good, Frankie!" he hisses out.

I move my hand toward my pussy and spread my juice from my opening to my clit as I rub it slowly.

I glance up at Cameron, his head thrown back, staring up at the ceiling. He's breathing through his nostrils to try and control himself as he softly thrusts into my eager mouth. He jolts sharply. "Fuck, stop, Frankie. I need to be inside you!" His voice pleads.

He pulls himself away. Grabbing his joggers, he searches his pockets for a condom as I lie back on the bed. I continue to stroke myself with my legs wide open on display. Cameron's eyes watch me, and as I lick my lips seductively, he rolls the condom on. "You're fucking incredible, you know that?"

Cam climbs over me, placing himself between my thighs, then he draws his lips to mine, giving me a slow, sensual kiss. I moan into his mouth and tighten my hold on his neck, pulling him closer still.

Cameron directs his cock to my opening and slowly pushes in, inch by agonizing inch; the action is slow and a stark contrast to the fast, rough pace in the changing room earlier. I've a feeling he's giving me what he wanted to earlier tonight.

I wrap my legs around his waist, my feet on his ass, and push him into me deeper, causing him to chuckle. "Fuck, that feels good, Cameron." I moan as he rolls his hips into me.

Every movement is slow and steady, it's loving and

deliberate. I meet Cameron's eyes, they're watching me just as closely. His eyes are filled with . . . love? My heart skips a beat as I slowly realize Cameron Donovan is making love to me. I gently touch his face. "Cam?" I question.

He gently shakes his head. "Don't, not now." His forehead meets mine; the look of vulnerability oozing from him.

I gently kiss his lips to give him the reassurance he craves. "Fuck, that feels incredible!" My pussy clenches against his cock as it continues rubbing me inside delicately, stretching me to make me feel whole.

Cameron's hand slips down my thigh as he grips it tightly as his pace picks up. "Fuck, Frankie," he growls.

"Feels so fucking good!" I moan in agreement. "Harder!" I demand.

His hand moves to my clit, causing my body to jolt and tense with pleasure. I throw my head back with the overwhelming sensations taking over me, my nipples rubbing against his chest as he begins to frantically push into me.

I scream out my release as Cameron's body stills and his mouth falls open above me. He releases a groan as his cum flows from him into the condom. "Fuck," he mutters through gritted teeth as he drops his head down to my neck.

I pull his mouth to mine for another kiss. "Beautiful, so fucking beautiful." His words warm me, and I feel treasured. I tighten my arms around his neck, causing him to chuckle. "I need to pull out and get rid of the condom, Frankie."

I shake my head. "Not yet." I'm not prepared to let him go, not yet.

Lying in Cameron's arms, I don't know when we fell asleep, but he'd spent so long stroking my skin and kissing me I was sure it must have nearly been morning.

But when I open my eyes to an almighty scream, I jolt upright in bed, causing Cameron to jump too. "What the fuck was that?"

"Shit," I panic as I quickly throw the sheets off of me and pull on my shorts and T-shirt.

"What the fuck's happening, Frankie?" Cameron is following my lead, pulling his joggers on.

"It'll be Aiden." I dart out the door and rush down the stairs. Romeo is awake on the couch, stroking Aiden's long blond locks. I scan the room for Bale, he's sitting up on another couch, completely unfazed, puffing on a cigarette.

I walk around to Aiden. Loud moans leave his mouth, his eyes are wide open with fear; he's shaking uncontrollably. "Aid, sweetie, it's me, Frankie. Come on, you're okay, you're safe." I stroke his hair like I've shown Romeo to do countless times. His moans are heartbreaking. "You're safe, Aid, he's gone. He's gone."

I glance at Cameron, and he moves from behind the couch to stand next to me. "Should I do something?" he asks me with desperate, pleading eyes. I shake my head.

"I'll go make drinks," Romeo suggests, his feet can't leave the room quick enough.

"He likes hot chocolate with marshmallows!" I shout after him.

Aiden's hand grips mine harshly, causing Cameron to tense beside me. I gently peek at him and shake my head. "He's gone, Frankie, I did it, didn't I?" Aiden's soft words break my heart.

"You did, Aiden, you were so fucking brave. I'm so

proud of you." He begins to wail and shake, rocking backward and forward.

"Fucking Jesus!" Bale bellows, throwing the blanket off of himself.

I spin around and eye him sharply. "What the fuck's your problem?"

"Him!" He throws an accusing hand at Aiden.

"You're kidding me, Bale. Have some fucking compassion!"

Bale's eyes flare. He scoffs. "Frankie, I've had to put up with this shit all fucking week! I thought bringing him here so he was close to you might fucking stop the dramatics."

I glare at him, my temper increasing. God, he's so heartless sometimes. "What are you talking about all week?" I stand, demanding to know what the hell's been happening.

Bale exhales and brushes his hand through his thick hair, sighing. "Mable had to ask me to have him for a bit. He's been struggling, Frankie. It's disrupting the kids; some poor little fuckers have started pissing the bed because of him. I told her I'd straighten him out before sending him home. Honestly, I'm at a fucking loss. I mean, what the hell am I meant to do with that?" He waves his hand at Aiden, sounding completely defeated. His words cause me to straighten my spine.

I think on what he's said, but before I can say anything, he continues, "He hasn't been taking his meds, Frankie. He's got it in his head he's better off without them."

Romeo returns with his hands full of drinks for us all, shifting uncomfortably. "I, erm, made us all hot chocolates,

Aiden." I smile at him sweetly. He's a lot more compassionate than Bale, that's for fucking sure.

I kneel in front of Aiden. "Aid, do you want to sleep with me? Will that help?" He nods slowly, and I catch a glimpse of Cameron tensing beside me. "Do you want your hot chocolate first?" He shakes his head and stands. I glare at Bale and smile at Romeo before making my way up the stairs. Aiden is trailing behind me like a lost puppy.

I'm just about to shut my door when Cameron appears. Aiden gets under the sheets like a zombie—he's completely oblivious to anything or anyone around him.

Cameron watches from the door as I get into bed, and his eyebrow raises in question. "Seriously?" I nod at him and pat the sheets beside me, showing him he can sleep on the other side. "Fuck." He chuckles to himself before moving around the bed and getting in.

I'm grinning internally at myself—Cameron Donovan is so desperate to be with me he's even prepared to share our bed and let Aiden have a sleepover. *Yeah, pussy whipped.*

"He's gone, Frankie, I did it!" Aiden tells me as he rolls away from me to face the door.

I stroke his hair gently. "He's gone, Aid, you did it. You're safe."

When Aiden's breathing becomes heavy, I turn and face Cameron. He's propped up on his elbow, watching me with eyes full of questions. I breathe out, "He suffers from night terrors." He nods for me to continue. "He's on medication for them and other things. But Bale just said he hasn't been taking them. I need to get him back on them, Cam. Mabel can't have him there if he's a threat to the other kids."

Cameron strokes my face gently. "You're amazing with him, Frankie." His eyes are full of love and pride. "Do the scars have anything to do with his terrors?" he whispers.

"Yeah, his mom used to whip the shit out of him when his dad wasn't abusing him and his siblings."

Cameron's face distorts into horror, and he swallows hard. "Fuck, that's bad." He scrubs a hand down his face as he watches Aiden breathing heavily. "You said his parents were dead?"

"Yeah, his dad. Fuck, Cam, he was so fucked up." I shake my head. "They were this posh upperclass family. Home tutored their kids and shit. But they were so fucked up." I glance back at Aiden to make sure he's sleeping. "His dad went too far one day and snapped. He killed his mom and sisters with a butcher knife. Aiden was hiding but came out halfway through and saw him slaughtering his little sister. He lost it, Cam. He just went wild and attacked his dad, hit him with a pan to start, then took the knife and went at it. It was a while before anyone found them." I swallow thickly with emotion. I can't imagine the trauma he must have endured, both before and after. "Aiden was in shock, put into a mental facility for kids before he got placed in foster care."

"Jesus!" Cameron hisses.

"He's fucked up, but he's our fucked-up, Cam. We're all fucked up some way or another."

Cameron nods his head and places a soft kiss on my forehead. "We'll sort it out, baby. I'll make sure of it." He squeezes me tighter, and I snuggle into his arms, feeling the safest I've ever felt in my entire life.

The sun beams through the room but it's not the light that wakes me, it's the door swinging open and hitting the dresser that startles me. "Wow, fuck. What the fuck is going on in here? You having a party without me?" Romeo chuckles, eyebrows dancing.

I slowly sit up. Cameron's head pops up from behind me, launching a pillow in Romeo's direction, causing him to chuckle. "Bale's ordering breakfast; be down soon." He turns on his heel and closes the door.

I stretch my body out while admiring a grinning Cameron. He nuzzles into my neck, leaving tender kisses behind my ear.

"I thought I was sleeping downstairs?" Aiden rubs his hair as he sits up, his scarred back exposed to us. Cameron's hold on me tightens.

"You had a night terror, Aid," I gently explain.

"Mm," he grumbles. "Been getting them a lot again lately."

My tone turns harsher. "Maybe if you'd stayed on your meds, you wouldn't be having them."

He scoffs back at me. "That's not going to happen!"

"Why the fuck not?" He's pissing me off. It took us ages to finally get him settled on something that suited him, and now he's screwing it all up.

He throws his head back on the propped-up pillows. "Because I'm not getting addicted to those things!"

"Addicted? Aiden, they're to help you!"

"Yeah. Well, you guys mean more to me than fucking pills, Frankie, so that's not going to happen. I'm coming off them all!" His head is downcast, his hair hanging in his eyes, shielding him. This is Aiden at his most vulnerable, and I hate it.

I jump out of the bed. "Off them all? Are you fucking insane?" I shake my head at him as Cameron starts getting dressed beside me. "You need them, Aiden. You can't just come off them." My voice is desperate.

"Yeah, I'm the insane one of the group, right? I'm good with that." He shrugs nonchalantly. "You guys are my family, Frankie, and I ain't doing nothin' that's going to jeopardize that!" he spits out.

I breathe deeply and pinch the bridge of my nose before softening my tone. "Aid, why would you think you would lose us?"

He huffs. "That's what happened to Nate." He slowly meets my eyes.

I move toward him slowly and kneel on the floor beside the bed so my eyes are level with his. I gently brush the hair from his face. "Aiden, that's not what happened to Nate. This is completely different; Nate chose illegal drugs, and his actions had consequences."

He snaps back just as quick. "You said he didn't mean what happened, that it wasn't his fault! You said we were family and nothing can change that. But where's Nate now, huh? Bale said he isn't family anymore. How the fuck does that work?! I'm not going to let myself get addicted to fucking pills, then lose you all when I do something stupid!"

His words are harsh, but they're actually pretty fucking true. We are family, and Bale needs to get a fucking grip and get over Nate's mistakes. Hell, I've had to.

"You know what, Aiden? You're fucking right. You're absolutely right, sweetheart. Bale is being a dick. He needs a little more time to calm down, and when he does, you'll see everything will be okay."

I quickly throw on some clothes and don't spare the room a backward glance as I storm downstairs to confront Bale.

Bale is sitting blowing into a coffee when I walk into the kitchen, not giving a minute to start my tirade. My chest pumping in temper. "You're the reason Aiden has stopped taking his meds!" I screech.

Bale glares at me and raises his eyebrow in response. "How d'ya figure?"

"He's got it in his head if he gets addicted to his meds, we're going to turn our back on him like we did Nate!"

Bale laughs a condescending laugh and throws his head back. "Fuck, he's lost it!"

"No, no, he hasn't lost it! You know his mind overworks things, you need to be more compassionate toward him, Bale. Your actions have consequences and the way you're treating Nate is fucking childish and ridiculous."

"Childish and ridiculous? Seriously? After what that prick did? He doesn't deserve to be a part of this family." His veins in his temple bulge in anger.

His words stun me. Sure, Bale is well known for not showing emotion, but this is something else, he's pure fucking hateful. I literally shout, "Enough, I've had E-fucking-nough of this Nate bullshit. It happened to me, Bale! *Me!* Not fucking you! I've fucking gotten over it so you can too!"

Bale chuckles, before turning his sinister eyes back to me. "You've gotten over it? Really, Frankie? Is that why you haven't breathed a word to your boyfriend about it? You don't just get over shit like that!"

My body sags. He's right I'm not over it. I never will be. But I won't let how I felt drag me down, I'm not going to go backward. I'm stronger than that! I brush my hand through my unruly hair.

"You make this fucking right, Bale!" I point at him harshly. "You give Aiden the reassurance he fucking deserves and needs!"

Bale picks up his coffee and walks out of the kitchen. My eyes follow him and meet with Cameron's, he was standing there the whole time and obviously heard everything. I can feel myself pale. He moves closer to me and pulls me into a tight hug, his gentle words caress my neck. "It's okay, you're okay. You don't have to explain a single thing." His gentle, thoughtful words bring tears to my eyes.

"Hey, where's breakfast?" Aiden's words break the tender moment, causing me to laugh.

"I got it!!" Romeo declares, coming through the patio doors that lead outside. He drops three brown bags on the worktop before pouring a coffee and returning to a chair outside, overlooking the pool.

"Fancies himself as a fucking mansion pimp or something out there." Cameron chuckles, tilting his head toward Romeo, whose arms are crossed, his legs up on the table, surveying the grounds. We all look at Romeo and break out in laughter.

Cameron busies himself in the kitchen while me and Aiden unpack the warm muffins. God knows where they got these from, but they smell delicious.

"So, I spoke to Bale, and he agrees that with you medically needing the pills, Aiden. If you did anything wrong, it wouldn't come back on you. You wouldn't get into trouble for it," I lie while Cameron watches me closely.

Aiden stops eating. "I don't know, it's risky, what if he changes his mind?"

"He won't."

"I've been thinking too, I know an amazing doctor. I'd be happy to pass your details on. He does free work and shit to help patients who've been in traumatic events. You know, like Army veterans or kidnappings, that type of thing. I'm sure if I spoke to him, he could offer you some advice. He gives therapy and recommends medications. He'd make sure you don't get addicted too," Cameron explains. I watch Cameron, who is struggling to meet my eyes.

Aiden's eyes light up. "Really?"

Cameron nods and shrugs. "Yeah, it's no big deal. He likes to help people."

"Wow, that would be great, wouldn't it, Aiden?" I coax.

Aiden takes another bite of the muffin, nodding. "So, what should I do about the pills?"

"I think it's best you go back on them. I'll sort things out with the doctor, then in between, you can be getting settled back with Mable, huh?" Cameron gently suggests.

Aiden nods his head faster. "Yeah, yeah, I'll do that. This is going to work." His whole demeanor has once again changed to being invigorated.

I move toward him and kiss the side of his head. "Yeah, it is, sweetie. Everything's going to be just fine, you'll see!"

He picks another muffin up, leaving the room to go outside. "Going in the pool before we head home!" he shouts over his shoulder.

Cameron comes around the counter and kisses my head. "Best go find a fucking doctor, then, hey?" He chuckles.

My heart warms. I cannot believe this is the same miserable, scowling fucker I met when I first arrived here. I stand on my tiptoes and kiss his lips gently, causing his lips to pull into a sweet smile. "Thank you!" I tell him genuinely.

23

CAMERON

The weekend went by way too fast. Having the guys over was great but seeing the trauma within Aiden was truly soul destroying. You'd have to be incredibly unbalanced to not be remotely moved by the haunting story that persistently rules his life.

I made it my mission to find a doctor to help him, and with the help of Neo, we managed to set one up using one of my father's old offshore accounts, so James won't be none the wiser.

Frankie and I discussed how we're going to act in public and we agreed we would keep our relationship hidden. The last thing we want is for James to be against it and risk him sending Frankie away or for him to try and split us up.

Making our way to school on Monday, I turn to Frankie, stroking my hand up and down her thigh. "It's going to kill me not being able to touch you at school today," I tell her. My whole body sags at the realization.

She turns her head to face me, sighing. "I know, you smell so fucking edible. I could literally jump you right now!" She beams, eyeing me up and down.

Fuck, she's hot! My dick jumps in my pants, completely down with her jumping me right now.

We pull up at the school, and I sigh out loud, removing my hand from her leg before the crowds start to gather. I push a hand through my hair in frustration. "I guess I'll see you in English?" I'm like a petulant child, that's for sure.

"I'm sure I'll see you before then, Cam, leave it with me!" Frankie winks before opening the door and leaving me wondering what the hell she means, but I'm sure as hell excited to find out. My girl is a dirty little minx.

My morning is spent avoiding Stacey and Taylor. Desperate for the day to move on so I can be in fucking English with Frankie. *Since when did I become a lovesick fucking puppy?* I'm making my way toward Chemistry when my phone buzzes in my pocket. I pull myself to the side and quickly glance at it. Seeing it's from Frankie, my heart races,

Hottie: I need help, in the principal's office. Please hurry!

Holy fucking shit, what the hell has she done now?! My heart pounds against my chest as I rush toward the reception area. I glance around for Mrs. Price, the secretary, but she isn't in the office. Spinning around, I wonder what the fuck to do before thinking to hell with it, and I push past her desk and head back toward the principal's office. I knock on his door and wait.

A sweet familiar voice speaks up. "Come in."

I open the door and my fucking jaw hits the floor. Frankie is on the principal's desk with her fucking cunt on display, her skirt tugged up to her waist, and she's rubbing herself. *What the holy fuck is happening?*

I spin around the room searching for the principal, my eyes bugging out. Feeling a combination of shitting myself and being fucking turned on.

Frankie chuckles, her sultry voice oozes from her. "Relax, Cameron. He's at a meeting and Mrs. Price has disappeared for half an hour. Now I've been very naughty and I'm very needy, so is there anything you can do to help me out?" She quirks a brow at me.

I roll my lip between my teeth. Sweet fucking Jesus!

I drop my bag and rush toward her. Dragging her heels to the end of the desk, I devour her pussy, and her elbows are on the desk helping her to sit up and watch me.

I spread her plush pink pussy lips and lap at her juices, my dirty girl is dripping for me.

Her head tips back as I suck her engorged clit, her moans causing my cock to push against my zipper. "Oh, fuck, Cam!" She swallows deeply. "I'm going to come!"

I abruptly release her clit. "Come on my fucking tongue, Frankie. I want to taste you all fucking day!" Her fists tighten on the desk as she starts thrusting her hips into my face. *Fuck, that's hot!* Yeah, she's fucking my face.

This is by far the most erotic thing I've ever done, and I know it's only the tip of the iceberg with Frankie Vadetta.

I push my fingers into her greedy pussy and hook them forward, hitting the spot I know will drive her crazy. She rides my face shamelessly causing my cock to bulge and drip pre-cum. I feel like I'm about to explode. Her back arches as she screams her release, the evidence dripping down my chin.

No sooner has she come do I grab her off the desk and spin her around. Leaning her over the desk and pulling her skirt up, I caress her ass cheeks in my palms. Her moans urge me on. I quickly find a condom from my wallet while fumbling with my belt and lowering my zipper, releasing my throbbing cock. I stroke it to relieve some tension while sheathing myself in a swift movement.

I guide my cock to Frankie's dripping pussy, stroking it up and down her ass cheeks and around her puckered hole, causing her to gasp. "You like taking it up the ass, Frankie?" She sucks in a breath.

Her head tilted to the side, and her reddened cheek against the wooden desk. "Yes," she manages to bite out between her moans. *Fuck yeah, that's hot!* My dirty girl, all fucking mine.

I tighten my hold on her hips as my cock finds her pussy hole. I slam into her, causing her body to move up the desk. Her hands clutch the end of the desk, turning white. "Ah, fuck, Cam!"

Hell yes! I pull back and slam back into her again, causing her to moan and pant. I grip her, with one hand on her hip bruising tight. Then I spank her ass with the other. "You're so fucking bad, Frankie!" *Spank!* Her pussy clenches me tightly with each spank. My balls tingle and my spine straightens. I work my hand around to her clit and press hard onto it, my thrusts pushing her further into my hand, effectively smacking her clit. Frankie's body tenses as she pushes her fist to her mouth. Holy shit . . . "Fuck, Frankie, fuck!" I bite my lip as my balls spasm, shooting ropes of cum out of my cock.

Our bodies sag together, completely sated.

How the fuck am I meant to go back to class after that?

———

Lunch soon comes around, and I'm grinning from ear to ear. This has by far been the best school day of my entire fucking life.

I've got a fucking spring in my step, and there's absolutely nothing that can change my good mood around.

I order my meal and sit in my usual seat, waiting for the guys to descend on the table. I scan the cafeteria and instantly my eyes land on Frankie's. She's watching me, so I wink at her, and she smiles a sweet, sexy smile before licking her lips seductively.

I shift in my seat as my cock starts to respond, making her bite her lip to stifle a giggle. Fuck, I wish she could sit over here with us, or me over there with her. I'm pulled out of my daze when Joel drops a tray of bread onto the table. "Hey, dude, how's your day going?"

I grin to myself widely with an air of confidence. "Good, yours?"

He watches me closely, then swings his head to Frankie's direction. "Oh my God, you did not?!" He laughs loudly.

I don't agree or disagree with him, I just continue to smugly smile.

My good mood automatically disintegrates when a body drops into my lap, and my body jolts in surprise before I realize what the fuck is going on. Fucking Stacey and her sickly-sweet scent.

Her nails work their way up my neck, and I grab ahold

of her wrist to stop her. "Stacey, stop this shit!" I snap, her pouty mouth turns up in disgust as she shuffles her ass on my lap. No doubt searching for my cock.

I push her hips from my lap. "Get the fuck off me; whatever we had is done. Over!" I hiss the words out at her.

Her hands go to her hips, and she tuts loudly. "What the hell, Cammy! I'm not finished yet!"

I glare at her, the cafeteria is growing quiet, and I know we're making a scene. "I'm done, Stacey, I don't want you touching me again! Fucking ever!"

Her eyes narrow on me. "Why?"

"Because I fucking said so. I don't need an excuse!" I glance at Joel who is sitting with his lunch, munching away with a smirk on his smug face.

"I said I'm not finished. So when you get your act together and you want to fuck, come find me!" She reaches out to touch my face with her long nails, but I pull away before she makes contact.

I narrow my eyes in disgust. "It's not going to happen, get the fuck over it!"

She pushes away from the table, with Taylor following behind her, and they leave the cafeteria, every eye watching them. "You'd better watch your back!" Joel points his fork at me. I laugh back at him before pushing my hand through my hair with tension. Peering over to Frankie, I smile softly at her, sending a small nod of reassurance her way, hoping she can see what she means to me through my actions. Because I sure as shit don't feel able to express the words.

FRANKIE

The week has been long and drawn out. Cam and I stole kisses and gropes between classes, and while at home, we had to play it cooler, knowing full well we had cameras around the mansion.

I suggested he come to my room to study. So when the door finally opens and the freshly showered bronze god stands in my doorway I'm practically salivating at the mouth and pussy because, let's be honest, I was fucking gagging for it!

"You look ready to eat me!" Cameron chuckles with a smug smile.

"Is that what you want? Me to eat you, Cameron?" I smile flirtatiously while getting to my knees on the bed. I drop my cami top straps and the top falls, uncovering my breasts, exposing the light red marks that Cameron left on me when we last had sex.

He sucks in a breath, and I can see his hard cock protruding from his shorts, making me lick my lips in anticipation.

Cameron walks toward me and stops above me, his rough hand brushes over the marks on my breasts. "Mine," he pants out.

I nod, loving the vulnerable glimmer in his eyes but seeing the determination behind his words.

"Turn around and remove the clothes." His voice is firm and authoritative, sending an excited shiver down my spine. His fists clench and unclench beside him, as if restraining himself.

I stand on the bed and turn around, dropping my shorts, leaving my bare ass on display for him. I gaze over my shoulder and see his Adam's apple bob, his eyes hooded with lust, wetness escapes between my legs. I lift the top over my head completely and drop it to the bed.

"Kneel." One word in his commanding tone and I almost combust. *Fuck, he's hot!* I kneel on the bed.

I hear rustling behind me, then Cameron throws a pack of condoms on the bed and a bottle of lube. *Oh, fuck, what's he got planned?* I bite my lip with both nerves and excitement.

I can hear Cameron dropping his shorts, he sucks in a breath as he trails his hand from the top of my neck down my spine, creeping lower to my ass. Both hands begin to caress my ass cheeks. "Fuck, Frankie, you've no idea what you do to me, baby." His words sound almost pained.

"Lean forward and spread your legs, put your cheek on the mattress."

I do as he asks, bending over, my ass in the air, my legs parted wider, and my face flush to the mattress. "So fucking hot!" he breathes out.

I hear him open the lube. Followed by a squirt. Then I

feel his cold, dripping hands around my pussy. "Does this feel good, Frankie? Me rubbing your greedy little clit?"

"Fuck, yes!"

"Move that pussy over my hand, Frankie, fuck yourself with my hand!"

He holds his right hand still as I thrust my body against his hand. Effectively fucking myself on him. I can hear him sucking in his breath and a harsh swallow. Then I feel him moving his body in time with mine, and the fact I know he's stroking his cock to the rhythm of my movements is such a fucking turn on.

My orgasm is building, I'm moaning and panting. "Oh fuck, Cam. Please don't stop!"

CAMERON

Watching Frankie's ass up in the air takes my breath away. My balls are tight before I even start rubbing my cock. I didn't realize I could be this restrained. It's hard work, and I'm impressed with myself, that's for fucking sure. All I really want to do is plow the fuck into her relentlessly.

Her slick pussy writhes against my hand, pushing her ass into my body with each movement. Her fucking asshole on full display, making me tense my own ass cheeks to keep my cum in check. There's only one place that's going tonight and it sure as fuck isn't on her ass.

"You gonna let me fuck your ass, Frankie?" I practically pant.

"Yes!"

Fuck, I nearly blow there and then, and I bite the inside of my cheek and stop my movements to gain control.

"You gonna let me fuck that ass bare, Frankie? Nothing between us?"

She nods. "Yes, just my ass, though. Nothing between us," she confirms.

I rub my hand over her puckered hole, she's relaxed and it's a fucking turn on knowing she's willingly going to do this with me. I've only fucked a chick's ass once before, and she was so fucking tense it was hard work and, in the end, I probably enjoyed it as much as her. Not a fucking lot.

I rub the lube around her tight hole. Glancing at Frankie, she's licking her lips, every fucking movement she does is so goddamn erotic and sensual, I'm so fucking lucky to have her. She's incredible.

"I want you to rub your clit, baby, then in your own time, push back on me, okay?"

She nods her head, then moves her hand between her thighs as I stroke my cock around her wet ass. When she gets a rhythm going, I move my cock to her greedy tight puckered hole. *Fuck, this is hot.*

She starts to moan and pushes back against me. The tip of my dick going into her hole has me sucking in a breath, forcing my cum to go down. As Frankie pushes back against me, I gently push my cock through her tight barrier, her legs spread wider as her hand becomes more frantic. "You're going to have to move soon, Cameron, I . . . I'm so fucking turned on . . . I'm not going to last long!"

"Fuck, Frankie, you want me to fuck your ass, baby? Say it! Tell me, dirty girl, you want me to fuck your ass," I spit out the words, desperate for her to let me unleash on her tight ass.

"Fuck my ass, Cameron, give it to me!" *Fuck yes!*

My back straightens as I lunge forward, jolting Frankie, causing her to scream into the mattress. My full cock sinks into her hole as I start pummeling her ass.

Her chants grow louder as her orgasm takes over her. "Yes, yes. Fuck yes!"

I throw my head back as I feel my balls tingling, my grip tightening on her hips, my mind swimming with the fact I'm going to come in Frankie's ass. Making her mine, my cum in her ass. "Fuuuck," I screech. White light blurring my vision, my heart skips out and I physically still at the impact of my orgasm.

I drop over Frankie's back, sending us both flattening to the mattress. "That was . . . hot!" She grins. *Fucking hot? It was insane!*

"Absolutely incredible." I pepper kisses down her back and around her neck.

Slowly I pull out of her ass, watching the movement with sick fascination, and as I see my hot cum drip from her ass, an overwhelming urge to see it dripping from her pussy comes over me. "Are you on the pill?"

Frankie's body tenses, making me frown. "Yes, why?" She turns over to stare at me.

I crawl over the top of her. Onto my elbows, kissing her face, making my way to her lips. "Just asking. I've got the overwhelming urge to watch my cum escape your pussy." I smile against her lips.

Frankie's hand grips my jaw. "I don't want that, Cam, I want to use condoms. I'm not ready for that. I'm sorry." I peer into her eyes, and they glisten, as if she's upset. I roll beside her and watch her closely, she's clearly worried. I'm not happy at that, but why the fuck would that bother me? It was just a crazy thought.

"Hey, it's okay." I laugh my suggestion off. "Your ass looked hot leaking my cum, but it's okay, we don't have to go bare. As long as I get you, I can live with that." I gently kiss her to reassure her, she kisses me back, and I relax against her.

I pull her into my side and snuggle my head into her neck. "You're everything to me, Frankie. I've never felt like this before, it makes me feel possessive and greedy, and I'm sorry if I push for more. Just promise me you'll bear with me?" I can't let my own crazy need for her push her away. I can't be without her, ever.

Frankie turns around to face me, her hand moving the loose hair from my forehead, then down to my jawline. "I feel it too, Cam. I don't mean to push you away. We've got to bear with each other, and we'll be okay, I can feel it." She smiles at me, and any doubt I had before about pushing her away or wanting too much is dispersed as her lips meet mine. The truth seeping from them.

24

FRANKIE

Saturday night soon comes around and we're on our way to another fucking party. Seriously, all these rich kids do is party and they're not even all that good at it.

I really wasn't in the mood for this, as it's growing increasing close to a date I've been dreading, and I guess I figured the distraction might do me good.

Joel has been bouncing in the front seat beside Cameron, chattering on about how Stacey has now moved onto some other poor unsuspecting jock who was quick to discover her less than stellar blowjob skills.

Cameron's eyes meet mine in the rear-view mirror; penetrating into me as if sensing I'm not myself. It should scare me how much we are entwined in one another's emotions but if anything, I find comfort in it. Except at this moment in time, I don't want him to sense I'm not myself, I need him to think I'm okay. I smile back, and I'm sure he can sense it's fake, his eyebrows pull together, studying me.

We enter the party that's already in full swing. Cameron's hand behind my back guides me to the bar. I wish I could hold him properly. As if sensing my thoughts, he dips his mouth to my ear. "I wish I could fucking hold you right now."

I smile up at him and nod in agreement, earning me a smug smirk.

A loud succession of laughs has me stilling in my spot, my back going ramrod straight as memories of the last time I heard that very same laugh overwhelm me . . .

I hand the beers over to the hot guys at the bar. "What do we owe you?" the hot friend asks.

"Oh, it's fine. My treat. Enjoy your night guys," I tell them with a wink. If I weren't unavailable, the brown wavey-haired, hazel-eyed sex on a stick would definitely be up my street. I shake my head with a laugh.

My phone buzzes in my hands again.

I glance at it and see that it's Bale, freaking the fuck out because Nate hasn't checked in with him yet. See, this is what happens when you have a relationship with someone in your crew, they screw up and automatically, it's your screw up too.

I roll my eyes as I push through the corridor that houses the restrooms and also our staff room. He's probably in here. As I push through the door that takes me to the staff room, a sickening feeling enters my stomach as a girly hideous laugh echoes through the corridor, and I'm almost close to not opening the door, worried at what I might be walking in on.

I push my anxious thoughts to the side and take a deep breath. I stride through the door with an air of confidence I don't feel, and sure enough, Nate is seated on the couch directly in front of me. My heart stutters at what I see, his head lolling to the side, and the laughter comes louder as I take in the scene surrounding me. Natalia Bennett is scrunched up next to Nate, her hands all over him, but he's completely oblivious because he's fucking high. Like, so fucking high he's almost at the golden gates. His nose is covered in coke!

My heart stops on the spot. I gasp for air. I feel my body pale, my vision clouding, noise I don't actually hear surrounds me. Despair, dread, betrayal, complete disappointment overwhelms me. He's been clean for months, months! I study him; he's a fucking mess.

The giggling moron beside him continues on, "I told you I'd bag myself someone with money, Frankie. Someone worth having!" She giggles. She's a bitch, a grade-A bitch! She knows we're together, yet she never let off trying to get Nate's attention, one way or another.

"You did this?" I choke out, almost shocked at how someone can be so cruel as to offer an open addict drugs. It's been common knowledge for a while now that Nate's got addictions. Fuck, everyone in every fucking club has been warned against giving him anything!

"He just wanted a little fun, didn't you, honey?" She preens against him with a spiteful smirk in my direction. Nate can barely fucking function. Me? I'm glued to the fucking spot in shock.

The door flies open and in walks Nate's cousin Vaughn. "Holy fucking shit! What the hell's going on?" His eyes wild with rage.

My words don't come out. I can't speak to explain a damn thing. My legs wobble, and I feel like I'm going to collapse. All the hard work, everything we've been through, gone. We've got so much to do; we were doing it. We were getting there. He's ruined it all, she's ruined it all!

"Fuck, Star. Star? Can you hear me, babe? Bale's going to hit the fucking roof!" I vaguely hear Vaughn pacing up and down before returning to me, rubbing his hand reassuringly down my back. "Star? Babe, do you think you can drive? Can you do the run tonight instead of Nate? I'll sort Nate, and you do the run, okay?"

I nod my head in agreement, taking the phone he thrusts into my hand. Glancing down at it, I see the details alight on the screen: Bugatti Chiron.

Like a switch has been flicked, I go into Star mode. Of course, I need to be on my game, we need this Bugatti. Bale has been after it for a while. We've already got new plates and a dealer lined up, and now more than ever we're going to need that money, because by the looks of Nate, I'm in this shit alone.

I nod in agreement to Vaughn and turn on my heels, the loud cackling giggles of Natalia Bennett causing my chest to tighten as I push through the doors, letting them slam behind me.

I crash into someone, sending the phone flying across the floor. I glance up into his eyes, the concern and panic evident, it's the guy from the bar, the hot one.

We exchange words, but I'm not even sure what we're saying. I swipe the wetness on my face, and I realize they're tears. Since when do I cry?

He hands me the phone back and when I glance down at the screen, I see the same guy's face staring back at me, a mirror image of him.

I stumble as realization hits home, this guy . . . this nice, caring guy . . . he's our hit. He's the owner of the Bugatti, Cameron Donovan. I tug on my hair and screech a "Motherfuck-

er!" before turning away and somehow making my way toward the club.

I turn around one last time to those concerned hazel eyes, the ones that have captivated me. "I'm sorry, Cameron."

"Frankie, Frankie! Are you okay? You're fucking pale, Frankie! Do you feel sick? Frankie, speak to me."

I shake my head and blink. My mind slowly coming back to the here and now, the giggling. Vaughn told me weeks ago she was in Trent Valley, and here she is.

CAMERON

I stroke Frankie's back. "Frankie, Frankie! Are you okay? You're fucking pale, Frankie! Do you feel sick? Frankie, speak to me."

I'd been talking to her, then she went fucking vacant, as though she was lost in her thoughts, her body tense, her face pale, and her breathing fucking erratic.

She's freaking me the fuck out.

As if suddenly hearing me, she shakes herself and stares up at me, a sickly-sweet smile crossing her face, making my nerve endings stand on edge.

"I'm fine, Cameron, better than fine, actually. I'm about to get a little justice." She smiles at me, and it doesn't reach her eyes. I dart my eyes to Joel, who shrugs but he's also watching her with concern closely, his eyebrows knitted together in confusion but also gauging her reaction.

Frankie moves around me and marches over to the loud crowd of giggling, she pushes past the group, placing herself in front of a couch. Me and Joel follow but hang back within the crowd.

On the couch are two guys I don't recognize, between them is a rough-looking chick. She sure as fuck doesn't seem like she belongs here, her cheap inflated fake tits are spilling out of her short fake designer dress, her long dark hair extensions are ragged and not the usual professionally done extensions you see around Trent Valley. Then the tattoos are a real giveaway; yeah, she isn't from round here.

Frankie stands above them, her arms crossed across her chest. She seems pissed but I'm not quite sure why. *Does she know this chick?*

The chick gazes up and the mere fact that the color drains from her face confirms she knows who Frankie is. *Shit, this isn't going to be good.*

I glance at Joel, shoving my phone at him. "Call Bale!"

"S-t-t-Star . . . Star?" the chick stutters her words out.

Frankie smiles, a condescending-as-fuck smile. "That would be me!" She holds her arms out in front to herself, as if presenting herself to the chick.

"Wh-what are you doing here?"

"Our last conversation went something like this, Natalia. 'I told you I'd bag myself someone with money, Frankie, someone worth having.' Does that sound about right? Well, tell me, Natalia, who did you bag?" Frankie's words come out through clenched teeth, making her words sound as though she's struggling to remain calm.

"I-I . . . that's not what I meant! Anyway, what are you doing here?" She tries to laugh her words off, trying to be friendly.

Frankie throws her head back and laughs, it's a forced fake laugh. Anyone that knows her knows that.

"Me?" She points to herself, her chest rising and falling

rapidly. "Me? I lost it all, remember? Thanks to *you*, Natalia!" She points in the chick's direction; she's now visibly shaking in fear of Frankie.

"N-no that was Nate! I just gave them to him, he paid me. A guy paid me to do it, I didn't know, I didn't realize," this Natalia chick spits out, panicking. It's obvious as fuck she's lying, and I don't even know this chick.

Frankie calmly steps back from Natalia, she appears controlled. My back straightens because this calm, controlled Frankie, reminds me of "Star." This isn't going to end good.

Frankie releases a slow cool exhale before calmly speaking. "You know our English TA taught me so much, Natalia, but there was this one quote that class concentrated on, how did it go?" She presses her finger to her lip as if remembering. "'There is neither happiness nor misery in the world; there is only the comparison of one state with another, nothing more. He who has felt the deepest grief is best able to experience supreme happiness.' Do you recognize that quote?"

Natalia shakes her head, gulping. A nervous flush breaking out up her neck into her cheeks.

"You should. You spent long enough drooling over the TA while he read the *Count of Monte Christo*. Have you felt deepest grief, Natalia?"

She shakes her head. "I'm sorry, Star, I swear I am!"

Frankie holds her hand up to shush her. "I have. Deepest grief and misery, Natalia, but it's true, it enables you to feel supreme happiness." Frankie's head drops down in thought before she turns her eyes to me. They hold mine, and I know she's referring to us.

I give her a small pleading head shake, whatever she

plans on doing needs to be stopped, and I'm hoping I can convey that in my eyes. She closes her eyes and turns back to Natalia, effectively shutting me out, and not acknowledging my silent plea.

"You know what else the Count was famous for?"

The room is deathly silent as Natalia shakes her head unsteadily.

Frankie smiles. "Tut tut, Natalia, you really should have paid more attention!" she mocks. "He's famous for revenge!"

Before Natalia can blink, Frankie has bent down to her boot and unsheathed a knife. She lunges at Natalia, holding her behind her head as she brings the knife down her face, from her forehead to her jaw, blood pouring from the open gouge. I fly toward them as the room erupts into screams and shouts. I push past people trying to get away from the scene.

The guys on either side of Natalia are trying to fight Frankie off of her but she's wild, crazy.

Her arms and legs flailing as they try to tackle her. "Fuck, get her arms, Joel!" I scream to Joel as I go for her waist.

"Don't you let her get away. Don't you fucking let her get away, Cameron. I swear I won't forgive you; I'll never fucking forgive you if you let her get away!"

Her words shock me, and I haven't a clue what the fuck is going on. "Joel, get the chick. Lock her in a bedroom, stay with her until Bale gets here. Don't let her out of your fucking sight, got me?!"

Joel nods as he throws the bleeding chick over his shoulder.

Frankie crumples in my arms, her body lax and heavy,

her fight gone. "It's okay, baby, I've got you." I speak softly into her ear as she turns her head into my neck, her chest heaving up and down. I close my hand around her head in comfort and lift her up around the waist. She wraps her legs around me like a child, and I carry her outside.

I head for my car, a screeching motorbike pulls beside me. "What the fucks going on?" Bale demands.

"Frankie attacked some Natalia chick? Joel's got her in a bedroom upstairs." I nod toward the house.

Bale's eyebrows shoot up. "She dead?"

I stumble. *What the fuck!* "What? No, she's not dead! She's cut up."

He rubs his forehead. "Shame. Don't worry, I'll sort it!" He winks and leaves me with a slap on the back. *What.the.fuck?!*

I place Frankie in the car and strap her in like an infant. I dash around to my side before she can get back out. My heart's pounding out of my chest as I start the engine.

"You okay?"

She turns her head to me and shakes it. *Fuck.* It hurts to see her like this, vulnerable and broken.

"What the fuck was all that about? I deserve to fucking know, Frankie!" I demand, my eyes must look wild right now.

"She drugged Nate, the night of the crash. She did it on purpose." Her voice is low and unsteady.

"She knew he was an addict?"

She nods her head and blows out a breath, her words sounding empty. "She wanted to screw things up for me. She's always been a bitch, she knew we were doing good, and she wanted to fuck things up. Nate was meant to be driving that night." She stares out the window, her voice solemn. "He could barely sit up. I took his place, and when you gave me the phone in the corridor, that was the first time I knew who the target was."

"That's how you knew my name? Why you apologized?"

She nods in agreement, her voice low. "You were so sweet and caring. That's why I couldn't leave your dad's chain, Cam. You didn't deserve any of that, I couldn't let you lose the chain too."

I pick up her hand and kiss her fingers. "I'm going to contact Neo when we get in. I'll make sure he knows to wipe any footage of what just happened, okay? He'll hack into all the phones that were there tonight."

Frankie nods and turns back to look out of the window, seemingly unfazed whether she's caught for cutting someone up or not. Well, lucky for her, I care enough for the both of us.

25

CAMERON

This week at school has been long and grueling with exams most days. Worst of all, Frankie seems to be distant. I'm not sure if it's the fight that's made her put the barrier up or something more, but when I try talking to her, her words are terse, and her responses are short.

I've got a sickening feeling of dread that she's purposely putting distance between us. I feel a combination of anxiety and anger bubbling inside. *Is she having second thoughts? Is she texting Nate? Where was she Wednesday when she told my mom she was at a non-existent study group? Why wouldn't she tell me? What the fuck is going on? Why the hell is she pushing me away?* I nibble on my lip in frustration.

My thoughts are banished when my phone lights up. It's almost midnight on Friday night and I'm lying in bed instead of being at a party with Joel. All because I want to feel close to Frankie, the girl currently locked in her room with a supposed headache.

I glance over at my phone, the buzzing lighting up the room again. Bale's name dances across the screen, and I wonder again how the fuck his name even got into my phone in the first place.

"Yeah."

"Hey, Cam, Frankie talk to you about tomorrow at all?"

I scrunch up my face. *Nope, haven't a fucking clue what he's talking about.* "Take the silence as a no, then." He chuckles to himself. "Listen, it's a big day for her tomorrow, she's going to need some support, me and the guys are throwing her a small party, and I think you should be there."

I'm at a loss for words, and haven't got a fucking clue what the hell is going on. But if she wanted me there, surely, she'd have mentioned it? Jesus, it hurts that she hasn't. *Why the hell is she pushing me away?*

"Listen, I know she's struggling at the minute, just try and be patient with her, Cam. I was hoping she'd have spoken to you before tomorrow but . . ." He pauses. " . . . just, she's struggling, man. I know she'd want you there, she needs you there."

I breathe out a deep breath. *What the fuck can I say to that?* "Sure, text me the time and address."

"Good man, see you there."

The phone line goes dead, and I run my hand down my face. *What the fuck am I letting myself in for now?*

I haven't seen Frankie all day, and I don't know whether to be pissed off or concerned. I make my way to the address Bale sent me; he seems convinced I need to be there for her so that's where I'll be.

FRANKIE

I've been dreading today, but the guys have kept me busy. Part of me feels awful for pushing Cameron out, but I don't feel strong enough to go through it all again. I'll explain to him at some point, but I just need today.

The guys have trimmed Bale's back garden up, and it's amazing. I gaze around at them and feel overwhelmed to have them here with me, even if a part of us is missing.

Bale clears his throat. "Frankie, someone here for you." He nods to the direction of the side gate, a figure looming in the shadows. I get up and make my way toward it.

Wearing a cap pulled down, covering his face, he slowly lifts his head and peers up at me. "Hey."

My eyebrows shoot up. "Nate, what are you doing here?"

He swallows harshly. "Bale called, said I could see you."

Wow, that shocks me. Perhaps he did listen to the shit I said about Aiden? "He did?"

Nate nods and fidgets on his feet. "I'd have seen you today one way or another, guess he figured he'd okay it first." He shrugs.

I twist my hands with a nervous energy. "How are you doing?"

He lifts his head up to meet my eyes. "Good, I've been clean a couple of months now. I'm still classed as a patient. But I've applied for a few jobs on the East Coast."

My heart swells for him. "Oh wow, that's, that's great, Nate." I genuinely mean it. He deserves to find his happiness.

"Thank you, for the cash. Vaughn said you'd been sending it; there wasn't enough in the house sale." I nod. I knew there wouldn't be and that's why I did it.

"And thank you for never giving up on me." He walks toward me and holds out a gift bag. I take it from him and nod while fiddling with my hands as he steps closer, his scent surrounds me. I acknowledge the fact that it actually doesn't do anything for me. Not anymore. He lifts my chin and peers into my eyes. "I'll love you always!"

A lone tear slides down my face. "I know. Me too."

He steps back and clears his throat, overcome with emotion. His words come out on a tremble. "I'd have been a good daddy, Frankie. I'd have done it for him."

"I know," I whisper. My eyes filling with tears.

"You look after our girl, Cameron Donovan!" he shouts as he walks away, and I turn to face Cameron, his eyes full of sympathy, love, and understanding.

He pulls me into his arms and hugs me tight, my heart pounding out of my chest. I close my eyes and embrace him. It feels like time has run away with us before he pulls away gently. "The teach?" He chuckles, breaking the moment and making me laugh.

"The TA actually, but yeah, that's Nate."

He smiles down at me. "You okay?"

"I will be." I nod.

He smiles and gently kisses my lips.

CAMERON

After knocking on the door and getting no response, I decide to just go in since I can hear music out the back.

I approach the patio and the guys' eyes are transfixed on something at the side of the house, so I follow their line of sight, it's Frankie talking to someone.

I approach cautiously, something tells me this is a private conversation, but I can't seem to help myself.

As I watch them interact, it's obvious Frankie is upset. Her shoulders sag and her head is hung low. The guy she's talking to seems familiar and it isn't until he looks at her fully that I realize it's her teacher, the guy that came to the court and then to the house to leave her a key to collect his belongings. She calls him Nate, and just like that, it all clicks together. *Holy fuck!*

As I'm standing, listening, I know he's seen me, and therefore, what he says, he knows I'm going to hear. "I'd have been a good daddy, Frankie. I'd have done it for him."

My legs almost buckle. *Oh, fuck no!* I glance back at the

guys, and they're surrounded by blue balloons, as if celebrating a birthday?

My mind quickly whirls back to conversations with Frankie, the one in the car weeks ago when she told me, *"Yeah well I lost more than you think."* The conversation with Natalia, *"Have you felt deepest grief and misery? I have."* The tattoo across her stomach with Nate's name, a reminder of their baby? A memory.

I pull her to me and hug her fucking tight. I never want to let her go, I never want her to feel pain again, no misery, or deepest grief. I kiss her on top of her head and make a silent promise to her. I'll always be there, and she'll always be mine.

We released balloons in honor of baby Max. I kept my thoughts and questions tucked away and just supported Frankie throughout the night.

She's quiet as I lead her to the room Bale is letting us stay in. We strip down and I lie on the sheets in my boxers as she tugs on my T-shirt, making me smile that she wants to wear my scent, and she rolls her eyes at my childish observation.

She lays her head on my chest, and I stroke her hair, her silky waves falling through my fingers.

"It would have been his birthday today," she whispers, and I nod, listening to her. "I lost him the night of the crash."

My arms tighten around her, the urge to vomit overwhelms me, but I swallow it down. All these months I've been fucking selfish, complaining about a fucking car and chain and she lost a fucking baby. I truly fucking hate myself here and now.

"Fuck, Frankie, I'm so fucking sorry!" I choke the words out because they simply aren't enough.

She shakes her head gently. "No, it's no one's fault, not really. I'd had cramps all day, when I found Nate drugged, I knew I shouldn't have been driving. But I did it anyway. I shouldn't have driven in the state I was in, let alone pregnant, Cameron." She takes a deep breath, my strong, strong girl.

"I crashed the car because I was so upset and overwhelmed, I couldn't think straight. I was panicking about how Bale was going to react to Nate, and if I'd be raising the baby alone."

She's crying softly and I squeeze her tighter. "The cramps got worse immediately after the crash. They were so intense they took my breath away, but I made myself go back for the chain and then the pain crippled me, I couldn't stand back up. I was arrested pretty much straight away, but I was losing a lot of blood, so they took me to the hospital."

I listen silently, stroking her back for support. "Bale came storming in not long after they told me I was in early labor and the baby's heart wasn't strong enough to survive. I gave birth with Bale beside me. Max was already asleep."

Fuck! Tears stream down my own face as I think about the strong, beautiful woman beside me and what she's been through yet come out the other side. She's truly amazing. She's my inspiration.

She swallows deeply. "We got to hold him, he was properly formed, just so tiny. Bale was a mess. That's why he's so protective over me." I nod. Understanding completely where Bale is coming from and also understanding his hate toward Nate, he obviously blames him for the events leading up to Max's birth.

Her hands tremble on my chest. "Bale blamed Nate. He wouldn't let him in the room to see me or Max. I had to beg him; it was awful, Cameron. Nate was such a mess, he crumpled to the floor, sobbing and saying he was sorry. The nurses had to pry Max from him."

She shakes her head at the memories, her voice a mere whisper. "He thought it was all his fault, it wasn't. The doctor explained I had a hereditary heart condition that I knew nothing about, and Max had developed it too. He wouldn't have survived, even without the crash."

"You're so strong, Frankie. So fucking strong!" I tell her with determination in my voice.

She chokes on her sob. "I went through a phase of not caring, I couldn't have cared less if they sentenced me to life in prison at the trial." My mind darts back to watching a very nonchalant Frankie in the courtroom, her whole demeanor being bored and carefree.

"You gave me something to care about, Cameron, *someone* to care about." Her head tilts up to look at me.

I gaze down at her and see the love in her eyes. "I love you, Cameron."

My chest feels tight. "Fuck, I love you, Frankie. So fucking much it hurts!"

"Yeah?" she questions with a quirk of her eyebrow.

"Fuck yeah!"

I kiss her. I kiss her like my life depends on it, like she's going to prison for the rest of her life. I kiss her with the desperation I feel for her.

26

CAMERON

'm relieved to find the house empty when we get back. My mom text to say we were all being subjected to another dinner get together tonight. Fan-fucking-tastic.

I follow Frankie upstairs to her room. She's been holding the bag that Nate gave her all the way home like her life depends on it. I fidget on my feet, unsure of what to do next. Clearing my throat, I man up. "You want me to stay while you open that? Or leave you to it?" I gesture at the bag on her knee.

Her beautiful eyes meet mine. "Stay. Please." I nod and sit next to her on the bed.

She breathes out and reluctantly opens the bag. Inside is a long box, she slowly pulls it out and opens the box. Sitting in the box is a knife, but it's the handle that's the important part, on the handle is an imprint of small fingerprints. Frankie's fingers graze over the fingerprints as she takes the knife out of the box with shaky hands.

"They're Max's fingerprints," she confirms through tears.

"It's beautiful!" I tell her. My throat tightening up with emotion.

Frankie swipes her tears away. "They're so tiny, aren't they?" I nod in agreement, studying at the tiny fingerprints on the handle.

"The knife thing is definitely you!" I smile.

It makes her chuckle through her tears. "Yeah, he knows I'm not a jewelry person. The way to my heart is a weapon, I guess." She grins.

"I love you, Frankie." I grab her face and kiss away her tears.

I clear my throat as I think of something I've been meaning to ask for a while now. "Hey, did you open the box you collected from Nate's?"

Her eyebrows furrow. "No, I didn't feel strong enough."

I look to her, and she nods her head in understanding as she gets up and goes to her closet. She comes back with the brown box, blue star drawn on the front. Her shaking hands stop herself from opening it, then she glances at me nervously. "Cam, I'm not sure what's in there. I don't know what you're going to see." She bites her bottom lip adorably.

I turn my body toward the box and try to act unfazed. "It's okay, I'll deal." *Fuck, there better not be fucking naked photos of them together.*

Frankie opens the box lid and gasps before sitting next to me and taking the items out one at a time. A small blue onesie with *My Dad's a Teacher* printed on it, a bundle of baby ultrasound scan photos. A framed photograph of Frankie and Nate makes my heart pound as I see the love in his eyes, his hands tight around her small baby bump. *Fuck, that's hard to see.*

Frankie continues sifting through the box of mementos, photos of her with all the guys, at various ages, her fiery, badass attitude clear as day. Small blue booties. A bundle of college certificates belonging to Nate and his brother, Ryan, the cop.

When Frankie reaches the bottom of the box, her eyebrows knit together. "What's wrong?"

Frankie pulls out a manila folder with writing on the front. *Nate, details on Frankie's father, as requested. Ry.*

Frankie eyes me, confusion evident on her face. "Nate must have asked Ryan for details on my dad's murder, he never mentioned it to me."

"Do you want to open it? I can do it for you if you prefer. Or we can leave it?" I suggest.

"No, I need to do this." Her voice is firm, confident, and controlled, there's almost like two versions of herself, the Frankie she shows me and the Star she shows everyone else, and right now, she's Star.

Frankie opens the file. Pages upon pages detailing her father's exploits with the Crew and the crime gangs run by Connor and Dominic. Her father, Jeremy Vadetta, was shot in the chest while fleeing an armed robbery at Hamilton Stockbrokers.

My chest hurts as I read the words. "Frankie. Hamilton Stockbrokers was my father's firm." Her eyes dart to mine in question. She turns the page to a photograph of her father's lifeless body, and she sucks in a gasp. I squeeze her hand in support.

Turning the page with shaky hands, the coroner's report details her father's demise. "I . . . I don't understand . . . it says my father's heart was healthy, how can it be healthy? Surely the report would pick up our hereditary heart condition?" Her eyebrows knit together in puzzlement.

"Maybe your mother had it, maybe she passed it down to you?" I suggest.

Frankie shakes her head in thought. "No, no, she didn't. The number of times she was in the ER, Cameron, I was there. I have literally held her hand when they told her she was lucky to be so fit and healthy, and they specifically said her heart was in amazing condition, given she took so many combinations of drugs. How can that be?"

I think for a moment. "Maybe you misunderstood the doctors when you had Max? Maybe you were confused, you went through a lot, Frankie."

"No, I had follow-up appointments about the heart condition, Cameron. Something's not right, I can feel it."

"Yeah, me too," I begrudgingly admit.

Frankie turns to the back page, a small bag attached to the folder with a memory stick inside it. Her hands shake as she detaches the bag.

I have a sickening feeling in the pit of my stomach. "Frankie, I'm not sure we should see what's on that. Maybe we should contact Bale?"

Frankie nods. "Yeah, I think you're right. I'll text him for a meet up."

FRANKIE

The rest of the day I'm anxious, a sickness brewing in my veins. Cameron and I are on edge with uncertainty. We agree to meet with Bale at his gym tonight, but first we have to endure another family meal.

The atmosphere in the dining room is its usual tension-filled debacle.

James dabs his napkin to his lips. "How has your week been. Frankie?"

I keep my eyes trained on my meal. My week's been utter shit. I celebrated what would have been my son's birthday, I'm unsure if he knows that or not, but I also don't care. "Fine," I reply in a clipped tone.

"Mm, interesting," he muses back.

Josie tries to make casual small talk. Asking about our school exams and if I've applied for any colleges yet or not, and I zone out. Nodding my head at appropriate times and smiling on cue.

Suddenly, Josie jumps up from the table. "Oh my goodness. How thoughtless of me. James, we almost forgot your medication!" Josie leaves the room, returning a few minutes later with James's medication. "I'm so sorry, darling, that's never happened before. We don't want that heart of yours packing it in, now do we?" She giggles to herself as James takes his medication.

Her words whirl around in my head. *"We don't want that heart of yours packing it in now do we?"* I glance at James in sheer panic. *It can't be? He can't be?!*

My eyes dart to Cameron's, his shocked face mirroring mine. His eyes drill into me, a subtle shake of his head instructing me not to act on Josie's words.

James's voice breaks me out of my trance. "Good thing I've got you around, Josie." He grins to himself. His smile resembling a wolf in sheep's clothing. My head pounds with tension and unanswered questions, my stomach roiling with the sickening answers I wish I could avoid.

I finally manage to exhale and relax into Cameron's Suburban, en route to Bale's gym. "Fuck, what the hell is happening!" Cameron spits out to himself, his fists tight on the steering wheel.

"I'm not sure. Do you think? Do you think he's . . .?" I can't say it, I can't say the words, there's no way he can be my father, surely?

Cameron takes my hand in his. "I don't know, Frankie, but things are slowly starting to come together, and I'm scared to think the answers are going to hurt you." He kisses my fingers in his signature sweet gesture.

When we finally arrive at the gym, I'm a bundle of nervous energy. We gather in Bale's office and explain to him and the guys what we've discovered in the report.

"Connor told me your dad and Jimmy were on that hit together. After your father was found, Jimmy disappeared.

We assumed he was laying low, which would follow protocol, but he never returned to us. No one thought anything different. He called in the job unsuccessful with a casualty. Everyone gave him slack, assumed he was grieving. Then he stepped away from the Crew and carved his own way," Bale explains.

"What exactly was the hit for?" Cameron asks.

"It was a stockbrokerage; the hit was to retrieve documents with account numbers detailing offshore accounts. They were to download the details onto a memory stick, and a buyer was already in place."

We all eye one another, slowly piecing together and drawing the same conclusions. "My father doesn't have the heart condition I have, Bale. But James is taking drugs for his heart at every meal. I'm starting to think he's my father, Bale. Fucking James!" My hands tremble and my heart is pounding in my chest, sure to burst through at any second.

"The stockbrokers they hit; that was my father's firm," Cameron confirms.

"Fuck!" Romeo bellows. "He's fucking planned this from the start. We knew he couldn't be trusted! Put the fucking memory stick in the computer!"

We watch on as Bale accesses the memory stick. He clicks on the first video, and I recognize the two men in the office instantly. Their faces are covered with balaclavas, but I know one is my father and the other one my uncle, I'm just not completely unsure which one is biologically which.

My eyes are glued to the man I grew up believing was my father as he places the memory stick in his pocket. I know it's him because as he leaves and walks past the camera, I see his Army dog tags dangling from his neck. "There, he's wearing his dog tags. But they weren't on his body; why weren't they on his body?" I ask with a shaky voice as I glance at each of the guys for answers.

Aiden flips through the file and his eyes cast over my father's lifeless photo, he shakes his head at me, confirming what I already know. They weren't on his body.

Cameron clears his throat, his voice soft. "Frankie, your uncle has the dog tags. I saw them in his office when I was a boy. He keeps them in his safe." My eyes bulge in temper, the bastard. *How dare he? How dare he decimate my father's achievements and steal his legacy.*

Cameron squeezes my shoulder in support, and I burrow my head into his neck, barely holding myself together.

"So, just to fucking confirm. They left the office with the memory stick, job successful. Jeremy had his dog tags on but was found dead without them. Anyone else thinking what I'm thinking?" Romeo rants.

"I'm thinking I'm going to fucking kill him!" I answer calmly. Cameron's grip on me tightens.

"There's one more video here, it's labeled *Office Backup*." Bale hovers the mouse, and eyes me as if asking for approval. I nod for him to go ahead and play it.

It's the office again, but my uncle is dressed smartly and completely open to the cameras. He pulls a small bag from his pocket and leans over the desk, and he places the item in the coffee cup before returning to his seat. Just in time as the office door opens and in walks a broad-shouldered man with a familiar smile. Cameron tenses beside me, and I feel his heart against my body,

"Th . . . that's . . . fuck. That's my dad!" He exhales.

Oh God, no! Jesus!

The two men laugh, and Cameron's father drinks from the coffee cup with an unsuspecting smile. My uncle is a murdering motherfucking prick, and he's going to fucking suffer. I can feel myself strengthen. I can feel myself become Star.

Cameron's father rubs at his heart and slowly makes his way out of the room as my uncle moves around the desk and starts to use the computer. Then as he peers up to the camera, the screen goes blank. He clearly believes he's wiped the footage.

"Motherfucker!" Cameron erupts and throws the table beside me against the wall. He tugs at his hair, panting. "Fuck!"

Aiden moves toward the door, I know the protocol . . . cover all exits, contain the threat. We can't risk Cameron going for James, not until we're ready. We need a plan.

CAMERON

Walking away from the gym with a plan in place helps give me some clarity. How Frankie can control her thoughts, feelings, and emotions is nothing short of spectacular. She is somehow able to compartmentalize them—she puts them all in a box and keeps them contained.

You would never believe she just found out that her father is not her father, but really her uncle. Her biological father murdered the man who brought her up, the man she loved and the man who loved her, they adored one another.

I've just discovered my father has been murdered by a man I once thought of as my mom's knight in shining armor. He swooped in and rescued her from the emotional and financial trauma of looking after mine and my father's assets.

At the time, she felt completely bombarded and out of her depth, yet James, an apparent work colleague of my father's, was happy to step in and help take control. Not only that but unbeknown to us at the time, he was taking control of my father's family on a whole. My mom had inadvertently signed us over to the man that had murdered her husband and his brother for his own financial and social gain, soon to be ruin.

My mom was having another break away, another spa retreat.

Normally I wouldn't question this, but given the recent events, I'm now able to think back on my family's relationship and figure out how fractured we truly are.

My mom had always been a homemaker when I was young, happy to be on hand and do the traditional meals together in the evenings. We enjoyed Thanksgiving together and she was home more than she was away, complete opposite of how we currently live. Another indication of perhaps things weren't as good in our home as she liked to portray.

I'd asked Neo to deal with the cameras for us, just in case James discovered we'd tampered with them. Clearly the man was far more in check with technology than what he led us to believe.

Frankie and I embrace our hands as we meet at the bottom of the staircase, and I kiss her lips gently. "You ready for this?"

"Absolutely!" she replies with the air of confidence I love. She squeezes my hand, in what should be worrying excitement, but I can't help but feel a small amount of excitement too. Because we were about to get answers, answers and fucking justice.

We walk into Jimmy's office hand in hand, without knocking. We sit next to one another, Jimmy's eyes trained on our hands, watching our every movement.

He chuckles to himself and then arrogantly relaxes back in the chair. "Something to tell me?" he muses with raised eyebrows.

"We're together," I reply in a snipped tone.

"I can see that." He leans back farther, trying to portray complete control.

Frankie decides to go in for the kill. "You know I have a hereditary heart condition, Jimmy, the same one as you." She watches him closely, like a predator watching its prey, and he swallows sharply. "My father and Jodie didn't have that condition. So, tell me, Jimmy, are you my biological father?" Straight to the punch.

He exhales. "When did you find that out?" he queries, not an ounce of compassion or care. His face is blank.

"The same time I found out you killed my father, robbed Hamilton, and murdered Cameron's father," she quips back with zero emotion.

Jimmy's chest rises rapidly, his breathing becoming erratic as he loosens the collar on his shirt. He waves his hand around, laughing to himself. "You have proof of these silly little accusations, do you?" He doesn't deny it, though, no outrage or remorse.

I lift my chin. "Oh yes. We've proof, plenty. Thanks to Ryan."

Jimmy throws his head back and laughs, he runs his hand through his hair. "Ryan Stone is dead; I made sure of that myself. He was sniffing around me like a restless puppy, so I made sure to put him down!"

Frankie gasps at the latest little cluster fuck he's dropped out before quickly masking herself once again. "But we do have proof. All the proof we need," Frankie replies with a tone of boredom.

"I've also discovered a little more interesting information," I add, while turning toward Frankie. "Last night, Neo searched into James's financial credentials and discovered a name on his bank statements that you know, Frankie." I eye her pointedly. "Tell me, Jimmy, why did you pay Natalia Bennett ten thousand dollars?"

Frankie sucks in air, her hand shaking in mine. I squeeze her tight to anchor her to me.

Jimmy chuckles to himself. "She was a little slut that was happy to suck my cock and drug Ryan's brother for me. I needed to make sure the little punk wasn't aware of his brother sniffing around me. It wasn't until I received the call that Frankie was in the hospital that I discovered the same little punk knocked up my daughter. I realized then that I had to bring her in to make sure she was none the wiser and keep an eye on things. To make sure she was distancing herself from them."

"You do realize you won't be leaving this room alive, right?" I ask him smugly.

"Really? And who's going to stop me? You? Really, Cameron? I practically raised you!" he spits; his temper now showing. And he expected what? Some fake loyalty? Because he supposedly raised me. He fucking put us in this position.

Frankie's firm voice cuts through my thoughts. "But not your own daughter, huh, Jimmy? You were willing to kill Nate? Just in case he suspected something. Do you hear how insane that is? I lost my baby that night!" Frankie bellows.

Jimmy's face contorts. "Like mother like daughter!" he spits out.

That's it, I fucking flip. I throw myself across the desk,

the scum bagging bastard! I smack his jaw so hard I swear it snaps. Frankie drags me back before my hands reach his neck.

The door opens and in strides Bale, Romeo, and Aiden. They stand along the back wall with their backs to the door, in complete silent support, a show of utter solidarity.

I stare back at the shit bag Jimmy is. Realization marring his features, color drains from his face, the fucker finally realizes he really isn't leaving this room alive.

I stroke Frankie's hand and pull the box from behind my back pocket. "Baby, I thought you'd like to do the honors." I nod encouragingly.

Frankie smiles as she opens the box, her knife from Nate. A touching tribute to the small life lost too early but one that will now help her to move on with clarity.

I move to stand and walk behind Jimmy, prepared to hold him in place, if necessary. A glance at Bale and a nod confirming my actions, I hold his shoulders down as my beautiful girl moves in front of him. She slices into his face with a maniacal grin. Jimmy tries to stand but I hold the prick down, and she lunges forward and stabs his thighs. His legs kick out, but she manages to hold them. His screams do nothing to douse my own rage.

Then she goes for his chest, Romeo moves toward us and holds his flailing legs down. Multiple stab wounds to his chest. Blood oozing from his wounds should sicken me, but I feel a sick sense of satisfaction for me, for Frankie, for our family.

Frankie moves to Jimmy's neck and with one final stab, she enters his jugular before pulling the knife out with a slick sickening pop. She wipes the knife on his shirt and smirks to herself, then her eyes meet mine and her smirk turns into a smile, a broad, natural, loving smile.

From the outside looking in, she would appear a deranged monster, but to me?

She's never looked so beautiful; she was born reckless and that's why I love my foulmouthed, tattooed, dirty girl.

EPILOGUE

EIGHT WEEKS LATER...

FRANKIE

I wake to kisses being peppered down my neck. I drape my hands around his shoulders and pull his lips toward mine with a smile gracing my own.

"Morning, beautiful." Cameron chuckles.

"Morning, Cam. Anything I can help you with?"

Cameron laughs, then licks his lips as he nudges my legs apart with his knee. "I'm sure you can figure it out." He smiles knowingly.

Cameron's cock enters me swiftly, my back arching to meet Cameron's smooth thrusts.

I'm currently on the implant, and I've gained confidence enough for Cameron not to have to wear condoms. His new favorite thing is to wake me up with a morning fuck and then watch in some fucked-up, possessive fascination when his cum runs out of me.

"Fuck, tell me you want my cum, Frankie. Tell me you need it!" he bites out.

His hips move side to side, forcing his cock deeper. "Fuck yes! I need it, Cam. Fuck, give it to me."

My nipples graze his chest, his head drops to stare at them as if sensing my need, and he hungrily sucks the piercing into his mouth as I move my hand to the other, squeezing it. "Fuck, that's hot, Frankie!"

My pussy clenches at his dirty words. "Cameron, harder!" His hips piston into mine. "Yes! Like that, Cam, don't stop!" I pant.

"Fuck, my dirty girl. Fuck!" His jaw clenches as I feel his spine straighten, and my pussy squeezes around his throbbing cock as my orgasm takes over me, my mind whirling with ecstasy. My breath taken as Cameron's cum fills me. My back arching, my head thrown back in awe.

His forehead drops to mine. "Fuck, that was amazing!"

I laugh at his observation, his body lowers to mine, and I stroke his back up and down. My thoughts wander to the day ahead. "What time are you meeting Bale?"

"Not until eleven. Give me five and I'll be good to go again!" He winks at me.

For the last few weeks, Cameron has been working out at Bale's gym, learning different martial arts disciplines. He's currently working out there as a hobby; his plans are to take over his father's business. Both Joel and Neo have offered to help, therefore, he will already have a trustworthy support system in place and their fresh young approach might be just what the company needs.

I've decided I'm going to be a trainer at one of Bale's

gyms. I'm also going to do evening courses when I leave school in social work. Ideally, I'd like to run a non-profit organization for youngsters of crime and violence, encouraging them to follow their dreams while offering emotional and physical support structures via the training I've received growing up.

Josie wasn't exactly distraught when she found out her husband had been murdered by some awful gang members from his past.

From all accounts, she'd been swept up in the marriage and soon regretted it but didn't want to cause her son anymore turmoil or heartache by admitting it.

I've grown to love Josie; she cares deeply for Cameron and me. She's also welcomed and supported our relationship, with a few rules.

One being we aren't allowed to sleep in the same bed, but hey . . .

I was born reckless, after all.

ACKNOWLEDGMENTS

Here I am again **TL Swan.**

How the hell did I do this? With your help, support and guidance. Thank you from the bottom of my heart. You've no idea the impact you have had on me and my fellow cygnets. We adore you, thank you for everything. This book really wouldn't exist without you.

To the Cygnet Inkers... thank you, thank you, thank you! For always being there. For answering my dumb questions, for pushing me on and more importantly for giving me your friendship. You girls mean the world to me.

To the Swan Squad, you girls make me smile every damn day! Patricia B, I feel so lucky to have you as a reader. Your posts and messages brighten my day. Never change.

Rhiannon Marina. Yet again you've been my go-to girl. Thank you for always supporting me, for answering my daft questions and lifting me up when I need it. Thank you Rhi.

To Nikila thank you for being you and pushing me on. Thank you for your friendship, I look forward to our messages and chats.

My friend Jaclyn, I cannot wait to see what the future holds for you. You've reassured me so much. I hope I can do the same for you.

Thank you to my Beta Readers, Libby, Chelsea, Rhiannon, Bex, Jennifer and J. You've been awesome. Thank you for answering a multitude of questions. We got there eventually.

To my friends Emma, Paula and Megan. Thank you for your support and encouragement. I can't tell you how much having you behind me means.

To Sarah and Meg, a friendship that has been drawn up through my first book CAL. Thank you lovely, for making me smile, especially on the days when I need it the most. Your photos and support are so meaningful.

To Katie Evans PA, who would have thought by you reading a book you'd now be such a hug part of my life? Thank you for all your help, support and chat. And most importantly, thank you for reading Born Reckless.

To my boys, thank you for everything. You are literally my everything.

As always...

To my hubby, the J in my BJ. Thank you for pushing me, listening to me and supporting me through this whole process. Without you I wouldn't be BJ Alpha.

Love you trillions!

ABOUT THE AUTHOR

BJ Alpha lives in the UK with her hubby, two teenage sons and three fur babies.
She loves to write and read about hot, alpha males and feisty females.

Follow me on my social media pages:
Facebook: BJ Alpha
My readers group: BJ's Reckless Readers
Instagram: BJ Alpha

ALSO BY BJ ALPHA

Secrets and Lies Series

CAL Book 1

CON Book 2

FINN Book 3

BREN Book 4

OSCAR Book 5

CON'S WEDDING NOVELLA

The Brutal Duet

Hidden In Brutal Devotion

Love In Brutal Devotion

Printed in Great Britain
by Amazon